AFTER THE END OF THE LINE

RAILROAD HAUNTINGS IN LITERATURE AND LORE

AFTER THE END OF THE LINE

RAILROAD HAUNTINGS IN LITERATURE AND LORE

EDITED BY
TIM PRASIL

BROM B<nes BOOKS

After the End of the Line: Railroad Hauntings in Literature and Lore is the fifth volume of the Phantom Traditions Library series, published by Brom Bones Books. These anthologies feature "forgotten" genres or sub-genres of popular fiction—from supernatural and fantasy tales to detective mysteries and science fiction—written primarily during the 1800s and early 1900s. Edited by Tim Prasil, each volume has a well-researched introduction, helpful and interesting footnotes, and an appendix that spotlights a work or two of relevant non-fiction from the same period. Learn more about the Phantom Traditions Library at BromBonesBooks.com.

The front cover illustration is from the front cover of *Scientific American* 64.15 [April 11, 1891], where it is captioned "The New 'Ghost' Express Train Between New York and Boston."

Introductions and notes © 2021 Tim Prasil.
All rights reserved.
No claim made on public domain material.

ISBN-13: 978-1-948084-10-9
ISBN-10: 1-948084-10-4

DEDICATION

To the citizens of Mrthyr Tydfil, Wales,
who, in February of 1804,
saw Richard Trevithick's steam-powered locomotive
run along rails, hauling iron and passengers.
It was a first, and it must have been astonishing.
But did any of them wonder: *Is it safe?*

CONTENTS

Introduction — Tim Prasil … ix

First Station: Danger Signals from Beyond

A Warning — Anonymous … 3
From "Beyond Gower's Land" — I.D. Fenton … 6
The Signal-Man — Charles Dickens … 8
The Ghost That Jim Saw — Bret Harte … 20
Under the Sheer-Legs — Henry Tinson … 22
A Railroad Ghost — Anonymous … 31
A Phantom Train — Anonymous … 32
An Interposition — Sarah G. Riker … 35

Second Station: Phantom Trains

The Phantom Train: The Dead Lincoln's Yearly Trip over the New York Central Railroad — Anonymous … 41
The Phantom Train; or, The Tunnel Clerk — Anonymous … 43
At Ravenholme Junction — Anonymous … 51
A Phantom Train: A Lightning Express Train That Made No Noise — Anonymous … 59
A Phantom at the Throttle — Anonymous … 60
A Ghost Train — W. L. Alden … 66
The Phantom Train — Mary R. P. Hatch … 74
The Phantom Train — Howard Wiswall Bible … 79

Third Station: Wraiths on the Rails

The 9.30 Up-Train — Sabine Baring-Gould	87
The 4.15 Express — Amelia B. Edwards	99
An Appalling Mystery — Anonymous	124
B 88 — Anonymous	129
The Engineer's Story — Eben E. Rexford	145
Untitled — Anonymous	148
Terror of Haunted Locomotives — Anonymous	149
Ghost Without a Head: A Midnight Phantom That Is Terrorizing Employees of the Lake Erie & Western Road — Anonymous	151
From *Real Ghost Stories* — W. T. Stead	153
A Ghost-Haunted Railway — Anonymous	155
A Railroad Ghost — Anonymous	156
The Ghosts of Sag Bridge — 213	161
Miss Slumbubble—and Claustrophobia — Algernon Blackwood	165

Appendix

Arrival and Departure of a Phantom Track Walker — W.W. Adair	179
About the Editor	187

INTRODUCTION

TIM PRASIL

It is currently understood that this is a hard headed, material, steam-engine and railroad age. All ghosts have fled, and all witches have been drowned.

The London Morning Chronicle, 1842[1]

When the passage above was printed, the railroad seemed to be whisking humanity into a shiny, mechanical future, leaving ghosts in the darkening, superstitious past. The sentiment survived as late as 1858, when a narrative titled "My Only Adventure" appeared in newspapers across the United States. The narrator opens his tale by saying that he has no ghost story to share: "Railways have put haunted chambers out of fashion. . . . Ghosts lived in old [stage]coaching days, and dwelt in quaint wayside inns; and I was never lucky enough to have my bed curtains disturbed by invisible hands." To be sure, the story is about that narrator surviving an invasion of completely *corporeal* criminals.[2] Why introduce it as decidedly *not* a ghost story? Did the author worry that, since *part* of the tale takes place at Christmas, readers might have expected it to end as a supernatural Yuletide yarn? The more likely answer is that the author simply wanted to affirm that ghosts had vanished in the smoke of the oncoming "steam-engine and railroad age."

By their very nature, though, ghosts materialize where they're least expected—they *refuse* to stay buried, especially in the past. Railroads and hauntings started to merge. One such case occurred in 1856, when several persons heard—but did not see—a phantom train pull into Staunton, Virginia. One report reads:

> Between the hours of eleven and twelve o'clock at night, the approach of a train of cars has been heard, the shriek of the whistle and the rumbling of the train increasing in distinctness

until the cars reached the Staunton Depot. Persons have gone to the Depot to find out the cause of the arrival at so unusual an hour, and when they got there found no train. The [station] agents say that no train is on the road at that hour of night, and yet the approach of one is unmistakably heralded by the rumbling and its arrival announced by the whistle.

This report concludes by saying a very similar mystery has occurred on "a Northern Railroad." In fact, heard-but-unseen trains became common enough to have been identified as a folklore motif,[3] and ghost reports in newspapers often feel much more like folktale than fact.

A very different case occurred in 1860. The *Burlington Hawkeye,* a newspaper in Iowa, reported on an unnamed train engineer who had been speeding along to reach the next stop. Suddenly, he saw a female figure on the track not far ahead! And there was *no way to stop in time!*

> The engineer remarked to the person on the engine, that that was the first person he had ever killed during his railroad experience. Arriving at the depot, he sent men with lights back to the spot where he saw the woman, but no sign or trace of anything was there. There was no body, no blood, no marks upon the track. Next morning the search was renewed with no success.

It's not an especially gripping *ghost* story. In fact, it only *became* a ghost story when, as the report was reprinted elsewhere, some editor added this spooky—if not a bit snarky—lead-in: "It is said that spectres, vampires and goblins are seen at night on the Chicago, Burlington and Quincy Railroad." With this editorial enhancement, the news report raced from Iowa to California one way and to England the other.[4]

Despite its simplicity, this story hints at two reasons why railroads and hauntings melded fairly quickly. First, while a remarkably convenient and efficient form of transportation, the iron horse was also a vehicle of death and destruction. Among many others catastrophes in the U.S., the Great Train Wreck of 1856 involved two trains colliding head-on in Pennsylvania, killing more than 50 and injuring more than 100. In 1863, around 75 passengers were killed when the weight of a train collapsed a badly-constructed bridge crossing Mississippi's Chunky Creek, and in 1876, another

Introduction

faulty bridge sent a train plummeting into Ohio's Ashtabula River with between 90 and 100 dead. Individual train wrecks would continue to claim even more American lives as the decades advanced.

Meanwhile, deaths from railway disasters grew throughout the United Kingdom: 18 people died in 1853, when one train rear-ended another in Straffan, Ireland (then governed by the UK); 23 died eight years later, when a similar event happened in a train tunnel near Brighton, England; 33 died seven years after that in a collision in Abergele, Wales; and about 70 died in 1879, when Scotland's Tay Bridge succumbed to stormy weather while a train traversed it. Needless to say, as railways stretched around the world, terrible train wrecks inevitably haunted them.

The second issue arising from that well-traveled report about the trainman and the insubstantial woman on the tracks is in what the incident suggests about the engineer. Since he seems to have been alone in seeing the figure, it's fair to ask if he had experienced an optical illusion, one brought on by the conditions under which train engineers work. These conditions are explained in an 1882 article titled "Superstitious Engineers." The anonymous writer states bluntly: "Like sailors, engineers are very superstitious." However, they have cause to be so:

> With only a fireman [controlling the steam] as a companion they are out in all kinds of weather, and I can tell you it is no pleasant thing for a man to ride at full speed on a dark night, peering out of a little window into a blackness made more black by the bright glare of the headlight. On all sides is darkness, and the little speck of monotonous track ahead is all that he can see. Certain engines, like certain ships, get bad reputations, and the men hate to run them. They consider them unlucky and believe they are bound to kill somebody, and so will refuse to drive them at top speed.[5]

Of course, believing some trains are unlucky is different from believing spirits can return to the mortal realm unsummoned.

However, the stereotype of engineers being superstitious also encompassed a belief in ghosts. This is illustrated in an 1894 issue of *Railway World,* a journal aimed at railroad professionals. "Important operations have been suspended by the vague report of a spectre," explains the unnamed writer, adding that managers should debunk these reports among their employees with a careful hand. "It does no good to ridicule superstition" or to "compel men to do what they dread.... What is wanted is to convince a frightened man that [a ghostly danger] is imaginary." For instance, one New Jersey apparition was exposed to be a white pig. Elsewhere, an eerie figure, which "rested in a gloomy attitude upon a graveyard gate," turned out to be a turkey. "The rumor that an apparition had been seen by one man," says the writer, "might lead others to abandon their work, and might render it difficult to get any labor performed after nightfall."[6] Railroad phantoms, then, could scare away profits.

The writer advising how to manage ghost sightings might have been pleased to read J.L.B. Sunderlin's "Railroad Superstitions," a 1912 reminiscence of times gone by. He opens by saying that "the railroad man of a decade ago, even, was a different man from the railroad man of today; for, as he has become educated he has shed many of his superstitious ideas." Sunderlin goes on to recount beliefs such as accidents coming in threes, the importance of nailing a horseshoe to the caboose or locomotive, and certain trainmen being gifted with the ability to "foretell dire and wondrous happenings." Included is a tale of "the wraith of an old trackwalker" running as fast as the train itself along the spot where he was killed. Neither a pig nor a turkey, however, this ghost story is explained by the shadow of a maple leaf clinging to the headlight.[7]

If all ghosts had truly "fled" before 1842—and if train engineers had truly ceased to be superstitious by 1912—then the mid-1800s to the early 1900s might be roughly marked as the first era of railroad hauntings. Luckily for us, engineers during those seventy years shared their ghostly tales, sometimes with news-hungry journalists. These reporters were joined by some of the era's ghost-story collectors. At the same time, this distinctive development in ghostlore was also inspiring fiction writers and poets. This, then, provides a timeframe for the variety of pieces collected in this anthology.

While gathering material, I noticed that motifs in the non-fiction narratives carried through to the literary works. This led me to organize the contents into three sections. I call the first "Warning Signals from Beyond," and you'll find that these warnings are communicated in a variety of ways. It might be an irresistible feeling—a compelling hunch—strong enough to induce an engineer to stop a train. It's a somewhat more traditional ghost in Charles Dickens' famous story "The Signal-Man," but the figure gives the focal character hard-to-decipher clues of future events. In Bret Harte's poem "The Ghost that Jim Saw," it's a vision of a house and a drunken man stumbling along the tracks. Newspaper accounts

Introduction

indicate that phantom locomotives soaring across the sky or even oddly moving lights could be interpreted as portents of tragedy.

Of course, the history of prognostication probably extends back even further than when Oedipus was prophesized to kill his dad and marry his mom. For centuries, it was said that dreams sometimes conveyed future events, and this idea still held interest in the 1800s. For instance, Catherine Crowe devotes an entire chapter to warnings gleaned through dreams in her 1848 book *The Night Side of Nature,* a remarkable compendium of "true" reports about otherworldly experiences. On the other hand, precognitive warnings experienced while fully awake come closer to what Victorians would refer to as "second sight." Crowe discusses this in her "Miscellaneous Phenomena" chapter, introducing it by saying that finding supporting evidence is a challenge because, "when the seers are of the humbler classes, they are called impostors and not believed; and when they are of the higher, they do not make the subject a matter of conversation, nor choose to expose themselves to the ridicule of the foolish." Being intimidated by skepticism certainly shows up in the pieces chosen for this anthology's first section, and they fit best with wide-awake "second sight."

Despite claiming she lacks abundant evidence, Crowe does offer a handful of accounts illustrating second sight. There's the houseguest who cut short his stay, claiming that "during dinner he had seen a female figure with her throat cut, standing behind Lady T.'s chair." Lady T. herself was then kept ignorant of this grisly vision—which might have been a terrible mistake—because, later that night, it was discovered that *she* had cut her own throat. Another of Crowe's examples concerns a man who saw "a dreadful face at one corner of the room. He described it as a bruised, battered, crushed, discoloured face, with the two eyes protruding frightfully from their sockets." The visionary face is so mangled that the man did not recognize it as *his own* after suffering a horrible accident the next day. Even a friend of Crowe's had a story to tell. Working in the medical field, he encountered a patient with "inflammation of the brain," a condition resulting from having seen her "Uncle John drowned in his boat under the fifth arch of Rochester Bridge!" Sadly, the niece died of her ailment. Worse yet, the following night, the uncle drowned "exactly as she had foretold."[8] In each of these cases, as happens with Oedipus, even the *foretold* calamity was not averted. I won't tell you if the same holds true for those you'll meet in the "Warning Signals from Beyond" section.

As suggested by the warning appearing in the form of a spectral train crossing the clouds, there is some overlap between the motifs. Nonetheless, the second section of this anthology, "Phantom Locomotives," spotlights a phenomena that doesn't predict the future. Instead, the trains here—like the one mentioned above as arriving at Stauton Depot—only mystify those in the present, even if they do so by reenacting the past.

In a sense, phantom trains are a modernization of earlier supernatural modes of transportation, especially phantom coaches and phantom ships. Since I hate to delay the start of your trip for *too* long, let's just take a glance at only those coaches. Several haunt England, but one of the most famous appears annually at Blickling Hall, once the residence of Anne Boleyn. Her ghost is said to be carried by coachmen and horses that are, in deference to the decapitated queen, also headless. Similar phantoms appear in Ireland, but they bring sad news. John O'Hanlon explains, "Headless apparitions of horses and coachmen are often seen driving from or towards grave-yards, during the dead hour of midnight. Such appearances, where found passing round a particular house, are regarded as ominous of some approaching disaster, and generally indicate a death warning to some member of the family." A few phantom coaches have traveled to the U.S., too. Henry S. Olcott notes one that had materialized in Vermont:

> On a cold winter night, just before bed-time, the [Eddy] family were gathered in the sitting-room, when they heard the noise of a carriage coming rapidly along the road from the northward. The circumstance was so strange, the ground being covered with snow which would prevent the sound of wheels being heard, that all went to the front windows to look....

There, the family distinctly saw a woman in Scottish apparel along with a driver atop an elegant coach. Speechless, they then noticed that the fence "and other objects, previously concealed behind the opaque bodies of the carriage and horses, began to show through, and in a moment the whole thing vanished into air, leaving the spectators lost in amazement."[9] In the end, this apparition proves to be an import of the Celtic harbinger of death that O'Hanlon mentions.

Such narratives, updated for the railroad age, *might* have been subtly reinforced by real events. At least as early as 1878, railroads in the U.S. were accused of running what were called "ghost trains," meaning freight was transported off-the-books with the profits pocketed by local management rather than passed on to company heads or investors. Does this explain the noiseless, smokeless train that a night tower attendant saw arrive, stop, and depart Watseka, Illinois, in March of 1907? Another tower attendant three miles south saw it come and go, too—but after telegraphing their despatchers, both men were told there was no such train. Perhaps not surprisingly, railroad officials denied the practice existed, but even rumors of goods being hauled on the sly might have inspired visions of trains that both were—and *weren't*—there. With more certainty, a new passenger train running between Boston and New York was announced in 1891. Its cars were painted a creamy white on the outside, and the appearance of this pale, giant snake—especially as it neared its final destination at 9:00 p.m.—led to it quickly being dubbed "the Ghost Train."[10] (Glance at the front cover of this book, and you'll see an illustration of it.) In other words, readers in the late 1800s were being told that *some "ghost trains" were real!*

Meanwhile, ghosts themselves were also appearing along the tracks. This brings us to the anthology's third section: "Wraiths on the Rails." Here, you'll meet a phantom hovering around a West Virginia railway tunnel. There's an engine that resonates with and echoes the suffering of those it has killed. There's a headless ghost seen by the crew of the midnight train while passing the spot where a conductor was decapitated while on duty. And these are what was being reported in newspapers—*not* what was being imagined by writers of fiction! Are they simply tall tales, perhaps told by railroaders with a twinkle in their eye? Are they better understood as railroad legend and lore? Or did they really happen? In a way, the uncertainty clouding the truthfulness of the articles in this section makes them more unsettling than the pieces of outright fiction there.

This isn't to say that the fictional wraiths on the rails aren't creepy, too. On one end of the spectral spectrum, there are demonic and vengeful ghosts. On the other extreme, there's a murdered railroad employee who manages to stick around long enough to thwart his killers' terrible train robbery. Somewhere in the middle, there are restless spirits "dragging the chains" of guilt due to their unsolved crimes. And I'm particularly a fan of Granny Whittaker's ghost cow.

Within these three sections, the individual pieces are arranged chronologically, meaning that the journey bounces between newspaper reports and short stories—with stops for memoir, travelogue, poetry, and a selection from a collection of "true" ghost stories. To make sure my reader knows what's what, I introduce each piece with a footnote stating the genre before the biographical data. I then did some mild editing to each work so that new readers will enjoy them without the little "distractions" of written language from the 1800s and early 1900s. In other words, I modernized once-hyphenated words, such as "to-night," while also dividing sentences and paragraphs that now feel unnecessarily long. Nonetheless, I worked to retain the charm of good, old-fashioned ghost-story telling.

But there's the engineer's whistle, and the conductor is calling out the first station. I depart here, so it looks like you'll have the compartment all to yourself. Enjoy your journey, and try not to think about what happened in this very compartment exactly one year ago today.

Oh, you haven't heard about that?

Well . . . I have to go now.

---

[1] Quoted in *The Madisonian*, Dec. 9, 1842, p. 2.

[2] "My Only Adventure," *Evening Star,* Feb. 13, 1858, p. 1. Along with this Washington D.C. journal, the tale appeared in South Carolina's *The Independent Press,* March 26, 1858, p. 1; Ohio's *Holmes County Republican,* July 15, 1858, p. 1; the *Saint Paul Weekly Minnesotan,* Aug. 14, 1858, p. 1, and others.

[3] *Lynchburg Daily Virginian,* June 28, 1856, p. 1. Ernest W. Baughman lists such auditory trains under E535.4(b) in his *Type and Motif-Index of the Folktales of England and North America* (Mouton & Co., 1966) p. 190.

[4] Quoted in *Daily National Democrat,* Dec. 29, 1860, p. 3. Along with this Marysville, California, journal, the report was reprinted in the English newspaper *Hereford Times,* Dec. 15, 1860, p. 11.

[5] "Superstitious Engineers," *Railway Age Monthly and Railway Service Magazine,* 3.4 [April, 1882] p. 249.

[6] "Superstition Among Railway Employés," *Railway World* 20.34 [Aug. 25, 1894] p. 669.

[7] J.L.B. Sunderlin,"Railroad Superstitions," *Railroad Association Magazine* 2.1 [Nov. 15, 1912] pp. 11-12.

[8] Catherine Crowe, *The Night Side of Nature; or, Ghosts and Ghost Seers* (T.C. Newby, 1848) Vol. 2: pp. 329-31.

[9] T.F. Thiselton-Dyer summarizes the Blickling Hall haunting and similar legends in the "Headless Ghosts" chapter of his book *The Ghost World* (Ward & Downey, 1893) pp. 147-51; John O'Hanlon, *Legend Lays of Ireland* (John Mullany, 1870) p. 90; Henry S. Olcott, *People from the Other World* (American Publishing, 1875) pp. 80-83. One of the best-loved and often-anthologized works of fiction related to this topic is Amelia Edwards' "The Phantom Coach," *All the Year Round,* Christmas issue [1864] pp. 35-48.

[10] "Ghost Trains," *Truth* 5.114 [March 6, 1878] p. 296; "Train Leaves No Sign," *Evening Statesman* [Walla Walla, Washington], March 4, 1907, p. 8; "McHenry's Ghost Trains," *The Indianapolis Journal,* Feb. 13, 1884, p. 7; "A Notable New Pullman Passenger Train," *Scientific American* 64.797 [April 11, 1891] p. 229.

FIRST STATION:

DANGER SIGNALS FROM BEYOND

A WARNING

ANONYMOUS[1]

I am not, nor was I ever, superstitious. I do not believe in dreams, signs, witches, hobgoblins, nor in any of the rest of that ilk, which antiquated maidens in olden time used to cheer the drooping spirits of childhood and send us urchins off to our bed, half scared to death, expecting to see some horrid monster step out from every corner of the room and, in unearthly accents, declare his intention to "grind our bones for coffee" or do something else equally horrid, the contemplation of which was in an equal degree unfitted to render our sleep sound or our rest placid. Somehow, the visitors from the otherworld that children used to be told of were never pretty nor angelic, but always more devilish than anything else.

But in these days, this has changed, for the ghosts in which gullible people deal now, are preeminently silly things. They use their superhuman strength in tumbling parlor furniture about the rooms, and in drumming on the floors and ceilings of bedrooms. The old proverb is that "every generation grows weaker and wiser." In this respect, however, we have reversed the proverb: a great many have grown stronger in gullibility and weaker in intellect, else we would not have so many spiritualists who wait for God and His angels to thump out their special revelations, or else tumble a table about the room to the tune of A B C.

I have known, as have many—probably all of my readers—a great many people who professed to have the firmest faith in prophetic dreams and signs, who were always pre-admonished of every event by some supernatural means, and who invariably are looking out for singular events when they have been visited by a singular dream. I have never believed in these things, have always laughed at them, and do so still. Yet there is one circumstance of my

---

[1] This is a chapter from a memoir titled *Reminiscences in the Life of a Locomotion Engineer* (Follett, Foster and Company, 1861) pp. 177-81. While not a ghost story, the piece reveals the staunch skepticism facing engineers who encountered supernatural phenomena—skepticism even from themselves.

life of this kind that is shrouded in mystery, that I cannot explain, that I know to be so—and yet that I can scarcely believe. A warning was given to me *somehow*, I know not how. Despite my ridicule of superstition and disbelief in signs or warnings of any kind, it so shook me and influenced me that I heeded it and, by so doing, saved myself from instant death. It also saved many passengers who, had they known of the "warning" which influenced me to take the steps which I did, would have laughed at me and endeavored to drive me on. The facts are briefly as follows—I tell them, not attempting to explain them nor offering any theory concerning them, neither pretending that angels or devils warned me, but only knowing that it was so:

I was running a Night Express train comprised of ten cars—eight passenger and two baggage cars—and all were well loaded. I was behind time and was very anxious to make a certain point. Therefore, I was using every exertion and putting the engine to the utmost speed of which she was capable. I was on a section of the road usually considered the best running ground on the line, endeavoring to make the most of it, when a conviction struck me that I must stop. A *something* seemed to tell me that to go ahead was dangerous and that I must stop if I would save life.

I looked back at my train, and it was all right. I strained my eyes and peered into the darkness, but I could see no signal of danger nor anything betokening danger, and there I could see five miles in the daytime. I listened to the working of my engine, tried the water, looked at the scales, and all was right. I tried to laugh myself out of what I then considered a childish fear.

Like Banquo's ghost, though, it would not down at my bidding. It grew stronger in its hold upon me. I thought of the ridicule I would have heaped upon me if I did stop, but it was all of no avail. The conviction—for, by this time, it had ripened into a *conviction*—that I must stop grew stronger, and I resolved to stop. Accordingly, I shut off and blew the whistle for brakes.

I came to a dead halt, got off, and went ahead a little way without saying anything to anybody what was the matter. I had my lamp in my hand and had gone about sixty feet, when I saw what convinced me that premonitions are sometimes possible. I dropped the lantern from my nerveless grasp and sat down on the track, utterly unable to stand.

There was a switch, the thought of which had never entered my mind as it had never been used since I had been on the road. It was

A Warning

known to be spiked,[2] but now was open to lead me *off the track*. This switch led into a stone quarry, from whence stone for bridge purposes had been quarried, and the switch was left there, in case stone should be needed at any time. But it was always kept locked, and the switch-rail spiked.

Yet here it was, wide open.

Had I not obeyed my pre-admonition—*warning*—call it what you will—I should have run into it, and, at the end of the track, only about ten rods long, my heavy engine and train, moving at the rate of forty-five miles per hour, would have come into collision with a solid wall of rock, eighteen feet high. The consequences, had I done so, can neither be imagined nor described. They could, by no possibility, have been otherwise than fatally horrid.

This is my experience in getting warnings from a source that I know not and cannot divine. It is a mystery to me—a mystery for which I am very thankful, although I dare not attempt to explain it nor say whence it came.

---

[2] A "switch" is a mechanism used to guide a train from one track to another. When a switch is "spiked," an iron spike is driven in to block the device from moving, ideally preventing trains from doing exactly what happens here.

FROM "BEYOND GOWER'S LAND"

I.D. FENTON[1]

As a people, the Welsh are much given to superstition, and many are yet pointed out said to be endowed with the power of prophecy or "second sight."[2] One instance, which occurred not many years ago in the neighbourhood, is firmly believed in. A farmer and his friend had been enjoying a day's fishing in the Tav, an excellent trouting stream that runs past the old Abbey of Whitland. As evening drew on, the sport grew slack, and at last the trout gave up taking at all, so the sportsmen put up their tackle, said "Goodnight," and departed on their several roads homeward.

The farmer, however, liked a pipe and was stopping with the intention of lighting his, when he became conscious of an indescribable sensation: the air seemed full of sound and yet was perfectly silent. As he stood perplexed, not to say alarmed, strange noises began to issue from the ground, the hill trembled beneath his feet, his pipe dropped from his hand, and he was on the point of running away, when a long whistling shriek accompanied by the sound of a thousand wheels burst from the hillside close behind him. A number of horses feeding close by pricked up their ears and galloped wildly down the hill, jumping right into the bed of the Tav, where they stood panting and frightened until the strange sound died away in the distance.

---

[1] This is extracted from a traveler's sketch of Pendine, Wales, which appeared in the *Once a Week* 11.281 [Nov 12, 1864] p. 575-80. Immediately afterward, Fenton discusses "corpse candles," which involve visions of funeral processions and sometimes burials that *presage* the actual events. In a sense, they—along with the spectral train witnessed by the farmer (and his horses) discussed here—are Ghosts of Things to Come.

[2] The notion that certain groups were proficient in second sight suggests an almost genetic basis. Along with the Welsh, Catherine Crowe says the Scottish Highlanders and the Germans exhibit it—as if the power resides in the gene pools of these ethnic and national groups. She also contends that second sight is passed down through certain families. *The Night Side of Nature; or, Ghosts and Ghost Seers*, (T.C. Newby, 1848) Vol. 1: p. 91 and Vol. 2: p. 328.

From "Beyond Gower's Land"

The farmer did not stay to pick up his pipe, but hurried home, brimful of the wonderful event and under considerable apprehension that some terrible calamity was going to happen to him or his family.

Sometime afterwards, the line for the South Wales Railway was surveyed and a tunnel at last completed, the mouth of which opened at the very spot from whence as was now explained a spectral train had issued, and upon the opening day, the farmer and a crowd of country folk were upon the spot to witness the effect, which certainly exactly answered the description given by him, even to the horses galloping into the Tav.

A couple of old men now living in Pendine positively affirm that they saw a spirit train crossing the plain, but as the bill to enable a company to open a line from Tenby to Narberth has just passed, I fancy there is little chance of this prophecy being fulfilled, at least for many a year.

THE SIGNAL-MAN

CHARLES DICKENS[1]

"Halloa! Below there!"

When he heard a voice thus calling to him, he was standing at the door of his box, with a flag in his hand, furled round its short pole. One would have thought, considering the nature of the ground, that he could not have doubted from what quarter the voice came, but instead of looking up to where I stood on the top of the steep cutting nearly over his head, he turned himself about and looked down the Line. There was something remarkable in his manner of doing so, though I could not have said for my life what. But I know it was remarkable enough to attract my notice, even though his figure was foreshortened and shadowed, down in the deep trench, and mine was high above him, so steeped in the glow of an angry sunset that I had shaded my eyes with my hand before I saw him at all.

"Halloa! Below!"

From looking down the Line, he turned himself about again and, raising his eyes, saw my figure high above him.

"Is there any path by which I can come down and speak to you?"

He looked up at me without replying, and I looked down at him without pressing him too soon with a repetition of my idle question. Just then there came a vague vibration in the earth and air, quickly changing into a violent pulsation, and an oncoming rush that caused me to start back as though it had force to draw me down. When such vapour as rose to my height from this rapid train had passed me and was skimming away over the landscape, I looked down again and saw him re-furling the flag he had shown while the train went by.

I repeated my inquiry. After a pause, during which he seemed

---

[1] This is probably the best-known piece of fiction about a railroad haunting. It was originally part of *Mugby Junction*, an anthology of train-related tales, appearing in one of the Christmas issues of *All the Year Round* [Dec. 10, 1866] pp. 20-25. This magazine was edited by Dickens.

The Signal-Man

to regard me with fixed attention, he motioned with his rolled-up flag towards a point on my level, some two or three hundred yards distant. I called down to him, "All right!" and made for that point. There, by dint of looking closely about me, I found a rough zigzag descending path notched out, which I followed.

The cutting was extremely deep and unusually precipitate. It was made through a clammy stone that became oozier and wetter as I went down. For these reasons, I found the way long enough to give me time to recall a singular air of reluctance or compulsion with which he had pointed out the path.

When I came down low enough upon the zigzag descent to see him again, I saw that he was standing between the rails on the way by which the train had lately passed, in an attitude as if he were waiting for me to appear. He had his left hand at his chin, and that left elbow rested on his right hand, crossed over his breast. His attitude was one of such expectation and watchfulness that I stopped a moment, wondering at it.

I resumed my downward way, and stepping out upon the level of the railroad and drawing nearer to him, I saw that he was a dark, sallow man with a dark beard and rather heavy eyebrows. His post was in as solitary and dismal a place as ever I saw. On either side rose a dripping-wet wall of jagged stone, excluding all view but a strip of sky. The perspective one way was only a crooked prolongation of this great dungeon. The shorter perspective in the other direction terminated in a gloomy red light and the gloomier entrance to a black tunnel, in whose massive architecture there was a barbarous, depressing, and forbidding air. So little sunlight ever found its way to this spot that it had an earthy, deadly smell. So much cold wind rushed through it that it struck chill to me, as if I had left the natural world.

Before he stirred, I was near enough to him to have touched him. Not even then removing his eyes from mine, he stepped back one step and lifted his hand.

This was a lonesome post to occupy, I said, and it had riveted my attention when I looked down from up yonder. A visitor was a rarity, I should suppose—not an unwelcome rarity, I hoped? In me, he merely saw a man who had been shut up within narrow limits all his life and who, being at last set free, had a newly awakened interest in these great works. To such purpose I spoke to him, but I am far from sure of the terms I used, for besides that I am not happy in opening any conversation, there was something in the man that daunted me.

He directed a most curious look towards the red light near the tunnel's mouth and looked all about it—as if something were missing from it—and then he looked at me.

That light was part of his charge? Was it not?

He answered in a low voice, "Don't you know it is?"

The monstrous thought came into my mind, as I perused the fixed eyes and the saturnine face, that this was a spirit, not a man. I have speculated since, whether there may have been infection in his mind.

In my turn, I stepped back. But in making the action, I detected in his eyes some latent fear of me. This put the monstrous thought to flight.

"You look at me," I said, forcing a smile, "as if you had a dread of me."

"I was doubtful," he returned, "whether I had seen you before."

"Where?"

He pointed to the red light he had looked at.

"There?" I said.

Intently watchful of me, he replied without sound, "Yes."

"My good fellow, what should I do there? However, be that as it may, I never was there, you may swear."

"I think I may," he rejoined. "Yes, I am sure I may."

His manner cleared, as did my own. He replied to my remarks with readiness and in well-chosen words. Had he much to do there? Yes—that was to say, he had enough responsibility to bear. But exactness and watchfulness were what was required of him, and of actual work—manual labour—he had next to none. To change that signal, to trim those lights, and to turn this iron handle now and then was all he had to do under that head.

Regarding those many long and lonely hours of which I seemed to make so much, he could only say that the routine of his life had shaped itself into that form, and he had grown used to it. He had taught himself a language down here—if only to know it by sight and to have formed his own crude ideas of its pronunciation could be called learning it. He had also worked at fractions and decimals, and tried a little algebra, but he was, and had been as a boy, a poor hand at figures.

Was it necessary for him when on duty always to remain in that channel of damp air, and could he never rise into the sunshine from between those high stone walls? Why, that depended upon times and circumstances. Under some conditions, there would be less upon the Line than under others, and the same held good as to

The Signal-Man

certain hours of the day and night. In bright weather, he did choose occasions for getting a little above these lower shadows. However, being at all times liable to be called by his electric bell—and at such times listening for it with redoubled anxiety—the relief was less than I would suppose.

He took me into his box, where there was a fire, a desk for an official book in which he had to make certain entries, a telegraphic instrument with its dial, face, and needles, and the little bell of which he had spoken. On my trusting that he would excuse the remark that he had been well educated—and, I hoped I might say without offence, perhaps educated above that station—he observed that instances of slight incongruity in such wise would rarely be found wanting among large bodies of men. He had heard it was so in workhouses, in the police force, even in that last desperate resource, the army. He knew it was so, more or less, in any great railway staff. If I could believe it, sitting in that hut—he scarcely could—he had been a student of natural philosophy and had attended lectures when young. But he had run wild, misused his opportunities, gone down, and never risen again. He had no complaint to offer about that. He had made his bed, and he lay upon it. It was far too late to make another.

All that I have here condensed he said in a quiet manner with his grave, dark regards divided between me and the fire. He threw in the word "sir" from time to time and especially when he referred to his youth—as though to request me to understand that he claimed to be nothing but what I found him. He was several times interrupted by the little bell and had to read off messages and send replies. Once, he had to stand outside the door and display a flag as a train passed and make some verbal communication to the driver. In the discharge of his duties, I observed him to be remarkably exact and vigilant, breaking off his discourse at a syllable and remaining silent until what he had to do was done.

In a word, I should have set this man down as one of the safest of men to be employed in that capacity, but for the circumstance that while he was speaking to me he twice broke off with a fallen colour, turned his face towards the little bell when it did *not* ring, opened the door of the hut (which was kept shut to exclude the unhealthy damp), and looked out towards the red light near the mouth of the tunnel. On both of those occasions, he came back to the fire with the inexplicable air upon him, which I had remarked without being able to define, when we were so far asunder.

Said I, when I rose to leave him, "You almost make me think

that I have met with a contented man." I am afraid I must acknowledge that I said it to lead him on.

"I believe I used to be so," he rejoined in the low voice in which he had first spoken, "but I am troubled, sir. I am troubled."

He would have recalled the words if he could. He had said them, however, and I took them up quickly.

"With what? What is your trouble?"

"It is very difficult to impart, sir. It is very, very difficult to speak of. If ever you make me another visit, I will try to tell you."

"But I expressly intend to make you another visit. Say, when shall it be?"

"I go off early in the morning, and I shall be on again at ten tomorrow night, sir."

"I will come at eleven."

He thanked me and went out at the door with me.

"I'll show my white light, sir," he said in his peculiar low voice, "till you have found the way up. When you have found it, *don't call out!* And when you are at the top, *don't call out!*"

His manner seemed to make the place strike colder to me, but I said no more than, "Very well."

"And when you come down tomorrow night, *don't call out!* Let me ask you a parting question. What made you cry, 'Halloa! Below there!' tonight?"

"Heaven knows," said I. "I cried something to that effect—"

"Not *to that effect,* sir. Those were the *very* words. I know them well."

"Admit those were the very words. I said them, no doubt, because I saw you below."

"For no other reason?"

"What other reason could I possibly have?"

"You had no feeling that they were conveyed to you in any—*supernatural* way?"

"No!"

He wished me goodnight and held up his light. I walked by the side of the down Line of rails—with a very disagreeable sensation of a train coming behind me—until I found the path. It was easier to mount than to descend, and I got back to my inn without any adventure.

Punctual to my appointment, I placed my foot on the first notch of the zigzag next night as the distant clocks were striking eleven. He was waiting for me at the bottom with his white light on.

The Signal-Man

"I have not called out," I said, when we came close together. "May I speak now?"

"By all means, sir."

"Good evening, then, and here's my hand."

"Good evening, sir, and here's mine."

With that we walked side by side to his box, entered it, closed the door, and sat down by the fire.

"I have made up my mind, sir," he began, bending forward as soon as we were seated and speaking in a tone but a little above a whisper, "that you shall not have to ask me twice what troubles me. I took you for someone else yesterday evening. That troubles me."

"That mistake?"

"No. That someone else."

"Who is it?"

"I don't know."

"Like me?"

"I don't know. I never saw the face. The left arm is across the face, and the right arm is waved—violently waved. This way."

I followed his action with my eyes, and it was the action of an arm gesticulating with the utmost passion and vehemence: *For God's sake, clear the way!*

"One moonlight night," said the man, "I was sitting here, when I heard a voice cry, 'Halloa! Below there!' I started up, looked from that door, and saw this *someone else* standing by the red light near the tunnel, waving as I just now showed you. The voice seemed hoarse with shouting, and it cried, 'Look out! Look out!' And then again, 'Halloa! Below there! Look out!' I caught up my lamp, turned it on red, and ran towards the figure, calling, 'What's wrong? What has happened? Where?' It stood just outside the blackness of the tunnel. I advanced so close upon it that I wondered at its keeping the sleeve across its eyes. I ran right up at it and had my hand stretched out to pull the sleeve away, when it was gone."

"Into the tunnel?" said I.

"No. I ran on into the tunnel five hundred yards. I stopped and held my lamp above my head and saw the figures of the measured distance and saw the wet stains stealing down the walls and trickling through the arch. I ran out again faster than I had run in—I have a mortal abhorrence of the place upon me. I looked all around the red light with my own red light, and I went up the iron ladder to the gallery atop of it, and I came down again and ran back here. I telegraphed both ways, 'An alarm has been given. Is anything wrong?' The answer came back, both ways, 'All well.'"

Resisting the slow touch of a frozen finger tracing out my spine, I showed him how this figure must have been a deception of his sense of sight. Such figures, I explained, originate in disease of the delicate nerves that minister to the functions of the eye and are known to have often troubled patients, some of whom had become conscious of the nature of their affliction and had even proved it by experiments upon themselves.

"As to an imaginary cry," said I, "do but listen for a moment to the wind in this unnatural valley while we speak so low and to the wild harp it makes of the telegraph wires."

That was all very well, he returned after we had sat listening for a while, and he ought to know something of the wind and the wires—he who so often passed long winter nights there, alone and watching. But he would beg to remark that he had not finished.

I asked his pardon, and he slowly added these words, touching my arm:

"Within six hours after the Appearance, the memorable accident on this Line happened, and within ten hours, the dead and wounded were brought along through the tunnel over *the spot where the figure had stood.*"

A disagreeable shudder crept over me, but I did my best against it. It was not to be denied, I rejoined, that this was a remarkable coincidence, calculated deeply to impress his mind. But it was unquestionable that remarkable coincidences did continually occur, and they must be taken into account in dealing with such a subject. To be sure, I must admit, I added—for I thought I saw that he was going to bring the objection to bear upon me—men of common sense did not allow much for coincidences in making the ordinary calculations of life.

He again begged to remark that he had not finished.

I again begged his pardon for being betrayed into interruptions.

"This," he said, again laying his hand upon my arm and glancing over his shoulder with hollow eyes, "was just a year ago. Six or seven months passed, and I had recovered from the surprise and shock, when one morning, as the day was breaking, I was standing at the door. I looked towards the red light and saw the spectre again." He stopped with a fixed look at me.

"Did it cry out?"

"No. It was silent."

"Did it wave its arm?"

"No. It leaned against the shaft of the light with both hands before the face. Like this."

Once more, I followed his action with my eyes. It was an action of mourning. I have seen such an attitude in stone figures on tombs.

"Did you go up to it?"

"I came in and sat down, partly to collect my thoughts, partly because it had turned me faint. When I went to the door again, daylight was above me, and the ghost was gone."

"But nothing followed? Nothing came of this?"

He touched me on the arm with his forefinger twice or thrice giving a ghastly nod each time.

"That very day, as a train came out of the tunnel, I noticed at a carriage window on my side what looked like a confusion of hands and heads, and something waved. I saw it just in time to signal the driver: *Stop!* He shut off and put his brake on, but the train drifted past here a hundred and fifty yards or more. I ran after it, and as I went along, I heard terrible screams and cries. A beautiful young lady had died instantaneously in one of the compartments. She was brought in here and laid down on this floor between us."

Involuntarily, I pushed my chair back as I looked from the boards at which he pointed to himself.

"True, sir. True. Precisely as it happened, so I tell it you."

I could think of nothing to say to any purpose, and my mouth was very dry. The wind and the wires took up the story with a long lamenting wail.

He resumed. "Now, sir, mark this, and judge how my mind is troubled. The spectre came back *a week ago*. Ever since, it has been there, now and again, by fits and starts."

"At the light?"

"At the danger-light."

"What does it seem to do?"

He repeated, if possible with increased passion and vehemence, that former gesticulation: *For God's sake, clear the way!* He continued, "I have no peace or rest for it. It calls to me for many minutes together in an agonised manner, 'Below there! Look out! Look out!' It stands waving to me. It rings my little bell—"

I caught at that. "Did it ring your bell yesterday evening when I was here and you went to the door?"

"Twice."

"Why, see," said I, "how your imagination misleads you. My eyes were on the bell and my ears were open to the bell, and if I am a living man, it did *not* ring at those times. No, nor at any other time, except when it was rung in the natural course of physical things by the station communicating with you."

He shook his head. "I have never made a mistake as to that yet, sir. I have never confused the spectre's ring with the man's. The ghost's ring is a strange vibration in the bell that it derives from nothing else, and I have not asserted that the bell stirs to the eye. I don't wonder that you failed to hear it. But *I* heard it."

"And did the spectre seem to be there, when you looked out?"

"It *was* there."

"Both times?"

He repeated firmly: "*Both times.*"

"Will you come to the door with me and look for it now?"

He bit his lower lip as though he were somewhat unwilling, but arose. I opened the door and stood on the step while he stood in the doorway. There was the danger-light. There was the dismal mouth of the tunnel. There were the high, wet stone walls of the cutting. There were the stars above them.

"Do you see it?" I asked him, taking particular note of his face. His eyes were prominent and strained, but not very much more so, perhaps, than my own had been when I had directed them earnestly towards the same spot.

"No," he answered. "It is not there."

"Agreed," said I.

We went in again, shut the door, and resumed our seats. I was thinking how best to improve this advantage, if it might be called one. He then took up the conversation in such a matter-of-course way—so assuming that there could be no serious question of fact between us—that I felt myself placed in the weakest of positions.

"By this time you will fully understand, sir," he said, "that what troubles me so dreadfully is the question, What does the spectre mean?"

I was not sure, I told him, that I did fully understand.

"What is its warning against?" he said, ruminating with his eyes on the fire and only turning them on me by times. "What is the danger? *Where* is the danger? There is danger overhanging somewhere on the Line. Some dreadful calamity will happen. It is not to be doubted this third time, after what has gone before. But surely this is a cruel haunting of me. What can I *do?*"

He pulled out his handkerchief and wiped the drops from his heated forehead.

"If I telegraph danger on either side of me, or on both, I can give no reason for it," he went on, wiping the palms of his hands. "I should get into trouble, and do no good. They would think I was

The Signal-Man

mad. This is the way it would work—Message: 'Danger! Take care!' Answer: 'What Danger? Where?' Message: 'Don't know. But, for God's sake, take care!' They would displace me. What else could they do?"

His pain of mind was most pitiable to see. It was the mental torture of a conscientious man, oppressed beyond endurance by an unintelligible responsibility involving life.

"When it first stood under the danger-light," he went on, pushing his dark hair off of his brow and then pulling his hands outward from his temples again and again in an extremity of feverish distress, "why not tell me where that accident was to happen—if it must happen? Why not tell me how it could be averted—if it could have been averted? When on its second coming, it hid its face. Why not tell me instead, 'She is going to die! Let them keep her at home!' If it came on those two occasions only to show me that its warnings were true—and so to prepare me for the third—why not warn me plainly now? And I, a mere poor signal-man on this solitary station! Lord help me! Why not go to somebody with credit to be believed and power to act?"

When I saw him in this state, I saw that, for the poor man's sake as well as for the public safety, what I had to do was to compose his mind. Therefore, setting aside all question of reality or unreality between us, I represented to him that whoever thoroughly discharged his duty must do well and that at least it was his comfort that he understood his duty, though he did not understand these confounding Appearances. In this effort, I succeeded far better than in the attempt to reason him out of his conviction. He became calm.

The occupations incidental to his post as the night advanced began to make larger demands on his attention. Finally, I left him at two in the morning. I had offered to stay through the night, but he would not hear of it.

That I more than once looked back at the red light as I ascended the pathway—that I did not like the red light and that I should have slept but poorly if my bed had been under it—I see no reason to conceal. Nor did I like the two sequences of the accident and the dead girl. I see no reason to conceal that either.

But what ran most in my thoughts was the consideration how ought I to act, having become the recipient of this disclosure. I had proved the man to be intelligent, vigilant, painstaking, and exact—but how long might he remain so, in his state of mind? Though in a subordinate position, still he held a most important trust, and would I, for instance, like to stake my own life on the chances of his continuing to execute it with precision?

I was unable to overcome a feeling that there would be something treacherous in my communicating what he had told me to his superiors in the Company without first being plain with himself. Instead, I ultimately resolved to propose a middle course to him. Otherwise keeping his secret for the present, I would offer to accompany him to the wisest medical practitioner we could hear of in those parts and to learn his opinion. A change in his time of duty would come round next night, he had apprised me, and he would be off an hour or two after sunrise and on again soon after sunset. I had appointed to return accordingly.

The next evening was a lovely one, and I walked out early to enjoy it. The sun was not yet quite down when I traversed the field-path near the top of the deep cutting. I would extend my walk for an hour, I said to myself, half an hour on and half an hour back, and it would then be time to go to my signal-man's box.

Before pursuing my stroll, I stepped to the brink and mechanically looked down from the point at which I had first seen him. I cannot describe the thrill that seized upon me, when, close to the mouth of the tunnel, I saw the appearance of a man with his left sleeve across his eyes, passionately waving his right arm!

The nameless horror that oppressed me passed in a moment, for in a moment I saw that this appearance of a man was *a man indeed* and that there was a little group of other men, standing at a short distance, to whom he seemed to be rehearsing the gesture he made. The danger-light was not yet lighted. Against its shaft, a little low hut, entirely new to me, had been made of some wooden supports and tarpaulin. It looked no bigger than a bed.

With an irresistible sense that something was wrong—with a flashing, self-reproachful fear that fatal mischief had come of my leaving the man there while bidding no one to be sent to overlook or correct what he did—I descended the notched path with all the speed I could make.

"What is the matter?" I asked the men.

"Signal-man killed this morning, sir."

"Not the man belonging to that box?"

"Yes, sir."

"Not the man I know?"

"You will recognise him, sir, if you knew him," said the man who spoke for the others, solemnly uncovering his own head and raising an end of the tarpaulin. "His face is quite composed."

"Oh, *how* did this happen—how did this *happen?*" I asked, turning from one to another as the hut was closed again.

"He was cut down by an engine, sir. No man in England knew his work better. But somehow he was not clear of the outer rail. It was just at broad day. He had struck the light and had the lamp in his hand. As the engine came out of the tunnel, his back was towards her. She cut him down. That man drove her and was showing how it happened. Show the gentleman, Tom."

The man, who wore a rough, dark uniform, stepped back to his former place at the mouth of the tunnel.

"Coming round the curve in the tunnel, sir," he said, "I saw him at the end like as if I saw him down a perspective-glass. There was no time to check speed, and I knew him to be very careful. As he didn't seem to take heed of the whistle, I shut it off when we were running down upon him. I called to him as loud as I could call."

"What did you say?"

"I said, 'Below there! Look out! *Look out! For God's sake, clear the way!*'"

I started.

"Ah! It was a dreadful time, sir. I never left off calling to him. I put this arm before my eyes not to see, and I waved this arm to the last. But it was no use."

Without prolonging the narrative to dwell on any one of its curious circumstances more than on any other, I may, in closing it, point out the coincidence that the warning of the engine-driver included. They were not only the words which the unfortunate signal-man had repeated to me as haunting him, but also the words which I myself—not he—had attached, and that only in my own mind, to the gesticulation he had imitated.

THE GHOST THAT JIM SAW

BRET HARTE[1]

Why, as to that, said the engineer,
Ghosts ain't things we are apt to fear;
Spirits don't fool with levers much,
And throttle-valves don't take to such;
    And as for Jim,
    What happened to him
Was one half fact, and t'other half whim!

Running one night on the line, he saw
A house—as plain as the moral law—
Just by the moonlit bank, and thence
Came a drunken man with no more sense
    Than to drop on the rail
    Flat as a flail,
As Jim drove by with the midnight mail.

Down went the patents. Steam reversed,
Too late! for there came a "thud." Jim cursed
As the fireman, there in the cab with him,
Kinder stared in the face of Jim,
    And says, "What now?"
    Says Jim, "What now!
I've just run over a man—that's how!"

The fireman stared at Jim. They ran
Back, but they never found house nor man—
Nary a shadow within a mile.
Jim turned pale, but he tried to smile,

---

[1] This poem comes from Harte's poetry collection *Echoes of the Foothills* (James R. Osgood, 1875) pp. 93-97.

The Ghost that Jim Saw

   Then on he tore
   Ten mile or more,
In quicker time than he'd made afore.

Would you believe it! The very next night
Up rose that house in the moonlight white,
Out comes the chap and drops as before,
Down goes the brake and the rest encore,
   And so, in fact,
   Each night that act
Occurred, till folks swore Jim was cracked.

Humph! let me see; it's a year now, 'most,
That I met Jim, East, and says, "How's your ghost?"
"Gone," says Jim; "and more, it's plain
That ghost don't trouble me again.
   I thought I shook
   That ghost when I took
A place on an Eastern line—but look!

"What should I meet, the first trip out,
But the very house we talked about,
And the selfsame man! 'Well,' says I, 'I guess
It's time to stop this 'yer foolishness.'
   So I crammed on steam,
   When there came a scream
From my fireman—that jest broke my dream.

"'You've killed somebody!' Says I, 'Not much!
I've been thar often, and thar ain't no such,
And now I'll prove it!' Back we ran,
And—darn my skin!—but thar *was* a man
   On the rail, dead,
   Smashed in the head!—
Now I call that meanness!" That's all Jim said.

UNDER THE SHEER-LEGS

HENRY TINSON[1]

I never heard of a man who had seen a ghost on a railway, till the instance which I am about to relate, though I don't know why ghosts should not be as plentiful on railways as anywhere else. Having for many years been assistant storekeeper at the London end of the Direct Meridian, I consider the locality of a locomotive depot favourable for ghosts. The long gloomy sheds and empty workshops, with uncouth machinery lying about and enormous engines imperfectly seen in the dim light, were after dark as vague and full of mystery as any old monastery or castle could ever be. In addition, it was difficult to put your foot on a spot where some poor fellow had not been killed or where, if an old hand as I was, you could not remember to have spoken to some stalwart driver or fireman before he started on the journey from which he never came back. Yet we had no ghosts about the place.

In a few years, we had a great change on the Direct Meridian: one of our principals retired, and his successor was a man who had risen from the ranks. Now this rising from the ranks is all very fine in theory, but on a railway at any rate, it does not answer. The men dislike serving under their old mates, who when promoted are often tyrants, taking a delight in going into a thousand little matters which a gentleman would never notice, and making the service almost intolerable. Otherwise, they are good kindly men enough, but obliged to see with others' eyes and hear with others' ears. Our new chief was one of the latter description. He was a most amiable man who did more mischief among his staff and whose name was used to sanction more injustice in the first twelve months after his appointment than would probably have been the case under a martinet in seven years.

Our station, being in London, was of course a very important

---

[1] This short story was published in *The St. James Magazine and United Empire Review* 2 [Christmas, 1875] pp. 41-47.

one, and a new superintendent was sent, by name Youles. He, too, had risen from the ranks, and the men who had fancied the previous "gaffer"—as chiefs are called on railways—a strict hand, soon found the difference, to their cost. The worst feature about this new master was his treachery. He would talk to the drivers in a hearty "hail fellow, well-met" sort of way that at first made them think there never was such a man, and he would promise his influence to get them everything they wanted.

But engine-drivers are a shrewd class, and it was soon found that, no matter what Youles said, if he did not have his own way or was not sufficiently cringed to, there was always some difficulty—never seeming to arise from him, however—which postponed a man's requests or got him into serious trouble. The old drivers, a set of north-countrymen, didn't care for him or any living thing, and would as soon have gone and told the Board of his tyranny as have smoked their pipes. This he knew, and so he avoided them accordingly. Towards the younger or more timid drivers, however, he was both deceitful and severe.

Sim Ferne suffered about the most from him. Sim was a poor, easy-tempered, nervous fellow, exactly the sort of man that Youles could terrorise. I am within bounds when I say that for three months Sim, who was a goods driver, never made a trip that he was not found fault with and bullied, for Youles did not feel it necessary to be smooth-faced with him. His nature was to bully, and he indulged it with all those he could frighten. And he did frighten Sim. I have seen the poor fellow wipe the tears from his eyes with the clean cotton waste I had just given him when about to start with his train. He has said, "Mr. Syres, he means my ruin. I shall be sacked without a character,[2] and then what will become of my children?" He had five very pretty little children, and when he used to see the three elder toddle off to Sunday school while he took the other two for a bit of a walk, I think he was the proudest and happiest of engine-drivers. Of course, I did my best to cheer him up, but everybody knew that what he said was true and that, do what he would, he would never do right.

At last, poor Sim took to drinking and came on duty once or twice obviously the worse for "beer." Youles positively chuckled at this. If the driver had gotten into scrapes before, you may be sure he did not keep out of them now. He learnt from a youth, Bill

---

[2] In other words, his employment would be terminated without his being given a character reference. These references usually came in the form of letters of recommendation, and Victorian society put a high value on them.

Soames's son—Bill Soames was another driver, and his boy was in the office with Mr. Youles—that his train tickets had a closer examination than those of the other drivers and that every trivial discrepancy in his entries was looked into and censured. With others, except a few timid fellows like himself, they were passed over.

It was dreadful to see how nervous Sim grew. His fireman has told me, over and over again, how he would sob like a child while talking of the persecution he suffered, how he would wish he was dead, and how he offered up strange wild prayers while on the journey.

It would take me too long to tell all the mischief Youles worked among the men and the dislike and dread everybody came to have of him. As storekeeper, I did not come much in contact with him, and so long as I kept things pretty straight, he had not much temptation to meddle with me. Things had gone on in this manner for some months. Two of our drivers had been dismissed, two or three had left for other lines, and many had been fined. Among the latter was Sim, who had been fined so repeatedly for coming on duty intoxicated that he would have been discharged, only Youles liked to play with a mouse before he killed it.

I remember very well one wet and windy afternoon about the beginning of February, when Sim came into my office for his stores, as he was booked to take out the 6.5 train. He had been drinking as usual, and I saw, in the pocket of the rough jacket he wore over his slop, a small bottle I knew he had lately been carrying full of gin. I was getting his stores together, when young Soames ran in with a message for me from Mr. Youles.

"Hollo, Sim!" he exclaimed, seeing the driver. "You are in for it again. Mr. Youles will be down on you this time."

"He *always* is down on me," said Sim. "I often wish I was a convict—or that he was."

"Well," said the young one, "I saw a letter on his desk, half-finished, to the chief. He is reporting you nicely, and I expect you'll have the sack. I'm off early tonight, for I'm going to the play." And with that the youngster scampered away.

Poor Sim said nothing, but looked at me as if he would look me *through*. I have seen but one man hanged, and I will take care to never see another. The look the poor wretch had given all around him when he came upon the scaffold was just like the desperate, hopeless look Sim Ferne gave me then. He went off to his engine, for he was always early. He did all he could to keep straight with his masters, and was often in the shed twenty minutes before his fireman, although it was the latter's duty to be there first.

About five-and-twenty minutes or perhaps half an hour after this, just as I was thinking of locking up, one of our fitters ran in. His face as white as a sheet.

"Mr. Syres!—" he exclaimed. "By George!— Mr. Youles is *killed!* He is smashed to bits at the end of the shops!"

Staying for nothing after hearing this, I ran out of the stores with no need to ask where the accident was, for every man and boy was running out of the shops towards the sheer-legs. The "sheer-legs" is an enormous tripod formed of three massive poles, united at the top and strong enough to bear our heaviest engines. When repairs to the lower parts of those engines are needed, they are slung under the legs by powerful chains, resting only on their fore or hind wheels as the case may be. These chains are worked by a "crab," which is easily turned by a couple of men at the handles. When the end of the engine is hauled up as high as is wanted, a bolt or pin is thrust into the wheel of the crab, which holds it from running down.

It was pitch dark, of course, but the lanterns from the shed and the portable gas lamps from the shops showed a crowd of sixty or seventy grimy fellows round the "legs." The foremen were shouting their directions, and everyone seemed scared. They made way for me, however, and I saw at once what had happened.

Mr. Youles had got under the engine, which was easy enough to do, probably to examine it. By some unaccountable mischance, the pin of the crab had given way. The tremendous weight of the locomotive—the *Mastodon,* one of our heaviest goods engines—had fallen upon him and crushed him to death at once. The front wheels were off, and it was the chimney end which had come down with such a fearful run. While the body of Mr. Youles was utterly smashed, strangely enough, his head—with its staring eyes and bushy red whiskers—protruded from under the framing and seemed to be looking at us with a horrible grin about the mouth, a grin which almost turned me sick.

The first thing to be done was to lift the engine. A couple of powerful "screwjacks," as they are termed, were at once placed under it, near the hind wheels. The foremen were busy in directing the labourers and keeping the crowd back when the time keeper and I left.

We thought we might as well go into the deadman's office to see that nothing of consequence was lying about and to lock the room. It appeared that, before Mr. Youles had gone his usual round, he had been burning his papers, for there was not a scrap of a letter of any kind, whether written or received by him, to be seen on his desk. In the fender, quite cold and black, was a heap of tinder which had recently been paper. This we noticed, and after locking the office door, we went home.

At the inquest, no one could account for the bolt slipping from the cogs. The general opinion was that it had not been pushed fairly home by the fitters who lifted the engine. This they strenuously denied, arguing that it would not have held all day unless they had done so. It was suggested, in reply, that any accidental jar might have loosened it a little and then the immense weight of the engine had pulled it down. At any rate, there was no doubt how Mr. Youles was killed, and a verdict of "Accidental death" was returned.

Nothing was ever heard of the report against Ferne, and while the new superintendent had his own likings and dislikings, as they all have, he did not meddle much with Sim. I saw the latter pretty often, for he had to come to me for his stores, and I was of the same opinion with the men—that Sim was going mad. Not only did he drink as much as before, but he grew very wild in his talk, and this not from drink. From some cause or other, the liquor he took never seemed to affect him now as it had once done. He never seemed tipsy, and although he talked strangely, it was not as a drunken man talks.

You could always excite him by speaking of Youles. I have said that Ferne was a quiet, timid fellow, and he was so, more than any man I ever saw. But if anyone mentioned our late gaffer, Ferne would rave about him, cursing and swearing so that it turned my very blood, though I had heard a good deal of bad language in my time. But strangest of all was the queer way in which he used to mutter to himself about the dead master. When anything started the subject accidentally, he would go on growling and muttering as if he could see Youles standing by his side. At last, from one thing and another, poor Ferne, instead of being the most popular man about the place, became to be so disliked and avoided that none of his mates cared to speak to him. This hurt him very much, I could see, but it was not to be wondered at.

The only man who really stuck to him was his fireman, Dick Farmer. Ferne had once done Dick a great service, and Dick never forgot it. In proportion, these two grew more friendly. In fact, the fireman twice fought men in the field at the back of our engine shed for insulting Sim. Neither of his antagonists came to work for a week afterwards.

Well, things had gone on much as usual for, I suppose, eight or nine months, when, on a drizzling, miserable December evening, I had to take a message to the coke-stage, which was about a quarter of a mile below my stores. Coming back, I had to pass the sheer-legs to the back of the shops. It was about six o'clock, and the drizzling rain was blown in my face by a bitter wind. It was very dark, too, but so many lights were about that no part was so black but that you could see to pick your way and see the wet glistening on the metals. I had just reached the corner of the shops, when an irresistible impulse made me turn round to look at the sheer-legs. I had passed them just before, and they were not more than fifty yards from where I stood. I knew that an engine was half suspended there, as was nearly always the case, but something made me turn round again. I saw the gigantic beams very distinctly, for a grate full of coals was burning close by, lighted for some men who were coming to work on the rails, and the sheer-legs were between me and the glare.

There hung the black, enormous locomotive, and below it—just where the front wheels had been—stood a man in a tall hat and a long great coat. I started with surprise, for the figure had not been there a moment before, as I could have sworn. There was something so horribly familiar in its outline that, after I had instinctively moved towards it, I recoiled in terror. I was collected enough, though I felt the drops of cold sweat on my forehead, to remember how accidental combinations of familiar objects, or changes in their position, had often imposed upon and terrified men. I moved first to the right, and then to the left, to see if by so doing I disturbed the figure. Not a bit—it was there still. As I looked, it took off its hat and passed its hand through its hair with a manner that was the manner of Mr. Youles, who was killed. Yes, the figure *was* Mr. Youles, as I had known him many months before. There he stood beneath the engine, looking up at the monstrous mass hanging above him, just as Youles must have looked up a moment before the iron avalanche crushed him.

So certain was I it was Youles, and so certain at the same time it could *not* be him, that I feared my brain was affected. I turned my eyes away from the sight with the same difficulty that a bird, as we are told, turns from the gaze of a serpent. I was conscious that I staggered in my walk. Then a voice on the bank by my side aroused me, a voice I almost dreaded lest my imagination had conjured up another spectre.

"Well, Mr. Syres, you have seen him at last, then?"

The voice was that of Sim Ferne, and it broke the spell. I looked round again, and there hung the locomotive. There the tall legs reared themselves. But all was dark, motionless, and void beneath them. Sim was descending a path down the slope, one by which the drivers often came to their work, and as I looked up at him, I saw he was perfectly sober and serious.

"Seen whom, Sim?" I exclaimed, feeling as I spoke that I would rather have met anyone rather than Ferne at that moment.

"Seen Youles, sir," returned the driver.

"Why, what do you mean?" I asked, not at all liking to own what I thought I had seen.

"Don't be offended, sir," continued Sim, "if I say that it is of no use your trying to deceive me. Youles walks there every night, I believe. I have seen him twenty times at least, but I did not think that any other eyes than mine *could* see him."

"Why not, Ferne? Why should you—" I began.

Without seeming conscious of what I was saying, he resumed: "He means something, Mr. Syres, depend upon it, by his showing himself to a second party. It is a warning. I always come this way when it is my turn to take my train after dark, because if I did not come and see him at the legs, I know he would come and see me."

"My good fellow," I said, "you are ill. You are not fit to take out your train. Go home now, lay up a day or two, and you will get your mind to rights."

"Is *your* mind wrong, Mr. Syres?" returned Ferne. "You know what you saw just now, and you are above denying it, sir. You are quite aware that you saw Youles under the engine. So did I—and, curse him! it is not the first time I have seen him there, the cowardly brute, and well he knows it. But I am all right. Goodnight, sir. Don't you forget that I said it was a warning."

He disappeared behind the building, and I returned to the stores, dwelling more on his strange manner and stranger words than even on the mysterious appearance which I had witnessed. I determined to question Sim a little more when he fetched his stores.

But his fireman came for them. We spoke as I was attending to him.

Dick said, "It is a queer job, this about the engines, sir. I wish we had knowed it earlier."

"What is wrong about them, Farmer?" I asked.

"Why, don't you know they have changed our engines?" exclaimed the man. "The *Colossus* has got a leaky tube, and so they have given us the *Mastodon*—the engine that killed Mr. Youles."

"Good Heaven!" I ejaculated, almost involuntarily.

"Yes, it's very unlucky," continued the fireman. "If I had knowed it before, Sim should never have—" Here, he checked himself as though afraid of saying too much. Bidding me goodnight, he left.

I left, too, almost immediately after. I had some doubt about telling my wife what I had seen. However, I decided upon doing so and found she considered it, using the very words of Ferne, *a warning*. As for myself, I hardly knew what to think of it all and lay awake half the night, nervous and excited.

In the morning, I went to work. I was passing the policeman at the gate.

He said, "A bad job, Mr. Syres, about poor Ferne."

"Why, what has happened?" I returned, and I felt myself trembling all over.

"*Killed,* sir, last night before he had got twenty miles on the road. He was under the engine, oiling her—for she had not been running for some time before—while they were in the goods siding at Baybridge, and by some accident which nobody can understand, she slipped forward a little. The connecting-rod struck him on the head and, of course, killed him directly."

I stopped to hear no more, but went on to the stores, where everyone was full of the accident. In the course of the morning, Farmer returned, another driver and fireman having gone on with the train.

Dick was very much distressed at the loss of his comrade, concerning whose death he gave just the same account as I had already heard. He could only suggest in explanation that the train, having been brought to a stand on an incline, some of the hinder trucks might have slipped a little and so given an impetus which moved everything slightly. This theory was eventually adopted at the inquest.

Farmer soon afterwards gave notice to leave, as he had obtained an engagement on an Indian railway, where he did very well. In fact, he was a first-rate hand and is now a foreman on the line he joined.

I had never mentioned to him what I had seen.

Just before he had left, however, Dick came to me to say that poor Sim had spoken a good deal about me on the last trip. He had said that I had seen the ghost of Youles.

I admitted this as I was sure there was more to be told.

Dick went on to say that, from the moment Sim found he was to drive the *Mastodon,* he coupled that fact with my having seen the ghost and made up his mind that he should never come back alive. If he really were killed, Dick was to be at liberty to tell me—as the only other person to whom the spirit of Youles had appeared—what Dick had long known: Sim had, in a fit of desperation, caused the death of the superintendent.

Sim had seen him standing under the engine, examining it with his lamp. No one was near, and all his insults and tyranny rushing at once into the driver's excited mind, he pulled out the bolt from the crab and let the engine down with a run. He had then gone into the office and burnt every scrap of writing he could see on Youles's table, so that nothing should remind his successor of the report against himself.

All this Dick had long known, but he would assuredly rather have died than reveal it, save at Sim's desire. Even now, it was perfectly clear that he failed to see any great harm in the murder of Mr. Youles.

I kept the secret until I left the line. I now venture to tell it and to declare—doubt it who may—that I have seen a railway ghost.

A RAILROAD GHOST

ANONYMOUS[1]

An Amsterdam (N.Y.) telegram says: Excitement runs high at Canaoharie, owing to the nightly appearance of a ghostly, mysterious light along the Central railroad track. The light starts from the old fort and is at first very small. It gradually increases in size and goes down the railroad track about three feet from the ground. The night watchmen say that a hand can be distinguished about it. Sometimes, the light goes bounding down the track and again rises thirty feet in the air. Several trains, including the Atlantic Express, have been stopped by the light, believing it to be a danger-signal. It appears about 10:30 p.m., just before the arrival of the fast mail.

Fifty persons lay in ambush in the vicinity recently in hopes of ferreting out the matter, but the light did not appear, but the night watchman and others vouch for the truth of its appearance. Usually railroad men are filled with fear and superstition and dread to approach the spot at night. Some say it is a forewarning of a railroad horror to be enacted in the vicinity.

---

[1] This report appeared in the *Wood County Reporter,* Sept. 6, 1883, p. 2. This newspaper was published in Grand Rapids, Wisconsin.

A PHANTOM TRAIN

ANONYMOUS[1]

"You ask if I have ever had an adventure on the railroad that would be interesting to the readers of the *Age*. I could wish you had left that question unasked, for it calls up an occurrence that for fifteen long years I have been doing my best to forget."

The engineer who made this remark is one of the oldest engineers running into Birmingham. His train had just pulled into the union depot, and the reporter had mounted the engine, which was being leisurely run into the round house. The engineer was attired in rough garments common to the guild while on duty. Underneath the tight-fitting cap perched on his head could be seen a plentiful sprinkling of gray hairs, betokening the decline of life.

"I would like to hear the story," insinuated the reporter as he seated himself in the cab and drew out his notebook and pencil, the time-honored though chestnutty earmarks of his profession.

"Well, you shall have it, although it is something I would willingly forget. But it seems impossible. Fifteen years ago, I was running on the East Tennessee road, between Knoxville and Chattanooga. The scenery between these two points is grand at points, the mountains being in sight nearly the entire distance. I had left Knoxville an hour late one afternoon in November, and at London, the telegraph operator handed me an order to make up the lost time as there was a large southern excursion onboard who wanted to make connection at Chattanooga for Atlanta.

"I had always been ranked as one of the coolest men on the road, as a man who never got excited, and I once ran over a burning trestle without a muscle changing. Yet this afternoon I was strangely nervous. For the first time in my life, I discovered I had nerves.

---

[1] Reprinted from the *Birmingham Age*, an Alabama newspaper, this interview appeared in Nebraska's *Omaha Daily Bee*, Oct. 23, 1888, p. 6. I also found it in New York's *The Sun*, Nov. 4, 1888, p. 7, and the *Chicago Tribune*, Nov. 5, 1888, p. 13. In the 1800s, it was common for newspapers to reprint articles from each other. In this way, ghost stories spread more widely than by word-of-mouth.

A Phantom Train

"'Jack,' I said to the fireman, 'I am all in a tremor. I am not superstitious, but I feel as if something was going to happen.'

"Jack burst into a loud guffaw. 'Why, cap'n, you nervous? That is too good,' and he laughed again.

"I said nothing else, but the uncomfortable feeling continued. I did not know it at the time, but I have since found out that even the iron nerves of an engineer must break down some time.

"Jack, in the meantime, was piling up coal in the furnace. 'Cap'n, you are cold,' he remarked after a few minutes' intermission. 'We'll have a better fire, and we'll be in Chattanooga in a jiffy.'

"The grim November twilight hung over the earth like a pall. We had passed Athens, and with only fifty-six miles to go to reach our destination. For the first time since I mounted an engine, I longed for the trip to end. I was looking straight ahead, where the iron bands far down the track seemed to unite into a single rail, when I was startled by an exclamation from Jack.

"'*Cap'n,*' he screamed, 'look there, my God, *look there!*' He was pointing with a trembling hand to the east, where in the distance the mountains loomed up grim and bare in their awful grandeur. The look of horror on the poor fellow's face was indescribable. But the sight I witnessed as I quickly turned my eyes to the east was enough to freeze the warm blood which courses through your veins, for there, above the mountain tops with a terrible distinctness, sailed a phantom engine drawing a phantom train. The puffs of smoke came regularly from the engine. I could see the glaring headlight, the lights in the coaches, all as plain as if the train was running on the side track by us. I stood there watching the strange sight too amazed to utter a word—how long I cannot say—but suddenly it disappeared, and I was recalled to myself by several jerks at the bell rope made by the conductor.

"I looked out and saw that we were at Cleveland.

"'What's the matter with you?' asked the conductor, coming to the engine. 'What do you mean by trying to run by Cleveland that way?' After a moment, he caught a glimpse of my face and added, 'Why, man, you look as if you had seen a *ghost!*'

"I looked at my watch and saw that it was exactly 6 o'clock. We had made up half an hour, and we pulled into Chattanooga an hour later, only a few minutes behind time.

"From the time of the appearance of the apparition to the time we pulled into the round house at Chattanooga, Jack had not spoken a word, but there was a fixed look on his face I did not like.

The affair was not discussed between us. Jack was strangely taciturn, and to tell the truth, I did not feel inclined to talk about the strange scene in the clouds.

"There is not a great deal more to tell. The run to Knoxville the next day was made without anything occurring worthy of comment. But on the return trip to Chattanooga on Friday, two days after we had seen the apparition—at 5:57 in the afternoon and two miles east of Cleveland—a wild freight thundered into us. I saw it too late to do any good, but I reversed my engine and then jumped. I happened to jump on the right side and escaped with a broken finger.

"But Jack, poor boy, had chosen the wrong side, and the immense locomotive crushed him to a jelly. I firmly believe that the accident happened at the very spot where Jack first saw the phantom engine and at the very minute, although two days later. Poor Jack, the discoverer of that wonderful sight, the warning was evidently intended for him.

"I did not make another run on that fated line. I asked to be excused from duty pending the investigation made by officials into the accident, and on the day the investigation was concluded and I was exonerated from blame, I walked into the superintendent's office and asked for my time.

"'You needn't feel badly about that accident,' remarked the superintendent kindly.

"'I don't,' I replied, 'but my nerves are shattered, and I want to change my location.'

"I saw a smile on the superintendent's face as I mentioned my 'nerves,' but he gave me my time without word. I spent five years in the Rockies in the vain attempt to drive that picture from my mind. Finally, I came back east, but the photographic camera could not fix an object more firmly than did the phantom engine in the mountains of Tennessee fix itself in my memory. I am only forty-five now, but you can see how gray I am. My hair was not turned white 'in a single night,' as the novelists tell, but in a few months after the occurrence, the change was effected as I used to think and worry over it a good deal, and that, too, when I was only thirty years of age."

For some minutes, the engine had been standing still in the yard, but the reporter did not notice when it stopped, so thrilling was the veteran engineer's story.

AN INTERPOSITION

SARAH G. RIKER[1]

There are people who sneer at the efforts of societies for psychical research. I don't.

There are persons who are always having either dreams that contain revelations or see apparitions or are conscious of something about to happen that *does* happen. I have no confidence in these people. If I believed in them, it would argue that in their makeup there is something especially amenable to some hidden law. But my own experience disproves this. I have had a manifestation—I know of no better name for it—of more consequence than any of these of which I have heard, yet I have had but *one* in all my life.

And this experience of mine, having come but once to me, in addition to indicating that my being is not unusually susceptible to such influences, points to the fact that others, either living or dead, do interfere at times in the current of our lives.

But it is not my intention to deliver a lecture. I propose to tell a story. I am a bachelor. I live at a club, associate almost entirely with men, and have no thought of marriage, and I may state here that I never expect to be married. I do expect, however, in another existence to be psychically united with one who will be, to me, my other self.

I was traveling and had been traveling for several days with but few and rather short stops. The season was summer, the time of day evening. My conveyance was a railroad train. I was sitting by an open window, looking out upon the fields flying by to the music of the car wheels dropping from the end of one rail and jumping onto another.

A favorite occupation of mine on a train has always been to imagine someone swimming along beside the train through the fields of grain that often line the track. On this occasion, we were passing numerous such fields, and my image of fancy was

---

[1] This short story comes from Maine's *The Ellsworth American,* March 2, 1910, p. 6. As with the article immediately before this, it was reprinted in several newspapers across the U.S. (along with its rather abrupt ending).

swimming along lustily. But as the twilight faded and objects were lost to view, lulled by the rattle of the train, I dropped asleep.

When I awakened, a train was beside the one I was on, moving in the same direction and going at the same rate of speed. Indeed, so exactly alike was the velocity of the two trains that I could see no gain or loss whatever to the train beside me. The window sashes of both trains were raised, and I could see the people of the other train, some reading, some lounging, some talking together.

But my attention was fixed on a lady who sat at the window opposite me. Her sash was up as well as mine, so that there was no obstacle, either transparent or opaque, between us. The distance between her and me, I suppose, was about three feet. She was looking at me with an expression on her face—especially in her eyes—that I never saw in anyone before and have never seen since, but I can't describe it. While I looked, she spoke to me.

"Leave the train at the next station and follow me," she said.

She put out her hand, but before I could grasp it, the two trains separated. In another moment, the one in which the lady sat seemed to enter a tunnel while mine went on in the open.

So vividly impressed was I that, when we slowed up a few minutes later, I took my grip[2] and, when the train stopped at a station, I stepped out. After a moment's delay, it went on and left me standing on the platform in a very singular mental condition.

"Will another train be along soon?" I asked of a station man.

"From the west?"

"No—from the east."

"No train from the east for four hours."

I was puzzled. I had been coming eastward.

"Is this track double beyond the station?" I asked presently.

"No double track on this line."

"What?"

"Single track from here both ways, all the way to the terminals."

An uncanny feeling came over me. I had seen a train on a track beside me, talked with a woman on that train, and had obeyed her instructions.

As soon as I could recover myself, I walked in a half-dazed condition into the station and sat down. I remember nothing but a clicking of a telegraph instrument. How long I sat there I don't know, but when I came to my usual consciousness, it was at hearing the telegraph operator cry out to a man outside:

"Great heavens! No. 23 has been wrecked on the bridge above!

---

[2] A "grip" is a mid-sized traveling case.

Bridge let the whole train down, with a terrible loss of life!"

Here was more to intensify that feeling of awe that had taken possession of me. A phantom woman on a phantom train had warned me of a real railroad accident in which I should probably have been killed.

From that day to this, I have treasured an image in my heart—the woman real, spiritual, or creation of my own brain. I have a theory of who she is or was. When I was a child, I played with a little girl who died. Did I discern anything in the features of the woman to remind me of the child? No. A grown woman bears little resemblance to a child. But would the spiritual child grow after death? Not bodily, yet, appearing to me, I might expect that she would show herself as she would have been, had she lived.

SECOND STATION:

PHANTOM TRAINS

THE PHANTOM TRAIN: THE DEAD LINCOLN'S YEARLY TRIP OVER THE NEW YORK CENTRAL RAILROAD

ANONYMOUS[1]

A writer in the Albany (N.Y.) *Evening Times* relates a conversation with a superstitious night watchman on the New York Central railroad. Said the watchman: "I believe in spirits and ghosts. I know such things exist. If you will come up in April, I will convince you." He then told of the phantom train that every year comes up the road with the body of Abraham Lincoln.

Regularly, in the month of April, about midnight, the air on the track becomes very keen and cutting. On either side, it is warm and still. Every watchman, when he feels this air, steps off the track and sits down to watch. Soon after, the pilot engine—with long black streamers and a band with black instruments playing dirges, grinning skeletons sitting all about—will pass up noiselessly, and the very air grows black. If it is moonlight, clouds always come over the moon, and the music seems to linger as if frozen with horror.

A few moments after, the train glides by. Flags and the streamers hang about. The track seems covered with a black carpet, and the wheels are draped with the same. The coffin of the murdered Lincoln is seen lying on the center of a car, and all about it in the air and on the train behind are vast numbers of blue-coated men, some with coffins on their backs, others leaning on them. It seems then that all the vast armies of men that died during the war are escorting the phantom train of the President. The wind, if

---

[1] This report was printed in South Carolina's *The Charleston Daily News,* Nov. 7, 1872, p. 3. It appeared in other newspapers, too, traveling as far as Portland, Oregon's *The New Northwest,* Dec. 6, 1872, p. 1. As mentioned in my Introduction, there are earlier reports of phantom trains, but this one—said to commemorate the anniversary of conveying Abraham Lincoln's body to his burial place in Springfield, Illinois—is certainly among the most famous.

blowing, dies away at once, and over all the air a solemn hush, almost stifling, prevails. If a train were passing, its noise would be drowned in the silence, and the phantom train would ride over it.

Clocks and watches always stop, and when looked at are found to be from five to eight minutes behind. Everywhere on the road, about the 27th of April, the time of watches and trains is found suddenly behind. This, said the leading watchman, was from the passage of the phantom train.

THE PHANTOM TRAIN;
OR, THE TUNNEL CLERK

ANONYMOUS[1]

"And I suppose you stopped to have a word with Uncle Ben as you came by," she said, turning over the letters.

"I only nodded a good-evening, but I mean to have a chat as I go back, if it's not too dark."

She laughed gaily. "Why, you're not afraid to go home after dark, are you? We don't have highwaymen hereabouts."[2]

"No, but I don't like to walk down the track unless I can see a very long distance ahead. After you descend the cut, it's a quarter of a mile to Uncle Ben's little house, you know, and how should I get out of the way if a train came by!"

She looked up at the big round-faced clock. "The freight passes down at eight, which will be in five minutes, and then the track is clear till nine, when the Express comes."

I shook my head dubiously. "Well, Miss Bessie, that may be very true, but I have a very well-defined dread of railroad tracks in the night, and you know there might be a special or something. In fact, it's much safer to avoid all possible danger."

She had found my letter by this time and now handed it over, and I made ready to leave.

This Miss Bessie, I should explain, was Miss Fenwick, who kept the post-office, ticket-office, store, and what not at the Glenrose Cut, as it was called, and was certainly a very charming young lady. I had been in the country about a month, keeping bachelor's hall in the woods and having a pleasant time altogether. But I had never yet missed my mail, and in this way, Miss Fenwick and I had become excellent friends.

---

[1] This short story was published in *Frank Leslie's Pleasant Hours* 21.3 [Oct., 1876] pp. 182-85.

[2] "Highwaymen" refers to robbers who typically rode on horseback and stole from travelers.

Uncle Ben, of whom she had spoken, was the tunnel clerk who passed nearly all his time at the mouth of the Glenrose tunnel, which began exactly where the open cut ended. She called him "Uncle," but he was no relation to her whatever—only the daughter of his old friend, Martin Fenwick, who had been killed years before in the tunnel—and about this people sometimes whispered a very melancholy story.

I went toward the door and just reached it, when Miss Fenwick called me back.

"Mr. Bruce, *please* say a word or two to Uncle Ben as you pass him. You can't imagine how lonely he is sometimes, and he likes you so very much, and he will appreciate it so much if you stop and chat with him for a minute."

There was a peculiar earnestness in her pleading that impressed me strongly. I felt that she was quite right, for the old man must be very lonely there, indeed, and it would be ungenerous in me, with so much idle time on my hands, to neglect her request. I consented at once.

"Certainly, Miss Bessie. You are quite sure there will be no train till nine, after the freight passes?"

"Hark!" she cried, listening as a whistle a short distance away shrieked twice. "Here is the freight now."

And then, almost in the same minute, with ponderous rumble and roar, the train flashed by.

"No other train now till the Express at nine," she continued. "There used to be an eight-thirty a great while ago, but it was abolished. Poor papa, I've heard, was killed on that train." She smiled sadly. "I'm glad it doesn't exist any longer, for whenever it came by, I should always be thinking of him. You *will* stop and sit with Uncle Ben, then? I am so glad, Mr. Bruce, for lately he has been in such low spirits and acting a little strange, and—and sometimes I am afraid he will drink a little brandy to cheer himself up. And you know brandy never does anybody any *real* good, does it?"

"Rarely, I'm afraid. But don't be disturbed, Miss Bessie—I mean to have quite a chat with Uncle Ben, and so goodnight. Don't worry about *anything*."

I took the side of the cut, going through cornfields and orchards, till I reached the declivity which led to the tunnel. Descending this brought me upon the track. It was quite dark, and I naturally experienced my usual nervous feeling as I walked along between the rails—a sort of cold chill in the back, as if a train were coming behind me.

There was a light in the little house where Uncle Ben passed his time. The windows were up, and I could just see the top of his gray head.

For a second, after stealing cautiously up, I watched him. He was sitting by the telegraphic instrument, which was whispering to itself in the usual manner. His legs were crossed, and his hands were in his pockets. He was looking down intently, thinking—thinking as deeply as man could.

But there was something else there, too—a black bottle and a common tumbler—and was there not a clouded stare in his eyes as he pondered and a flush upon his forehead and cheek?

I rapped on the windowsill, and he started and glanced across. He seemed amazed at the sight of me.

"Good evening," he said. "Come in. Bless me, you're the first visitor I ever had at this time o' night, and—*ha, ha!*—I was almost disposed to take you at first for a—" and he crossed the threshold.

When I was seated, I explained that Miss Fenwick had mentioned his loneliness, and I thought there really must be a great deal of truth in her conjecture, judging especially from his remark as I entered.

He laughed a little oddly, then sighed and poured some brandy from the bottle into the glass.

"Lonely enough sometimes, indeed," he said, "but here's a lively companion, if you like his society, you know. Try him, and judge for yourself."

I declined, whereupon he added a few drops more to the liquor and drank it himself. Then he fell to chatting very rapidly and with a strange, incoherent merriment. He told me many things of his solitary life. But I was not interested. I was troubled, for I could see that, though the man was not absolutely tipsy, he was peculiarly affected by the liquor—affected as men are who use it habitually and are not at any time either sober or drunk. Upon this topic of drinking, I began cautiously to question him, and it came out that he had employed stimulants, I gathered *immoderately,* for the last three months, and then I felt sorry enough for poor Miss Fenwick.

After a time, I cast about me for an excuse to go, and so looking at the clock, I remarked that it was half-past eight.

Immediately, he turned pale and became restless, staring up and sauntering about the room, and twice again he applied himself to the accursed brandy.

He took up his lantern and put on his hat and went toward the door and came back and then went again.

"I can see my way up the track," I said. "I will go now and, perhaps, drop in tomorrow."

Suddenly, he seized me by the arm as I was about to pass out the door and, bending a lurid glare upon my face, exclaimed:

"Are you *mad?* Don't you hear the whistle of the *train?* It will pass in two minutes—and *then* you can go!"

"Train!" I repeated, astonished beyond measure. "The track is clear till the Express passes at nine. Collect your wits. You have been drinking too much."

"*No!* There is a train at half-past eight! Hark—the whistle again, and I must show the light! She goes by on the north track."

He ran out, holding the lantern high over his head.

"I hear no whistle—and see nothing," I answered, standing by his side and peering into the darkness.

"*Ha,* that's what they *all* say!" he cried, "but *I* hear it—and see it both! Look, she's coming now—don't you see the light in front of the locomotive and the hot coals falling beneath—and don't you hear the rattle and roar—and *there,* there's the whistle *again!* All's clear!" he shouted, waving the lantern and following with his glittering eyes the imaginary train as it tore by. "Safe tonight, and all's well—and—*ha ha!*—let's have something more to drink."

He re-entered the little house. I was too much startled to stand upon further ceremony, and so I left him. Walking rapidly along the track, I gained the acclivity, ascended, and took my way through the woods homeward.

Next day, I went to the station as early as I could arrange it. At the moment I entered the store, I saw that Miss Fenwick knew I wished a private conversation with her. She effected the opportunity, and I spoke directly to the point.

"I fear your Uncle Ben is doing very wrong. I have found out a great deal more than I ever suspected, Miss Bessie."

She was pale and tremulous, and utterly cast down. "I gathered as much from what he said when he came home," she answered, "and I don't believe I slept an hour last night."

After a little further conversation, she grew more confidential. She told me the history of Uncle Ben's life and of his friendship for her father. Both poor, they had worked together on this railroad—the one as tunnel clerk, and the other as engineer. When people would ask Martin Fenwick if he was not sometimes afraid as he drove his engine through that somber tunnel, he would say, "Ben's there," with a smile that showed his faith in their affection for each other. And Martin Fenwick's wife would often say, "I am never troubled about the tunnel as long as I know Ben's in his box." But one night Ben was too late, and there was an accident. Martin Fenwick was killed. And nevermore, from that time, was Ben the same man.

This Miss Fenwick told me at much greater length, and she added: "Uncle Ben has taken care of me since my mother died, and he loves me as the dearest thing on Earth. But he changes every day, and sometimes I feel the strangest dread of him—a presentiment of horror mingled with another feeling that I cannot understand or describe. I know his delusion with respect to the phantom train, but how is it to be cured? Immediately after the accident so long ago, it took possession of him in his illness. When he recovered, it disappeared, only to return at intervals. Now, of late, it—it"—her voice faltered—"it never goes away from him at all!"

When I left her that day, I wondered if Uncle Ben's cure were utterly impossible. To consult a physician would be to reveal his secret, and he would lose his position.

What if I undertook the cure myself? I resolved to try.

That very evening, I once more sought him in his little house. Having found all things nearly as before, I came directly to the point with regard to the brandy drinking, saying that it would injure his mind as well as body if he did not cease. I gave him several good reasons for this opinion.

But he answered that he was so lonely and melancholy, and it was too late to relinquish his habit now. We argued very calmly, and so the time rolled on to nearly half-past eight. Exactly as before, he became fidgety and kept his eyes fixed upon the clock.

"She'll be here in five minutes," I heard him mutter.

The proper way to deal with a monomaniac, I had always read, was to practically exhibit the absurdity of his fancy while pretending, at the same time, to hold it with himself. I knew that even some of the most outrageous lunatics still possessed a strong sense of the ridiculous.

So I said: *"Who'll* be here?"

He looked embarrassed and uncomfortable, but I repeated the question more emphatically.

"The train at 8:30. You know well enough."

"So much for your brandy, Uncle Ben," I rejoined, assuming a smile. "You see impalpable trains, but we sober fellows have a keener faculty yet. We are made of such ethereal matter that we can allow your trains to run over us without harm."

He picked up the lantern, and his face grew dark. "The whistle! I must show the light. She goes by on the north track." He hastened toward the door.

I followed after and ran out upon the track.

"Get off the track, or you are lost!" he shouted. "She is coming *now* and will cut you *down*. For the sake of Heaven, *clear the way!"*

I watched him as, with outstretched arms and wide eyes, he followed the progress of the spectral cars—and they came and passed and were gone—and, of course, I still remained on the track unhurt. I walked over to him, pretending to laugh heartily.

For a minute or two, he seemed bewildered—and then suddenly burst out laughing, too.

"You are right," said he. "And I'll swear I thought I saw it. Well, it must have been the brandy, and so no more for me. I swear it!"

Next day, I took the opportunity at the moment it presented itself of having another conversation with Miss Fenwick. There was another person with her—a young man of the name of Warden, who was evidently her lover.

They told me very frankly the little history of their love, which— of course, being true—had not run by any means as smoothly as could be wished. In fact, Uncle Ben did not like this Mr. Warden at all, and only because Miss Fenwick liked him. What was sadder yet, the young man had very little money, so a consummation of their hopes seemed very far away indeed.

Uncle Ben had told Bessie of the previous night's incident— how he had been cured of his delusion. He had then asserted his determination to drink no more. It was something sweet and good to receive the pretty woman's sincere gratitude for what I had done on her behalf, and I was repaid a hundred times.

And now all that remained was to assure myself that the old man's cure was complete. That day, there was a dreadful storm of wind and rain. Ceaseless cataracts poured from the black and angry skies. The streams were swollen. Every little pool in the roads became a torrent. Even in the fields, the furrows were deep with water and the ripe corn was beaten down and destroyed.

However, I fought my way manfully to the cut, descended the side, and gained the railroad track.

The light was burning in the clerk's hut. As I entered, he was sitting thoughtfully as usual and the little telegraphic instrument clicked as of old.

But there was no bottle of brandy there.

The Phantom Train; or, The Tunnel Clerk

I hardly remember what we talked of, but it was nothing referring to the matters of the previous visits. I watched him steadily and noted that he still furtively glanced, now and then, at the clock.

To keep him occupied, I remember saying, "This night's tempest will be trouble at the bridges and culverts, Uncle Ben!"

"Ay, and no train will be on time for the next three days," he answered, "and we shall have specials flitting by like shooting stars!"

It was twenty minutes past eight. He got up slowly and seized the lantern.

I felt some dismay, as you may readily suppose. The cure had been no cure at all.

"Don't look so disheartened!" he laughed. "There's no 8:30, I'm aware. You convinced me last night, and tonight, I am going to convince *myself!*"

"What do you mean?"

"When the phantom train comes by, I mean to stand in her way—just as *you* did!"

This relieved me at once. Evidently some small remnant of his delusion yet remained, which he wished to be free of, and I readily acquiesced in his desire.

Slowly, the hands of the clock moved to twenty-seven minutes past eight. He was standing at the open door, the lantern in his hand, quiet and still smiling.

Suddenly I heard the long-drawn ominous whistle of a locomotive!

A chill seized me! An icy finger seemed to be tracing out my spine! Was this fancy, and *I* mad now?

"Do you hear nothing?" I called out.

He pointed to his ear. "Nothing *tonight!*" he said, a faint sadness in his voice.

Oh, heaven! *I* heard—or was mad! Nearer and nearer came the fifing and drumming of a train! I threw myself upon the ground and listened at the iron rail, and the rumble and roar approached, and the hoarse puffing of the engine became distinct, and the earth shook beneath the monster's giant tread!

Uncle Ben walked over to the north track!

"Come back!" I screamed, for scream it was. "I hear *a train coming,* as I'm a living man!"

He shook his head, and in the glare of the lantern, I still saw his melancholy smile of unbelief.

"The phantom train!" he answered, and he turned his eyes down the track. "Yes, I see her coming as of old—so many, many nights—and the hot coals are falling beneath—and it is the same. But *she is not there!*"

And I, too, saw and stared like one in a dream, and I heard the frantic shrieks of the engineer's whistle, and I cried aloud.

But Uncle Ben still stood on the track, the light in his hand and the weird smile on his face.

And then there were shrieks and other lights as the train flashed by. Something warm spurted in my face—blood!—and I fell senseless.

Days afterward, I learned all. It was a special train, and its coming had been announced all along the line. But Uncle Ben had not heard the click of his telegraphic instrument *since* before dark that terrible evening. When they examined his body, they found cotton pressed into his ears. I understood why he had put it there—to shut out the roar of his phantom train if it should seem to pass that night.

The story is too sad to be further dwelt upon. The sequel was pleasanter, for some twelve months after the catastrophe I have related, passing through that part of the country, I stopped an hour at the little hotel recently established. Who should be master and mistress but Mr. and Mrs. Warden, the latter, of course, my sweet friend Bessie Fenwick. They were just married and were succeeding in their enterprise finely.

Though I supped with them, none of us had the courage to refer to the sad fate of poor Uncle Ben.

AT RAVENHOLME JUNCTION

ANONYMOUS[1]

"Were you ever out in a more wretched night in your life?" asked Harry Luscombe in a tone of disgust as we were trudging wearily along after a full half-hour of absolute silence.

The rain was certainly coming down "with a vengeance," as people say. We had been out all day fishing in some private waters about ten miles from home. A friend had given us a lift in his trap the greater part of the way in going, and we had arranged to walk back, never dreaming that the sunny day would resolve itself into so wet an evening. Fortunately, each of us had taken a light mackintosh, and we had on our thick fishing boots—otherwise, our plight would have been much worse than it was.

"Wretched night!" again ejaculated Harry, whose pipe the rain would persist in putting out.

"But surely we cannot be far from the Grange now?" I groaned.

"A good four miles yet, old fellow," answered my friend. "We must grin and bear it."

For ten more minutes, we paced the slushy road in moist silence.

"I wouldn't have cared so much," growled Harry at last, "if we had only a decent lot of fish to take home. Won't Gerty and the governor chaff us in the morning!"

I winced. Harry had touched a sore point. I rather prided myself on my prowess with rod and line, yet here was I, after eight hours' patient flogging of the water, going back to the Grange with a creel that I should blush to open when I got there. It was most annoying.

By-and-by we came to a stile, crossing which we found a footpath through the meadows, just faintly visible in the dark. The footpath, in time, brought us to a level crossing over the railway. But instead of crossing the iron road to the fields beyond, as I expected

---

[1] This short story comes from *The Argosy* 22 [Dec., 1876] pp. 462-68.

he would do, Harry turned half round and began to walk along the line.

"Where on Earth are you leading me to?" I asked as I stumbled and barked my shins over a heap of loose sleepers by the side of the rails.

"Seest thou not yonder planets that flame so brightly in the midnight sky?" he exclaimed, pointing to two railway signals clearly visible some quarter of a mile away. "Thither are we bound. Disturb not the meditations of a great mind by further foolish questionings."

I was too damp to retort as I might otherwise have done, so I held my peace and stumbled quietly after him. Little by little, we drew nearer to the signal lamps, till at last we stood close under them. They shone far and high above our heads, being in fact the crowning points of two tall semaphore posts. But we were not going quite so far skyward as the lamps, our destination being the signalman's wooden hut from which the semaphores were worked. This of itself stood some distance above the ground, being built on substantial posts driven firmly into the embankment. It was reached by a flight of wooden steps, steep and narrow. We saw by the light shining from its windows that it was not without an occupant.

Harry put a couple of fingers to his mouth and whistled shrilly. "Jim Crump," he shouted, "Jim Crump—hi! Where are you?"

"Is that you, Mr. Harry?" said a voice, and then the door above us was opened. "Wait a moment, sir, till I get my lantern. The steps are slippery with the rain, and one of them is broken."

"You see, my governor is one of the managing directors of this line," said Harry in explanation while we were waiting for the lantern, "so that I can come and go, and do pretty much as I like about here."

"But why have you come here at all?" I asked.

"For the sake of a rest and a smoke, and a talk with Jim Crump about his dogs."

Two minutes later and we had mounted the steps, and for the first time in my life, I found myself in a signalman's box.

It was a snug little place enough, but there was not much room to spare. There were windows on three sides of it, so that the man on duty might have a clear view both up and down the line. Five or six long iron levers were fixed in a row below the front window. The due and proper manipulation of these levers, which were connected by means of rods and chains with the points and signals outside— and the working of the simple telegraphic apparatus which placed

At Ravenholme Junction

him *en rapport* with the stations nearest to him, up and down—were the signalman's sole but onerous duties. Both the box and the lamps overhead were lighted with gas brought from the town, two miles away.

"I have been wanting to see you for the last two or three weeks, Mr. Harry," said Crump, a well-built man of thirty with clear resolute eyes and a firm-set mouth.

"Ay, ay. What's the game now, Crump? Got some more of that famous tobacco?"

"Something better than the tobacco, Mr. Harry. I've got a bull terrier pup for you. Such a beauty!"

"The dickens you have!" cried Harry, his eyes all a-sparkle with delight. "Crump, you are a brick! A bull terrier pup is the very thing I've been hankering after for the last three months. Have you got it here?"

"No, it's at home. You see, I didn't know that you were coming tonight."

Harry's countenance fell. "That's a pity now, isn't it?"

"It don't rain near so fast as it did," said Crump, "and if you would like to take the pup with you, I'll just run home and fetch it. I can go there and back in twenty minutes. It's agen' the rules to leave my box, I know, and I wouldn't leave it for anybody but you—and not even for you, Mr. Harry, if I didn't know that you knew how to work the levers and the telly a'most as well as I do myself. Besides all that, there will be nothing either up or down till twelve-thirty. What say you, sir?"

"I say go, by all means, Crump. You may depend on my looking well after the signals while you are away."

"Right you are, sir." And Crump proceeded to pull on his over coat.

"I wish I could make you more comfortable, sir," said Crump to me. "But this is only a roughish place."

Harry and I sat down on a sort of bunk or locker at the back of the box. Harry produced his flask, which he had filled with brandy before leaving the hotel. Crump declined any of the proffered spirit, but accepted a cigar. Then he pulled up the collar of his coat and went.

In the pauses of our talk, we could hear the moaning of the telegraph wires outside as the invisible fingers of the wind touched them in passing.

"This is Ravenholme Junction," said Harry to me.

"Is it, indeed? Much obliged for the information," I answered drily.

"About two years ago a terrible accident happened close to this spot. No doubt you read about it at the time."

"Possibly so. But if I did, the facts have escaped my memory."

"The news was brought to the Grange, and I was on the spot in less than three hours after the smash. I shall never forget what I saw that night." He smoked in grave silence for a little while, and then he spoke again. "I don't know whether you are acquainted with the railway geography of this district, but Ravenholme—I am speaking of the village, which is nearly two miles away—is on a branch line, which diverges from the main line some six miles north of this box. After zigzagging among various busy townships and hamlets, it joins the main line again about a dozen miles south of the point where it diverged. Thus, it forms what is known as the Ravenholme Loop Line. None of the main line trains run over the loop. Passengers from it going to any place on the main line have to change from the local trains at either the north or south junction, according to the direction they intend to travel."

I wondered why he was telling this.

"You will understand from this that the junction where we are now is rather an out-of-the-way spot—out of the way, that is, of any great bustle of railway traffic. It forms, in fact, the point of connection between the Ravenholme Loop and a single line of rails that turns off to the left about a hundred yards from here, giving access to a cluster of important collieries belonging to Lord Exbrooke. The duty of Crump is, by means of his signals, to guard against the possibility of a collision between the coal trains coming off the colliery line and the ordinary trains passing up and down the loop. You will readily comprehend that, at a quiet place like this, a signalman has not half the work to do, nor half the responsibility to labour under, of a man in a similar position at some busy junction on the main line. In fact, a signalman at Ravenholme Junction may emphatically be said to have an easy time of it."

I nodded.

"Some two years ago, however, it so fell out that an abutment of one of the bridges on the main line was so undermined by heavy floods that instructions had to be given for no more trains to pass over it till it had been thoroughly repaired. In order to prevent any interruption of traffic, it was decided that, till the necessary repairs could be effected, all mainline trains should work over the

Ravenholme Loop for the time being. As it was arranged so it was carried out."

"Well?"

"The signalman at that time in charge of this box was named Dazeley—a shy, nervous sort of man, as I have been told, lacking in self-confidence and not to be depended upon in any unforeseen emergency. Such as he was, however, he had been at Ravenholme for three years and had always performed the duties of his situation faithfully and well. As soon as the mainline trains began to travel by the new route, another man was sent from headquarters to assist Dazeley—there had been no night work previously. The men came on duty *turn and turn about,* meaning twelve hours on and twelve hours off. The man who was on by *day* one week was on by *night* the following week."

"Go on."

"It is said that Dazeley soon began to look worn and depressed, and that he became more nervous and wanting in self-confidence than ever. Be that as it may, he never spoke a complaining word to anyone, but went on doing his duty in the silent depressed way habitual with him. One morning, when he was coming off duty—it was his turn for night work that week—his mate was taken suddenly ill and was obliged to go home again. There was no help for it—Dazeley was obliged to take the sick man's place for the day. When evening came round, his mate sent word that he was somewhat better, but not well enough to resume work before morning, so Dazeley had to take his third consecutive 'spell' of twelve hours in the box. You see, Ravenholme is a long way from headquarters, and in any case, it would have taken some time to get assistance. Besides that, Dazeley expected that a few hours at the very most would see his mate thoroughly recovered. So nothing was said or done."

I was growing interested.

"The night mail from south to north was timed to pass Ravenholme Junction, without stopping, at 11.40. On the particular night to which we now come—the night of the accident—it is supposed that poor Dazeley, utterly worn out for want of rest, had lain down for a minute or two on this very bunk. He had dropped off to sleep, his signals standing at 'all clear,' as was usual at that hour. Had he remained asleep till after the mail had passed, all would have been well, everything being clear for its safe transit past the junction. Unfortunately, the night was somewhat foggy, and the engine-driver, not being able to see the lamps at the usual distance, blew his whistle loudly. Roused by the shrill summons, Dazeley, as it is supposed, started suddenly to his feet. His brain being still muddled with sleep, he grasped one of the familiar levers, and all unconscious of what he was doing, he turned the mail train onto the single line that led to the collieries."

"Oh!"

"The consequences were terrible. Some two or three hundred yards down the colliery line, a long coal train was waiting for the mail to pass before proceeding on its journey. Into this train the mail dashed at headlong speed. Two people were killed on the spot, and twenty or thirty more or less hurt."

"How dreadful!"

"When they came to look for Dazeley, he was not to be found. Horror-stricken at the terrible consequences of his act, he had fled. A warrant for his arrest was obtained. He was found four days afterwards in a wood, hanging to the bough of a tree—dead. One of his hands clasped a scrap of paper on which a few half-illegible words had been scrawled, the purport of which was that, after what had happened, he could no longer bear to live."

"A sad story, truly," I said as Harry finished. "It seems to me that the poor fellow was to be pitied more than blamed."

"Crump's twenty minutes are rather long ones," said Harry as he looked at his watch. "It is now thirty-eight minutes past eleven. No chance of getting home till long after midnight."

The rain was over, and the wind had gone with it. Not a sound was audible save now and again the faint moaning of the telegraph wires overhead.

Harry crossed to the window and opened one of the three casements. He said, "A breath of fresh air will be welcome. The gas makes this little place unbearable." Having opened the window, he came back again and sat down beside me on the bunk.

Hardly had Harry resumed his seat, when all at once the gas sank down as though it were going out, but next moment it was burning as brightly as before. An icy shiver ran through me from head to foot. I turned my head to glance at Harry, and as I did so I saw, to my horror, that we were no longer alone. There had been but *two* of us only a moment before. The door had not been opened, yet now we were *three*. Sitting on a low wooden chair close to the levers, and with his head resting on them, was a stranger, to all appearance *fast asleep!*

I never before experienced the feeling of awful dread that crept over me at that moment, and I hope never to do so again. I knew instinctively that the figure before me was no corporeal being, no creature of flesh and blood like ourselves. My heart seemed to contract, my blood to congeal. My hands and feet turned cold as ice. The roots of my hair were stirred with a creeping horror that I had no power to control. I could not move my eyes from that sleeping figure. It was Dazeley come back again—a worn, haggard-looking man, restless, and full of nervous twitchings even in his sleep.

"Listen!" said Harry to me almost inaudibly.

I wanted to look at him—I wanted to see whether he was affected in the same way that I was—but for the life of me, I could not turn my eyes away from that sleeping phantom.

Listening as he bade me, I could just distinguish the first low dull murmur made by an oncoming train while it is still a mile or more away. It was a murmur that grew and deepened with every second, swelling gradually into the hoarse inarticulate roar of an express train coming towards us at full speed. Suddenly the whistle sounded its loud, shrill, imperative summons. For one moment, I tore my eyes away from the sleeping figure. Yonder, a quarter mile away—or it might have been a half mile, but being borne towards us in a wild rush of headlong fury—was plainly visible the glowing Cyclopean eye of the coming train. Still the whistle sounded, painful, intense—agonised, one might almost fancy.

Louder and louder grew the heavy thunderous beat of the train. It was close upon us now. Suddenly the sleeping figure started to its feet. It pressed its hands to its head for a moment as though lost in doubt before giving one wild, frenzied glance round. Then it seized one of the levers with both hands, pulling it back and holding it there.

A sudden flash—a louder roar—and the phantom train had passed us and was plunging headlong into the darkness beyond. The figure let go its hold of the lever, which fell back to its original position. As it did so, a dreadful knowledge seemed all at once to dawn on its face. Surprise, horror, anguish unspeakable: all were plainly depicted on the white, drawn features of the phantom before me. Suddenly it flung up its arms as if in wild appeal to Heaven, then sank coweringly on its knees and buried its face in both its hands with an expression of misery the most profound.

Next moment the gas gave a flicker as though it were going out, and when I looked again, Harry and I were alone. The phantom of the unhappy signalman had vanished. The noise of the phantom train had faded into silence. No sound was audible save the unceasing monotone of the electric wires above us.

Harry was the first to break the spell. He said, "Today is the eighth of September, and it was on the eighth of September, two years ago, that the accident happened. I had forgotten the date till this moment."

At this instant, the door opened, and in came Jim Crump with the puppy under his arm. Struck with something in our faces, he looked from one to the other of us and did not speak for a few seconds.

"Here be the pup, sir," he said at last. "And a reg'lar little beauty I call her."

"Was it not two years ago this very night that the accident took place?" asked Harry as he took the puppy out of Crump's arms into his own.

Crump reflected for a few moments. "Yes, sir, that it was, though I'd forgotten it. It was on the eighth of September. I ought to know, because it was on that very night my youngster was born."

"Were you signalman here on the eighth of September last year the year after the accident?"

"No, sir, a man of the name of Moffat was here then. I came on the twentieth of September. Moffat was ordered to be moved. They said he had gone a little bit queer in his head. He went about saying that Dazeley's ghost had shown itself to him in this very box and that he saw and heard a train come past that wasn't a train, and I don't know what other bosh. So it was thought best to remove him."

"We thought just now—my friend and I—that we heard a train coming," said Harry as he gently stroked the puppy. "Did you hear anything as you came along?"

"Nothing whatever, sir. Had a train been coming, I must have heard it, because I walked from my house up the line. Besides, there's no train due yet for some time."

Harry glanced at me. He was evidently not minded to enlighten Crump as to anything we had seen or heard.

Five minutes later we left, carrying the dog with us. Whether or not Harry said anything to his father I don't know. This, however, I do know. Within six months from that time, certain alterations were made on the line which necessitated the removal of the signalman's box at Ravenholme Junction to a point half a mile further south. But I have never visited it since that memorable night.

A PHANTOM TRAIN
A LIGHTNING EXPRESS TRAIN THAT MADE NO NOISE

ANONYMOUS[1]

[Hanover (N.H.) Special.]

John Saunders and Hiram Townsend were riding home from this village last night, when they came to a crossing over the railroad track.

"There's a train coming!" said Saunders, pointing up the track in the direction of East Berlin.

The men pulled the horses in by the side of the track to let the train go by. It appeared to be surrounded by a thick mist, although the night was clear and the stars were shining. The engineer could be seen looking out of the window of the cab, but there was no noise as the train drew near. The fireman kept pulling on the bell rope as is customary when nearing a crossing, but not a sound came forth.

The phantom engineer was recognized by several parties as Tom Williams, who was killed on this section of the road a few weeks ago while running on the midnight express.

---

[1] Another example of how newspapers once spread ghost stories, this article—apparently originating in New Hampshire—comes from the Kansas newspaper *The Iola Register,* Jan. 1, 1886, p. 3. Like their counterpart, heard-but-unseen phantom trains, these seen-but-unheard ones were common enough to have been included in Ernest W. Baughman's *Type and Motif-Index of the Folktales of England and North America* (Mouton & Co., 1966) p. 190. It's given the motif designation E535.4(a).

A PHANTOM AT THE THROTTLE

ANONYMOUS[1]

Mountain engineers are perhaps the most fearless class of men in the world, says the *Denver News*. Journeys of so perilous a nature that the blood of all ordinary men curdle at the bare thought of undertaking are successfully made by them. Those men who ride hundreds of miles through the mountains are seldom frightened, but today there resides in Denver a man who would not "pull" a train over Marshall pass for a cool million, and when the name of that famous place is mentioned, he involuntary clenches his hands and pales visibly.

Several years ago, there was a story circulated that three times a week a phantom train went steaming over the pass and that ghostly forms could be seen through the car windows. Although the statements in regard to it were incoherent, engineers began to regard a certain portion of the track with suspicion and usually hugged the rails there as close as possible.

One morning, a freight "runner" pulled into Green River and informed the operator that he had seen the train, and so earnestly did he plead with the master mechanic that he was given an engine on the Salt Lake division. Other experiences were related, and it became almost a weekly occurrence that some engineer would report having seen a train of which the dispatcher had no record and could not account for. In nearly every instance, the engineers who complained were those who pulled the night passenger train, which reached Green River at 7 o'clock in the morning.

One engineer who had twice seen the much-talked-of train

---

[1] This article comes from Nebraska's *Omaha Daily Bee*, May 19, 1889, p. 6. I also found it in West Virginia's *Wheeling Sunday Register*, June 30, 1889, p. 7. In the Omaha paper, the story is presented as if it were as factual as the article right beside it: a report on the opening of Johns Hopkins Hospital. However, such pieces seem less like standard news and more like folklore. In fact, a shorter version of Nelson Edwards' adventure found its way into Charles M. Skinner's *Myths and Legends of Our Own Land* (J.B. Lippincott, 1896) Vol. 2: pp. 192-95.

pulled out of Salida as white as the snow on the ground, and the following morning, the fireman brought the engine into Green River, the brakeman firing[2] and the engineer in an insensible condition. He had seen the phantom train and that was his last trip on the road.

FEARLESS AND COOL.

The regular train was then placed in the hands of an old and tried engineer by the name of Nelson Edwards, who had as a fireman Charles Whitehead. Both men were cool and calculating, well educated, and generally considered the most fearless men in the employ of the Rio Grande—men who had caught runaway trains on the mountain side without so much as a flush suffusing their cheeks. For nearly two months they were on the train, back and forth every other day, and while alternating crews had changed several times, they had not as yet seen the mysterious train, the sight of which had been the cause of so many engineers quitting that division.

One evening, just at dusk, while the fireman was lighting his lamp, the engineer, Edwards, experienced a strange feeling creeping over him, and as he pulled into the canyon the silence seemed deeper than usual, the night darker, and the air colder. Several times before they reached the grade, the "popping" of the safety valve caused him to start. But soon they were winding in and about the labyrinth of small canons and over deep arroyos. As his trained eye swept the glittering rails ahead, he forgot his uneasiness. Engineers seldom speak to their firemen—as a rule they are too busy because the constant watching requires that their minds should be on their work. Tonight, Edwards was more like a sphinx than usual, for it had been reported that there was a bridge in danger of going down and a defective rail in one of the canons. Ever and anon, he slackened the speed of his train as a matter of safety.

THE DANGER SIGNAL.

The engineer passed under a snow shed,[3] and the strange roar so peculiar on such occasions followed. While in the shed, from far away, there came the long, warning whistles of an approaching train. Edwards remarked to his fireman that No. 8 was following

---

[2] He was "firing" in the sense of "fired up" or in an agitated state.

[3] A "snow shed" is a tunnel-like structure built to protect trains against avalanches of snow, something especially prudent in the Rocky Mountains.

too close. Again, when about five miles farther on, he recognized the same whistle, this time nearer, and at short intervals, the signal was heard coming rapidly nearer.

"It must be a wild train," Whitehead grumbled, as the engineer reached for the rope and gave two short, sharp whistles, only to hear the long, dangerous answers.

Again in a snow shed, it occurred to him that he had to "saw by" an eastbound freight at the next switch, twenty-five miles further up the mountain, and as he left the shed, the bell sounded three times, and he brought his train to a standstill as quickly as possible. In the crisp night air, he could hear the doleful sounds of the followers as the piston rods traveled back and forth in the cylinders, but a sound more ominous than that was the long-drawn whistles of the engine that was rapidly overhauling him.

The conductor ran forward at this juncture and asked: "What did you stop for?"

"What did you pull the bell-cord for?" rejoined Edwards.

"You're crazy," the conductor said. "Now pull her wide open and light out for the switches because we've got to pass No. 19 there. Besides, there's a wild train a-climbing up on us. D'ye hear?"

RACING FOR LIFE.

Edwards drew back the lever with a strange feeling. He opened the throttle, the wheels slipped on the rails, but as they caught the sand, the long, heavy train began to move forward slowly. Both men in the cab could hear the sand grind beneath the enormous weight of the engine. The train increased in momentum as it moved forward, and in about five minutes was running as fast as practicable on that portion of the road.

The following train was approaching nearer and nearer. Again, the short series of warning whistles was heard, which Edwards answered, but only to hear the wild train give the danger signal again. He looked out of the window as he was rounding a curve and noticed the other train rapidly approaching. Cold beads of sweat stood out on his forehead as he pulled the throttle wide open.

Faster and faster the speed of the train increased, and more dangerous was the track. They were now in the very worst portion of the pass, where the snow banks were the most treacherous, and just in this part of the track was where the broken rail was reported. Every time the engine struck a curve, it seemed as though it was impossible for the small flanges to hold the engine to the rails. The cars were rocking violently. The train was lurching frightfully. The passengers were rudely awakened from their slumbers by the train striking a snowdrift. The speed of the train was so great that it broke the drift easily and was soon roaring through a snow shed. How the fireman labored. His shirt was wet with perspiration, for the hungry furnace consumed the coal so quickly that the stack belched fire.

AWAITING DEATH.

The passengers, having been warned of the impending danger, had dressed themselves.[4] The women were wringing their hands in despair, strong men were trembling, and the thought of every person on the train was of the man whose hand rested on the throttle of the engine ahead. Would he be able to outrun the pursuing train and break all the snow banks, or would the rear train dash into the coaches and kill all the passengers? Who was their engineer? Was he competent? The curtains were all thrown up, and a few daring men clung on the platform and glanced anxiously back. The conductor started suddenly as he caught a glimpse of the driving wheels of the rear train. They were fully ten inches larger than those on the engine ahead.

With hand tightly clenched on the throttle, Edwards' eye rapidly swept the track. He was a good engineer, for even under that awful strain, he had presence of mind to shut off his steam in order to save it when running down grade without brake pressure. Never once while running did he allow power to take the place of speed, a fault of most engineers under excitement.

At this time, the snow began to descend. In the peculiar light that settled on the earth caused by the snow, Edwards saw something in a backward glance he took that made his blood freeze and almost caused his heart to cease beating. On the top of one of the cars of the rear train was the tall white figure of a man gesticulating wildly. At the same time, he could see a white form in the cab. A terrible thought flashed through his mind—the train, the peculiar condition—*it was the phantom train!*

THE SPECTER STILL GAINING!

Without further parley, regardless of the broken rail, he dropped the lever another notch, and then as quickly as possible but cautiously, he opened the throttle valve. His trained ear caught every sound his engine made, and under the intense excitement, he once thought he heard the pistons grinding and the axle pound. What a wild ride it was in the night. It would be impossible to pass

---

[4] In other words, they put on their outerwear in preparation to leave the train.

a broken rail at the terrific speed they were traveling. He was leading the race by about two hundred yards now, and as his train approached a point where the track reversed and ran parallel, he nerved himself for the trial.

He rounded the curve safely, and started, and was moving back on the serpentine curve with the rapidity of lightning. As he passed the other engine, he saw two extremely white figures in the cab. The specter engineer turned a face to him like dough and laughed. The ghostly fireman reached for the cord, and again a series of short, sharp whistles sounded.

Onward the train plunged into the night, roaring through snow sheds and over iron bridges that trembled beneath the sudden shock. So fast was the train traveling that the rush of air could be heard by the passengers. Wherever there was a snow drift, the train would break through it like a hurricane. Faster and faster, for now they were mounting to the highest point of the pass where it was coldest, steam was not so plentiful, and soon Edwards had the lever in the corner and the throttle wide open. The greatest speed his engine was capable of had been attained, and Edwards could but watch the rails in front of him and keep his hand on the throttle.

The phantom train was gaining. He could go no faster—he was helpless. Around the shelves of the high mountains and along the ridge of lofty hills, over deep arroyos and through long snow sheds, the race continued. The very landscape was closing behind the train like a cloud. The mountains seemed to recede rapidly, but all the while, the specter train was gaining ground. The wind arose and sighed, and from the north, heavy clouds began to drift southward. The pilot struck a slight snow bank and hurled it a hundred feet high.

THROUGH THE TEMPEST.

A terrific storm was soon in progress, the furies of which seemed to concentrate on the fleeing passenger train. On into the night, the train swept, specter and passenger like bolts of lightning pursuing one another through the sky.

Edwards sighted a bridge that was reported weak, passed it safely, and, having by this time crossed the summit, was now on the down grade. Steeper it became, and when one particularly heavy hill was reached, for the first time in his life, Edwards was guilty of running the grade without applying the air brakes. Soon he sighted the switch. No. 19 was not there, and with a madness born of excitement, he went tearing by like the wind. Another series of

A Phantom at the Throttle

short, sharp whistles, and an instant later the engineer saw a red lantern swinging in the right of way. He was running down grade, and the thought of No. 19 ahead, the mysterious train behind, and being a trained mechanic, he instinctively applied the air.

The wheels stopped revolving, but the train was still running over the snowy rails. Far ahead, he observed light, shadowy, fantastic forms, and as the train drew nearer, he saw that they were spirits! They appeared to be repairing the track. The next minute, flying toward the ghosts on the track, Edwards passed through the crowd of ten or twelve and reached the curve beyond. He ventured a backward glance. He watched the phantom train run to a broken rail, the engine running off onto the ties, and one second later, the heavy freight pitched the embankment.

A moment later, it vanished.

Afterward, in the frost of the fireman's window, writing was discovered. It had been scribbled in a peculiar hand:

> Yeers ago a frate train was recked as yu saw—now that yu saw it, we will never make an other run. The enjine was not oundor cantrol and four sexshun men wor killed. If yu ever ran on this road again yu will be recked.

Edwards passed No. 19 at the second switch, reached Green River at 6 o'clock the next morning, an hour ahead of time, and left the Rio Grande that day. The following evening, he went to Salt Lake and went back to Denver over the Union Pacific, on which he is now running and is considered one of the most trustworthy men in their employ. The phantom has not been seen since that eventful night.

A GHOST TRAIN

W. L. ALDEN[1]

"Do you mean to tell me," I asked the stationmaster, "that you really believe that a train has a ghost, and that ghostly trains run over actual railways at night?"

"If you were a railroad man," replied my friend, "you'd see the foolishness of asking such a question! Do I believe in ghost trains? You might as well ask me if I believe in Pullman cars.[2] Why, man! Every railroad man knows that ghost trains are liable to be met with almost any night. I don't say that they are common, but I do say that there are lots of men who have seen 'em and have just as much reason for believing in 'em as they have for believing in any regular train."

"Have you yourself ever seen a ghost train?" I asked.

The stationmaster chewed his cigar for a moment in silence. Then he said: "Seeing as it's you that asks me, I'll tell you something that I haven't told any man for more than ten years, unless he happened to be an experienced railroad man. You see, I got tired of having people doubt my word and insinuating that I was a lunatic or had been drinking too much whisky. You'll perhaps think the same, but what I'm going to tell you is a cold fact, and there ain't a bit of lying, or poetry, or political argufying, or any of those sort of imaginative things about it.

"You know the road from here to Tiberius Center? It's pretty near a straight line, but when I first came into these parts, the trains used to run from here to Tiberius Center by a mighty roundabout way. The line, as it was originally laid out, ran in a sort of semi-

---

[1] This short story comes from Washington D.C.'s *Evening Star,* Jan. 25, 1896, p. 16. About the same time, it also appeared in the English magazine *The Idler* 8.48 [Jan., 1896] pp. 556-62.

[2] Named for George Pullman (1831-1897), these cars came to dominate passenger rail service in the U.S. during the late 1800s and early 1900s. In contrast to the bare accommodations of earlier decades, Pullman cars offered riders luxury and privacy along with the chance to sleep in pull-down beds. The Pullman Company manufactured the cars and managed their operation while paying to have them coupled to trains run by other railroad companies.

A Ghost Train

circle, taking in half a dozen small towns lying northwest of this place. After a while, the company surveyed the new line and bored the big tunnel through the Blue Eagle mountain. The old line wasn't entirely abandoned until about two years ago, but after the tunnel was finished, there was only one passenger train each way daily on the old line, and a freight train three times a week.

"I had a brother who lived up at Manlius, a town on the old line about seventy miles from here. That is to say, Manlius was his post office address, but he lived in a house that was three miles from the station, and there wasn't any town of Manlius, except the station house and a little shanty that was used as a post office. I was a kind of a general assistant at this h'yer station where we are now, and there not being very much work on hand, I got two days' leave and took the train up to see my brother. It was just about a year after the new line had been opened, and as the company meant to abandon the old line, they hadn't put any repairs on it worth speaking of, and it was about the roughest road you ever traveled over.

"As a rule, I never troubled myself about railroad accidents, knowing that they're bound to come and you can't help yourself. Still, I was a little scared. There had been a terrible bad accident on that very road just before the expresses quit running over it. A train with a Pullman car full of passengers went off the track just as she had struck a bridge over the Muskahoot River, and as the bridge was over eighty feet high—and the river was over twenty feet deep—nobody ever saw hide or hair of that train or of anybody connected with it from that day to this.

"Well, I got up to my brother's along about 8:00 or mebbe 8:30 in the evening. I found him gone away and the house locked up. I hammered on the doors and tried the windows till I had settled that there wasn't anyone at home and that I couldn't break in. Then I meandered back to the station, calculating to pass the night in the woodshed and take the train back to Jericho the next day.

"It had been snowing hard, and there was near a foot of snow on a level, let alone the big drifts that were here and there. I was pretty well fagged out when I got to the station, which, of course, was shut up for the night, and if it hadn't been that I had a quart of whisky in my pocket, I should have come near freezing to death. I went into the woodshed and got round behind the wood, where the wind couldn't reach me. After cussin' my brother for a spell on account of his having gone off and shut up his house, I made my preparations for taking a nap.

"Just then, I heard the rumble of a train. This naturally

astonished me, knowing as I did exactly what trains were running on that road and that there wasn't any sort of train due at that station for the next fifteen hours. However, the train kept coming nearer and nearer, and pretty soon, I heard the grinding of the brakes, understanding that the train was coming to a stop. I didn't lose any time in getting out of that woodshed and going for that train.

"I could see it standing close to the water-butt about fifty yards down the road, and I knew, of course, that the engineer was taking in water. When I reached her, I saw that the train consisted only of a baggage car and a Pullman sleeper. I swung myself up on the rear platform of the sleeper and pushed the door open with a good deal of trouble, for the woodwork seemed to have swelled and there wasn't anybody to help me from the inside of the car.

"When I got inside, I looked around for the passengers, but there wasn't a single one. Neither was there any sign of the porter, who ought to have been there to ask me for my ticket and to pretend that I was making him a lot of trouble by asking for a bed. You know the ways of porters and how they always make you feel that, if you don't give them a pretty big tip, you are a good deal worse than a slave driver. The car was lit up after a fashion by a single oil lamp, and all the berths looked as if the passengers had just jumped out of them and the porter hadn't been round to make up the beds. I couldn't think what had become of the passengers, seeing as they couldn't have gone into the baggage car, and it didn't seem probable that a whole carful could have distributed themselves at way stations. However, that wasn't any affair of mine.

"I opened both doors of the car to let a little air blow through, for it was very musty, and then I picked out a good berth and calculated to turn in for the night. I soon found that those berths weren't fit for any Christian to sleep in, for the bed clothes were as damp as if they had been left out in a rainstorm. Where the water had come from that had soaked them, I couldn't imagine, for it hadn't rained any for a week. It stood to reason that the snow couldn't have drifted into the car, shut up as tight as it was. Then it puzzled me to imagine why the porter hadn't taken the wet clothes away and what had become of him anyhow. The whole business was enough to throw a man off his balance. I gave up thinking about it, and going into the washroom, I sat down in the wash basin, which was the only dry seat in the car. Leaning up against the corner, I tried to get a nap.

"By this time, the train had left the station several miles behind and was running at a rate that I knew would have been risky on any road, let alone as rough a road as the one we were on. At first, I didn't mind this, the running of the train not being my business. But pretty soon I found that I could not keep in my seat without holding on with both hands. I've been in cars that have done some pretty tall running and over some mighty rough ground, but I never before or since knew a car to jump and roll and shake herself generally as that car did. I began to think that the engineer was either drunk or crazy and that the passengers had got so scared that they all left the train. To tell the truth, I would have been glad to have left the train myself, but I never was fond of jumping, and if there is any man who says that he likes to jump from a train that is doing forty or fifty miles an hour—why, just don't believe him.

"All of a sudden, I thought of the bell cord, and I decided that I would pull it and stop the train. Then if any conductor appeared I would tell him who I was and inform him that, if he didn't make his engineer run the train in a decent way, I would take good care that the division superintendent should know all about the thing. So I got hold of the bell cord and gave it a fairish sort of pull—not the very hardest sort of a pull, you understand, but just a moderate pull. The cord *broke* in my hand as easy as if it had been a piece of thread, and all chance of stopping the train that way disappeared. I looked at the bell cord and saw that it was as rotten as a politician's conscience, so I just broke off a piece of it about two or three yards long and put it in my pocket, intending to show it to the division superintendent as a specimen of the way in which Pullman car conductors attended to their business.

"All the time, the train was rushing ahead at a speed that would have been counted worth noticing even on the New York Central.[3] When she struck a curve—and there were lots of them—she just left the track entirely and swung round that curve with her wheels in the air. And when she did strike the track again, you can bet that things shook. Of course, I don't mean that the train actually did leave the track, but that was the way it would have seemed to you if you had been aboard that car. I went to the forward door to see if there was any chance of getting into or over the baggage car and so

---

[3] In 1893—three years before this story was published—the Empire State Express, run by the New York Central Railroad, was said to have broken the speed record by traveling faster than 100 miles per hour. (This was challenged shortly afterward and has been ever since.) The news traveled as far as Los Angeles, where it appeared in *The Herald,* May 12, 1893, p. 1. There, the announcement notes: "The passengers say the train ran smoothly but the telegraph poles looked like pickets in a fence. There was no unusual swinging or jolting."

reaching the engineer, but it would have taken a monkey in first-rate training to have climbed over that baggage car without breaking his neck at the rate we were running.

"I went back into the sleeper again and, holding onto a berth, tried to light up a cigar. Somehow, the match didn't seem to take much interest in the thing. I felt confident that, in a few minutes more, the car would leave the track and go to everlasting smash. I remember feeling thankful that I had gone over my accounts just before leaving Jericho and that nobody could fail to understand them.

"Just then I thought of the brake. If I should go out on the platform and put the brake on, the engineer would feel the drag on the car and would stop the train, unless he was stark mad. At any rate, the thing was worth trying. I got out on the platform, hanging on for all I was worth to the handrail, until I got hold of the brake wheel. It was as rusty as if it had been soaking in water for a week, but I didn't mind that. I jammed that brake down good and hard, but the brake chain snapped almost as easy as the bell cord, and there was an end of that plan for stopping the train. Of course, I knew that a brake chain sometimes snaps and you can't prevent it, but it was curious that both the bell cord and the brake chain on that car should have been good for nothing.

"Well, I got back into the car again. I took a middling good drink of the whisky, and it sort of warmed up my courage. I never was a drinking man, even in my young days, for I despise a drunkard, especially if he is a railroad man. But I hadn't had above six or seven drinks that day, and I knew that another moderate one wouldn't do me any harm.

"I was beginning to feel a little better, when I remembered that I had never heard the whistle of the locomotive since we had started from Manlius station. That showed me that the engineer wasn't either drunk or mad, for in either case he would have blown his whistle about two-thirds of the time, there being nothing that a crazy man or a drunken engineer finds as soothing as a steam whistle. I couldn't explain our flying around curves and other level crossings without sounding the whistle except on the theory that the engineer had dropped dead in his cab. But then there would have been the fireman. Both of the men couldn't very well have died at the same minute, and if there was anything the matter with the engineer, the fireman would naturally either have stopped the train and tried to get help—or he would have run it very cautiously, that not being his usual business, and would have been very particular

A Ghost Train

about whistling at the proper places. Not hearing the whistle was, on the whole, more astonishing to me than finding a Pullman car without a passenger or without a porter—and with the bed clothes soaked with water—and the bell cord almost too rotten to bear its own weight.

"There wasn't a thing to be seen through the car windows, for they were thick with dirt. So, wanting to get some idea of the locality that we had got to, I went out on the rear platform again, and getting down on the lower step, I leaned out to have a look all around. Just then we started around another curve, and what with my fingers being a little numb—and what with the swaying of the car—I lost my hold and was shot off that train like a mail bag chucked onto the platform when the Pacific Express goes booming by.

"Luckily, I fell into a snowbank and wasn't seriously hurt. However, the shock stunned me for a while. When I came to, I found that I had no bones broken and that my skull was all right. I picked myself up and started to walk down the track till I should come to a house. After walking about half a mile, as I should judge, I came to East Fabiusville, where there is a little tavern—and mightily glad I was to see it! I knocked the landlord up and got a bed. It was noon the next day before I woke up.

"There wasn't any train to Jericho until after 8:00, so not having anything to do, I looked up the landlord. I found he was an old acquaintance of mine, by the name of Hank Simmons. When I told him that I had come to Fabiusville by a night train, he sort of smiled. I could see he didn't believe me.

"'I don't say that the train stopped here,' I said, 'for the last I saw of it was a mile or so up the road, where I fell off the rear platform into a snowbank. But all the same, I did come most of the way from Manlius last night in a Pullman sleeper.'

"'Then you must have come on what the boys call the ghost train,' says Hank.

"'What train's that?' says I.

"'Why, it's the ghost of the train that went off the bridge on the Muskahoot River. The boys do say that, every once in a while, there is a train made up of a locomotive, a baggage car, and a Pullman sleeper. It comes down the road hustlin' and goes off the Muskahoot Bridge into the river. I never saw no such train myself, but there's lots of folks living along this road that have seen it, and you'd have hard work to convince 'em that it isn't the ghost of the wrecked train. Come to think of it, that there train was wrecked just a year ago last night, and it's probable that her ghost was out for an airing, as you might say.'

"Well, when I came to think the thing over, I came to the conclusion that Hank was right and that the Pullman with the wet bedclothes and the rotten bell cord was nothing more or less than the ghost of a car. However, I didn't say much more to Hank about it at the time, for the less a man talks about seeing ghosts the better it is for him, if he wants to be considered a reliable man. But as soon as I got back to Jericho, I went to see the division superintendent and told him the whole story.

"'See here,' he said when I had got through, 'I suppose I ought to report you, but considering that you were not on duty last night—and that you're not a drinking man as a general thing—I shan't say anything about it. But if you'll take my advice, you'll not tell that ridiculous story to anybody else.'

"'Then you think I was drunk and dreamed the whole thing, do you?' I asked.

"'I don't *think* so—I'm *sure* of it,' says he. 'I've just been over the division reports, and no such train as you describe has been seen at any station. Besides, I know where every Pullman car in the company's service was just at this identical time, and it's impossible that a Pullman should have been on the Manlius branch last night. No train of any kind went over that branch between 8:00 last night and 7:00 this morning.'

"'Then I wish you'd explain how I traveled from Manlius station to East Fabiusville last night between 9 and 12. I can prove by the conductor of the up-train that he let me off at Manlius after 8:00 last night, and I can prove by the landlord of the Fabiusville Tavern that I put up at his house just before 12:00. A man, whether he is drunk or sober, can't travel seventy miles in three hours unless he does it on a railroad train.'

"The superintendent was a mighty smart man, but this conundrum of mine was more than he could answer. So he only smiled in an aggravating sort of way and said: 'You'd better take my advice and keep quiet. You know how down the directors are on any man that drinks too much whisky. If you go about talking of this adventure of yours, the chances are you'll lose your place.'

"Just then I happened to think of the piece of bell cord that I had taken from the car. I put my hand in my pocket, and there it was, sure enough. I held it up and said to the superintendent: 'There's a piece of the rotten bell cord that I told you about. Perhaps you'll say I dreamed six feet of cord into my pocket.'

"The superintendent took it, and I could see that he was

considerable staggered. 'You say you got this out of the Pullman sleeper that you dreamed about?' he asked.

"'That's just exactly and precisely the identical place where I got that cord aforesaid,' says I, as solemn as if I was on my oath.

"'Well!' says he, 'I take back what I said about your having been drunk. That there cord hasn't been in use in any car on this road for more than a year. The last car that had a cord like that was the one that went into the Muskahoot River. That's a cotton cord, and we don't use anything but hemp nowadays.'

"'Then you think that I was on a ghost train, after all?' says I.

"'I think,' says he, 'that the less you say about it the better—that is, if you care to follow my advice. If you keep on talking about it, you'll have half the trainmen on the division watching for ghosts and neglecting their regular duties.'

"Of course, I promised to do as the superintendent said, and I never mentioned the ghost train until this particular superintendent had skipped to Canada with over $100,000. He was a most amazing smart man, and if I had gone against his wishes, I wouldn't have stayed in the company's service very long.

"However, when I did begin to tell the story, nobody believed me, except now and then by an old train hand who had seen ghost trains himself and knew all about 'em. I've told you the story as straight as a die, and you can take it or leave it just as you choose. As Horace says, 'There's more things in heaven and the other place than any philosopher ever dared to dream about.'"[4]

---

[4] Alden is having a final bit of fun with names here, since in Act 1, Scene 5, of Shakespeare's play, Hamlet—not Horace—says *something close to* this phrase to Horatio. Earlier, the author played with ancient Roman politicians by naming locations Tiberius Center, Manlius, and East Fabiusville.

THE PHANTOM TRAIN

MARY R. P. HATCH[1]

It was in the fall of 1881, Sept. 20, that a party of five including myself, started on a trip to Dixville Notch, a wild and romantic pass situated some fifty miles north of the White Mountains. Circumstances prevented our setting forth at the proposed hour, so it was nightfall ere we passed through Colebrook.[2] Indeed, lamps were lit in many of the stores and dwellings. Upon inquiry we learned that we were still ten miles from the Notch. We decided, however, to go forward, although our horses were tired and did not pull well together, being both off horses which had never before been driven side by side.

The twinkling lights grew less frequent and finally disappeared altogether, which led us to conjecture that we were now in the Dixville region. The stars came out, and the moon gave a faint light, but this only served to make more apparent the gloom of the impenetrable forests and rocky cliffs. As we observed all this, we regretted that we had not remained at Colebrook until morning, for the road—if not actually dangerous—was dreary enough.

We seemed as much out of the world or, at least, from the abodes of man as though we had been traveling days instead of hours. The cry of a loon or some other bird of night occasionally broke over the silence which settled over us, for the gentlemen were too much engaged in their efforts to keep the horses in the narrow path to indulge in any but laconic remarks. Miss Alden and I, with tightly clasped hands, sat rigid and still, waiting for the carriage to be overturned or hurled downwards into the darkness.

"Aren't you afraid?" exclaimed Miss Alden.

"No, I feel as safe as though I were in my mother's lap,"

---

[1] This short story comes from a Minnesota newspaper called *The Princeton Union,* Nov. 11, 1897, p. 6.

[2] Dixville Notch, the White Mountains, and Colebrook are authentic locations in New Hampshire.

The Phantom Train

returned Charlie, but immediately before the laugh subsided, he drew up the horses so suddenly, Mr. Ackley got down and discovered that he had narrowly escaped being thrown down a precipice.

"Shall we go on?" I asked anxiously.

"We can't turn around, and I suppose we must," returned Charlie.

The gloom increased, the darkness thickened. Trees grew thick on either side of the road. The curtains of our carriage were down, and Miss Alden and myself were thus enveloped in total darkness. As for my little boy, he had fallen asleep.

Suddenly we heard the shrill whistle of a locomotive, and the thunder of a train broke the silence. Our horses quivered with fright so that their harness shook, and they began plunging and rearing. Bending forward to peer out, we saw the lights of a passing train high up on the crags. Another whistle, a rumble, and it had vanished.

"Heavens!" exclaimed Charlie, "we have seen the phantom train!"

"Phantom train?" repeated Miss Alden, "I see nothing remarkable about it."

"Nothing remarkable—when there is not a railroad track within twenty miles of here? That train," said Charlie, "if it did not float in the air, ran over the points of stones bristling several feet apart and at an altitude that surveyors have thus far not interfered with."

"Is this true?" I asked.

"It is indeed," he replied. "I have heard of this train, but never believed in its existence until now. It only appears one night in a year, and I suppose we have chanced upon that night. Luckily or *unluckily*."

Absurd as the story has always appeared to me, I did not—in the uncanny darkness which surrounded us—find it too strange for belief. Indeed, had we not seen with our own eyes the phantom train?

"Shall I tell you the story as I heard it?" asked Mr. Ackley.

"Oh no, not until we are out of this gloom," said I.

"If we *ever* are," said Miss Alden.

We went on, past one or two lumbering camps, untenanted and solitary. Just as we began to feel hopelessly shut in by dangers, seen or unseen, we entered a cleared space and, in a moment, drew rein at a large, pleasant, well-lighted hotel: the Dix house.

The change was wonderful. Out of the dreadful darkness into

the cheerful house and the pleasant parlor where quite a number of guests, remnants of the summer visitors, were sitting cozily together.

"See it? Yes, I see it every 20th of September for years till the landlord took to having me here to tell the story of his company," broke from one corner of the room.

We observed a tall, weather-beaten old man who looked strangely out of place in the midst of the group of well-dressed city people.

"Hezekiah Winters," said one gentleman, rising and placing chairs for Miss Alden and myself, "was about to tell of the Phantom Train which is popularly supposed to appear every 20th of September."

"Let us not interrupt his recital," said Mr. Ackley as we all exchanged glances.

"You see," said the old man, "I was hostler down to Cohos, and I was a-tendin' to my duties when into the stable comes a young man, genteel but sorter dissipated lookin' and with somethin' in his eye that I didn't like the looks of.

"This young feller says to me, 'They tell me at the house that I can't get to Dixville tonight, but I'll go if the devil will help me, and I believe he will!'

"'They say he helps his own,' says I perlitely, but he didn't seem to mind what I said.

"'You see,' says he, 'there's a young lady with me, an' her mother is very sick. If we can get through the Notch tonight maybe she will see her mother before she dies. We've *got* to go—an' we *will* go!'

"'But there ain't no train, and there ain't no team that goes this time er night,' says I. I turned round to card one o' the hosses, and when I looked 'round, he wa'n't there. I was surprised because, you see, the stable doors opened and shut terrible hard and squeaked on their hinges.

"Well, he was gone. *Vanished* like. I went up to the house, an' the cook an' the chamber maid was a-talkin' about a lady in the parlor.

"'She's handsome as a drawn picture,' says Mary, 'and her feller is handsome, too. They're a runaway couple, I b'lieve.

"'Handsome!' said the cook, 'He's too wicked lookin' to be handsome!'

"'I wish I could see her,' says I, for you see I pitied the girl if she was going to run off with *that* man.

The Phantom Train

"'Well, come with me,' says Mary, 'I guess you can get a look at her, for I am jest a-goin' to ask her if she wants anything.'

"I followed Mary as fur as the parlor door, but in a minute, she comes out lookin' scared.

"'She ain't there,' says she.

"Well, ladies and gentlemen, no one ever set eyes on them after that, but strange sights and strange sounds was heard that night by more'n one. Miss Higgins, the milliner, was waked by a noise like a train passin' her window, and Dick Henderson was run over by a train and had his leg broke. There wa'n't no track, mind you, where they found him, and a good many folks said Dick was too drunk to know what hurt him.

"But old Mr. Fellows is the soberest man you ever saw, and he heard a train a-tootin' and bellerin' that night like all possessed. I heered him tell on't down to the store. He thought the day of judgment had come. And the Widder Storm, a mother in Israel, if there ever was one, says she was a-comin' from a sick neighbor's and saw right before her an ingine, but she didn't see no one else till the car passed her and then, sittin' by the winder that was all lit up, she saw a beautiful young lady and she was a-cryin'.

"She felt so sorry for her, the Widder Storm did, that she never thought of there bein' no track for the car till she got home, and then she said she shook like a leaf and she remembered that the smoke had a dreadful curious smell.

"Just a year from that night I happened to be camped out in Dixville Woods, and 'long towards midnight, I saw passin' high up on the peakid rocks a train tearin' along at a terrible rate. It was all lit up, but there wa'n't only the ingine and one car. 'Twas too fur off to see inter the windows, but I knew it was the same train. That feller was attendin' of the ingine, and the pretty girl was cryin' inside. I was sure on't, for when a man calls on the devil as he did, he's sure to git help, and he's pretty sure to git more'n he wants on't.

"Wall, the next year, me an' Jim Gallagher thought we'd get nigher, if we could. We set out to climb the rocks 'long in the afternoon, but sure's your born, we never got no higher, though we climb an' climb. When night came, we was in a different place, but no higher. By an' by, the train came tearin' along. It looked wickeder this time. The ingine seemed possessed an' belched an' blowed an' quivered an' throwed fire—and this time, I could just make out the figger of a man walkin' on the car. I looked 'round at Jim an' he laid on the ground rollin' an' twistin' as though he was in a fit. I shook him pretty rough, an' he set up and gasped.

"'Wall, Ki,' says he, 'I never believed nothin' before that you ever see it, but that's a phantom train, sure 'nough. Where's it goin' to?'

"Sure's the world I never thought of that, but Jim's a readin' feller, you see. At the rate that train traveled, it could go 'round the world pretty quick or down to Chiny, and 'round t'other way, for it don't need no rails, you see. But who was the feller an' who was the girl, an' was it a lie about her sick mother? I've figgered on it pretty stiddy, but I don't git no nigher the truth.

"Wall, two or three years after, a tall, melancholy man came to the Phenix to inquire after his daughter.[3] Said he'd tracked her so fur. Said he supposed she'd gone off with a stranger to him. His daughter got acquainted with him at school. Course, no one could tell anything about her. And there wa'n't no one could bear to tell him the terrible stories goin' 'bout the phantom train, so he went back to Canady."

---

[3] While "the Phenix" might refer to the Concord's popular Phenix Hotel, another Phenix Hotel was located in Newport, both cities in New Hampshire.

THE PHANTOM TRAIN

HOWARD WISWALL BIBLE[1]

My story tells of Daniel Lee,
    A trapper and guide,
Whose cabin nestled 'neath a tree
    Upon the mountain side.

The day broke full of sleet and rain.
    By night, it turned to snow.
As Dan set out to meet the train,
    At midnight from the Bow.

The Bow was where the track came round
    And crossed the road from camp,
And o'er the deep snow-drifted ground,
    It proved a weary tramp.

'Twas but a lonely flagging stand
    Deep in the frosted wood,
And there, a lantern in his hand
    That stormy night, Dan stood.

The icy blasts blew fiercer still
    Like to a thousand gales,
And yet no train came to fill
    The silent, empty rails.

Then, without whistle, bell, or ray,
    The engine's head all black,
A train came slowly on its way
    Along the empty track.

---

[1] This poem was taken from *Metropolitan* 39.5 [March, 1914] p. 19.

Howard Wiswall Bible

Dan saw no light, nor heard no roar,
    The mighty train was still,
And as he stepped aboard the car,
    He felt a gruesome chill.

Without the rumbling wheels' refrain,
    Without the whistle's shriek,
The silent train went on again
    Through midnight cold and bleak.

Upon the icy vestibule,
    With hand upon the door,
Dan quaked, to damn himself a fool,
    Then entered, quaking more.

For all about sat one-time men,
    Without the break of life,
And living Dan encountered them
    With ghostly horror rife!

Deep stunned by fear, he sat beside
    The door that he came through,
And terrified, he made the ride
    An hour, maybe two.

Then by his side, a child of five,
    A doll pressed to her breast,
Said, "Tell me, please, are you alive?"
    And all he said was—"Yes."

Now, that one word was like the cheer
    On Resurrection Morn,
For from all sections crowded near
    Those from whom life was torn.

The lifeless child, without a stir,
    Spoke further in dead tone
And told how mother waited her
    To bid a welcome home.

The Phantom Train

She said to him, "Please go for me,
    And give my mamma this,"—
And then the doll fell on his knee—
    "And say I sent a kiss."

In frenzy, Dan sprang to the aisle
    And shouted to the dead:
"Is this the place the good revile,
    About which I have read?"

Then from the middle of the car
    The old conductor spoke,
Each as from a sepulcher
    The horrid stillness woke.

"This train," said he, "is Number Four
    And runs through ev'ry night.
For nine and twenty years or more,
    She's held the track by right.

"Upon this run, nigh ten o'clock,
    Perchance a minute past,
We hastened on from block to block,
    A-running somewhat fast.

"To pick up time we'd lost by storm
    That filled the cuts with snow,
When rounding out from Piney Thorn,
    A landside shot below.

"The train, the passengers, and crew—
    A grim and gory mass.
Not one alive of all we drew
    From first to second class.

"And now the train you're traveling by
    Is still old Number Four,
And while a phantom, yet she'll try
    To make the run once more.

"I ask no ticket, nay, or pass.
    All that I ask, you see,
Tell how, despite her tangled mass,
    Old Number Four ran free.

"Tell to the masters of this line
    Their record is preserved.
Tell them we made the run on time
    With ev'ry rule observed."

Then with his ghostly lamp aswing,
    He slowly passed away.
Yet let the lantern's glimmer bring
    Each form within its ray.

Faster and faster grew the pace
    With hurl and lurch and swerve—
Wilder and wilder waxed the race
    O'er bridge and switch and curve.

Towns flew by like a twinkling eye
    In silence deathly still,
By where the northbound train should lie
    At foot of Dead Man's Hill.

Grim was the run through the Great Divide,
    Where mountains towered high,
For echoes caught the phantom's glide
    Like souls in their last cry.

And then the gruesome Moon arose
    With ghastly light so white
To show what kindly dark would close
    From eyes of Man that night.

Sometimes, Dan slumbered in a faint.
    Sometimes, he sat upright.
And then again he heard the plaint
    Of dying souls in flight.

The Phantom Train

So silver rays of day drew near
    To cap a sleeping town,
And Dan, in throes of mortal fear,
    Toward the door bore down.

Then from the platform, misty white,
    Where hurried footsteps led,
He leapt afar into the night
    While on the phantom sped.

And all was still and peaceful, too.
    The snowclad town asleep
Was resting 'neath the winter's hue
    In mantle cold and deep.

But hark! Dan heard a message flight
    Down from the icy wires
And crawled toward the station's light,
    A crawl of seeming hours.

There sat a man with nerve astrain
    And face of deathly hue,
Receiving word about a train
    An hour overdue.

The night train down from Crossway Bow
    That o'er a precipice fell
And carried all—both high and low—
    To Heaven or to Hell!

THIRD STATION:

WRAITHS ON THE RAILS

THE NINE-THIRTY UP-TRAIN

SABINE BARING-GOULD[1]

In a well-authenticated ghost story, names and dates should be distinctly specified. In the following story, I am unfortunately able to give only the year and the month, for I have forgotten the date of the day, and I do not keep a diary. With regard to names, my own figures as a guarantee at the end of this paper as that of the principal personage to whom the following extraordinary circumstances occurred, but the minor actors are provided with fictitious names, for I am not warranted to make their real ones public. I may add that the believer in ghosts may make use of the facts which I relate to establish his theories, if he finds that they will be of service to him, when he has read through and weighed well the startling account which I am about to give from my own experiences.

On a fine evening in June, 1860, I paid a visit to Mrs. Lyons while on my way to the Hassock's Gate Station, on the London and Brighton line. This station is the first out of Brighton.

As I rose to leave, I mentioned to the lady whom I was visiting that I expected a parcel of books from town and that I was going to the station to inquire whether it had arrived.

"Oh!" said she readily, "I expect Dr. Lyons out from Brighton by the 9.30 train. If you wish to drive the pony chaise down and meet him, you are welcome, and you can bring your parcel back with him in it."

I gladly accepted her offer, and in a few minutes, I was seated in a little low basket-carriage, drawn by a pretty iron-grey Welsh pony.

The station road commands the line of the South Downs from Chanctonbury Ring, with its cap of dark firs, to Mount Harry, the scene of the memorable battle of Lewes. Woolsonbury stands out

---

[1] The oldest work of fiction in this anthology, this was originally published in *Once a Week* 9.218 [Aug. 29, 1863] pp. 253-57. It was reprinted in Baring-Gould's collection *A Book of Ghosts* (Methuen, 1904) pp. 327-40.

like a headland above the dark Danny Woods, over which the rooks were wheeling and cawing previous to settling themselves in for the night. Ditchling Beacon—its steep sides gashed with chalk-pits—was faintly flushed with light. The Clayton windmills, with their sails motionless, stood out darkly against the green evening sky. Close beneath opens the tunnel in which, not so long ago, had happened one of the most fearful railway accidents on record.[2]

The evening was exquisite. The sky was kindled with light, though the Sun was set. A few gilded bars of cloud lay in the west. Two or three stars looked forth—one I noticed twinkling green, crimson, and gold like a gem. The harsh, grating note of the corncrake came from a nearby field of young wheat. Mist was lying on the low meadows like a mantle of snow, pure, smooth, and white—the cattle stood in it to their knees. The effect was so singular that I drew up to look at it attentively. At the same moment, I heard the scream of an engine, and on looking towards the downs, I noticed the up-train shooting out of the tunnel, its red signal lamps flashing brightly out of the purple gloom which bathed the roots of the hills.

Seeing that I was late, I whipped the Welsh pony on and proceeded at a fast trot.

At about a quarter mile from the station, there is a turnpike.[3] Beside it is an odd-looking building tenanted by a strange old man usually dressed in a white smock, over which his long white beard flowed to his breast. This toll-collector—he is dead now—had amused himself in bygone days by carving life-size heads out of wood, and these were stuck along the eaves. One is the face of a drunkard, round and blotched, leering out of misty eyes at the passers-by. The next has the crumpled features of a miser worn out with toil and moil. A third has the wild scowl of a maniac, and a fourth the stare of an idiot.

I drove past, flinging the toll to the door and shouting to the old man to pick it up, for I was in a vast hurry to reach the station before Dr. Lyons left it. I whipped the little pony on, and he began to trot down a cutting in the green-sand, through which leads the station road.

---

[2] The narrator is near the border of West and East Sussex counties in England. Though Baring-Gould bumps the date a bit *earlier,* the location would have reminded the original readers of the two trains that collided in Clayton Tunnel on August 25, 1861, given that the piece was first published two years *after* that tragedy. The accident left 23 dead and 176 injured, making it the worst British rail disaster to that point.

[3] In this case, "turnpike" means a tollgate.

The 9.30 Up-Train

Suddenly, Taffy stood still, planted his feet resolutely on the ground, threw up his head, snorted, and refused to move a peg. I "gee-up-ed," and "tsh-ed," all to no purpose. Not a step would the little fellow advance. I saw that he was thoroughly alarmed: his flanks were quivering, and his ears were thrown back. I was on the point of leaving the chaise, when the pony made a bound on one side and ran the carriage up into the hedge, thereby upsetting me on the road.

I picked myself up and took the beast's head. I could not conceive what had frightened him. There was positively nothing to be seen except a puff of dust running up the road, such as might be blown along by a passing current of air. There was nothing to be heard except the rattle of a gig or tax-cart with one wheel loose—probably a vehicle of this kind was being driven down the London road, which branches off at the turnpike at right angles. The sound became fainter and, at last, died away in the distance.

The pony now no longer refused to advance. Nonetheless, he trembled violently and was covered with sweat.

Dr. Lyons noticed this when I met him at the station.

"Well! upon my word you have been driving hard!" he exclaimed.

"I have not, indeed," was my reply. "Something frightened Taffy, but what that something was, is more than I can tell."

"Oh, ah!" said the doctor, looking round with a certain degree of interest in his face, "so you met *it,* did you!"

"Met *what?*"

"Oh, nothing. Only I have heard of horses being frightened along this road after the arrival of the 9.30 up-train. Flys never leave the moment that the train comes in, or the horses become restive—a wonderful thing for a fly-horse to become restive, isn't it?"[4]

"But what causes this alarm? I saw nothing!"

"You ask me more than I can answer. I am as ignorant of the cause as yourself. I take things as they stand and make no inquiries. When the flyman tells me that he can't start for a minute or two after the train has arrived—or urges on his horses to reach the station before the arrival of this train, giving as his reason that his brutes become wild if he does not do so—then I merely say, 'Do as you think best, cabby,' and bother my head no more about the matter."

"I shall search this matter out," said I resolutely. "What has

---

[4] A "fly" is a horse-drawn vehicle, including a for-hire public conveyance that is like a Hansom cab.

taken place so strangely corroborates the superstition that I shall not leave it uninvestigated."

"Take my advice and banish it from your thoughts. When you have come to the end, you will be sadly disappointed, and you will find that all the mystery evaporates, leaving a dull, commonplace residuum. It is best that the few mysteries which remain to us unexplained should still remain mysteries, or we shall disbelieve in supernatural agencies altogether. We have searched out the arcana of Nature and exposed all her secrets to the garish eye of day, and we find, in despair, that the poetry and romance of life are gone.

"Are we the happier for knowing that there are no ghosts, no fairies, no witches, no mermaids, no wood spirits? Were not our forefathers happier in thinking every lake to be the abode of a fairy, every forest to be a bower of yellow-haired sylphs, every moorland sweep to be tripped over by elf and pixie? I found my little boy one day lying on his face in a fairy-ring, crying: 'You dear, dear little fairies, I *will* believe in you, though Papa says you are all nonsense.' In my childish days, I used to think, when a silence fell upon a company, that an angel was passing through the room. Alas! I now know that it results only from the subject of weather having been talked to death and no new subject having been started.

"Believe me, science has done good to mankind, but it has done mischief, too. If we wish to be poetical or romantic, we must shut our eyes to facts. The head and the heart wage mutual war now. A lover preserves a lock of his mistress's hair as a holy relic, yet he must know perfectly well that, for all practical purposes, a bit of rhinoceros hide would do as well—the chemical constituents are identical. If I adore a fair lady and feel a thrill through all my veins when I touch her hand, a moment's consideration tells me that phosphate of lime No. 1 is touching phosphate of lime No. 2— nothing more. If for a moment I forget myself so far as to wave my cap and cheer for King, or Queen, or Prince, I laugh at my folly next moment for having paid reverence to one digesting machine above another."

I cut the doctor short as he was lapsing into his favourite subject of discussion and asked him whether he would lend me the pony-chaise on the following evening that I might drive to the station again and try to unravel the mystery.

"I will lend you the pony," said he, "but not the chaise, as I am afraid of its being damaged should Taffy take fright and run up into the hedge again. I have got a saddle."

The 9.30 Up-Train

Next evening, I was on my way to the station considerably before the time at which the train was due.

I stopped at the turnpike and chatted with the old man who kept it. I asked him whether he could throw any light on the matter which I was investigating.

He shrugged his shoulders, saying that he "knowed nothink about it."

"What! Nothing at all?"

"I don't trouble my head with matters of this sort," was the reply. "People do say that something out of the common sort passes along the road and turns down the other road leading to Clayton and Brighton. But I pays no attention to what them people says."

"Do you ever hear anything?"

"After the arrival of the 9.30 train, I does at times hear the rattle as of a mail-cart and the trot of a horse along the road, and the sound is as though one of the wheels was loose. I've a-been out many a time to take the toll, but—Lor' bless 'ee!—them sperits, if sperits them be, don't go for to pay toll."

"Have you never inquired into the matter?"

"Why should I? Anythink as don't go for to pay toll don't concern me. Do ye think as I knows 'ow many people and dogs goes through this heer gate in a day? Not I. Them don't pay toll, so them's no odds to me."

"Look here, my man!" said I. "Do you object to my putting the bar across the road, immediately on the arrival of the train?"

"Not a bit! Please yersel'. But you han't got much time to lose, for theer comes thickey train out of Clayton Tunnel."

I shut the gate, mounted Taffy, and drew up across the road a little way below the turnpike. I heard the train arrive—I saw it puff off. At the same moment, I distinctly heard a trap coming up the road, one of the wheels rattling as though it were loose. I repeat deliberately that I *heard* it—I cannot account for it—but, though I heard it, yet I *saw* nothing whatever.

At the same time, the pony became restless. He tossed his head, pricked up his ears—he started, pranced, and then made a bound to one side entirely regardless of whip and rein. He tried to scramble up the sandbank in his alarm, and I had to throw myself off and catch his head. I then cast a glance behind me at the turnpike. I saw the bar bent—as though someone were pressing against it—then, with a click, it flew open and was dashed violently back against the white post to which it was usually hasped in the daytime. There it remained, quivering from the shock.

Immediately, I heard the rattle-rattle-rattle of the tax-cart. I confess that my first impulse was to laugh, the idea of a ghostly tax-cart was so essentially ludicrous! But the reality of the whole scene soon brought me to a graver mood, and remounting Taffy, I rode down to the station.

The officials were taking their ease as another train was not due for some while, so I stepped up to the stationmaster and entered into conversation with him. After a few desultory remarks, I mentioned the circumstances which had occurred to me on the road and my inability to account for them.

"So that's what you're after!" said the master somewhat bluntly. "Well, I can tell you nothing about it. Sperits don't come in my way, saving and excepting those which can be taken inwardly. And mighty comfortable warming things they be when so taken. If you ask me about other sorts of sperits, I tell you flat I don't believe in 'em, though I don't mind drinking the health of them what does."

"Perhaps you may have the chance, if you are a little more communicative," said I.

"Well, I'll tell you all I know, and that is precious little," answered the worthy man. "I know one thing for certain—that one compartment of a second-class carriage in the 9.30 up-train is always left vacant between Brighton and Hassock's Gate."

"For what purpose?"

"Ah! that's more than I can fully explain. Before the orders came to this effect, people went into fits and that like in one of the carriages."

"Any particular carriage?"

"The first compartment of the second-class carriage nearest to the engine. It is locked at Brighton, and I unlock it at this station."

"What do you mean by saying that people had fits?"

"I mean that I used to find men and women a-screeching and a-hollering like mad to be let out. They'd seen some'ut as had frightened them as they was passing through the Clayton Tunn'l. That was before they made the arrangement I told y' of."

"Very strange!" said I meditatively.

"Wery much so, but true for all that. *I* don't believe in nothing but sperits of a warming and cheering nature, and them sort ain't to be found in Clayton Tunn'l to my thinking."

There was evidently nothing more to be got out of my friend. I hope that he drank my health that night. If he omitted to do so, it was his fault, not mine.

As I rode home, revolving in my mind all that I had heard and seen, I became more and more settled in my determination to thoroughly investigate the matter. The best means that I could adopt for so doing would be to come out from Brighton by the 9.30 train in the very compartment of the second-class carriage from which the public were considerately excluded.

Somehow, I felt no shrinking from the attempt. My curiosity was so intense that it overcame all apprehension as to the consequences.

My next free day was Thursday, and I hoped then to execute my plan. In this, however, I was disappointed, as I found that a battalion drill was fixed for that very evening, and I was desirous of attending it, being somewhat behindhand in the regulation number of drills.[5] I was consequently obliged to postpone my Brighton trip.

On the Thursday evening about five o'clock, I started in regimentals, with my rifle over my shoulder, for the drilling ground, a piece of furzy common near the railway station.

I was speedily overtaken by Mr. Ball, a corporal in the rifle corps, a capital shot and most efficient in his drill. Mr. Ball was driving his gig. He stopped on seeing me and offered me a seat beside him. I gladly accepted as the distance to the station is a mile and three-quarters by the road and two miles by what is commonly supposed to be the short cut across the fields.

After some conversation on volunteering matters, about which Corporal Ball was an enthusiast, we turned out of the lanes into the station road, and I took the opportunity of adverting to the subject which was uppermost in my mind.

"Ah! I have heard a good deal about that," said the corporal. "My workmen have often told me some cock-and-bull stories of that kind, but I can't say has 'ow I believed them. What you tell me is, 'owever, very remarkable. I never 'ad it on such good authority afore. Still, I can't believe that there's hanything supernatural about it."

"I do not yet know what to believe," I replied, "for the whole matter is to me perfectly inexplicable."

"You know, of course, the story which gave rise to the super-

---

[5] Our narrator appears to be part of the Volunteer Force. In 1857, with its armed forces dispersed across a vast empire and tensions with France on the rise, Great Britain formed this organization. The regiments were localized, often growing from rifle clubs, and members trained part-time, standing by in case of emergency. In 1908, the corps evolved into the Territorial Force and, in 2013, the Army Reserve.

stition?"

"Not I. Pray tell it me."

"Just about seven years agone—why, you must remember the circumstances as well as I do—there was a man druv over in a light cart. From where, I can't say, for that was never exactly hascertained, but from the Henfield direction. He went to the Station Inn and threw the reins to John Thomas, the ostler. This man bade him take the trap and bring it round to meet the 9.30 train, by which he calculated to return from Brighton. John Thomas said as 'ow the stranger was quite unbeknown to him and that he looked as though he 'ad some matter on his mind when he went to the train. He was a queer sort of a man with thick grey hair and beard, and delicate white 'ands, jist like a lady's.

"The trap was round to the station door, as hordered, by the arrival of the 9.30 train. The ostler observed then that the man was ashen pale—that his 'ands trembled as he took the reins. The stranger stared at him in a wild habstracted way, looking as if he would have driven off without tendering payment had he not been respectfully reminded that the 'orse had been given a feed of hoats. John Thomas made a hobservation to the gent relative to the wheel which was loose, but that hobservation met with no corresponding hanswer. The driver whipped his 'orse and went off. He passed the turnpike and was seen to take the Brighton road hinstead of that by which he had come. A workman hobserved the trap next on the downs above Clayton chalk-pits. He didn't pay much attention to it, but he saw that the driver was on his legs at the 'ead of the 'orse.

"Next morning, when the quarrymen went to the pit, they found a shattered tax-cart at the bottom, and the 'orse and driver dead, the latter with his neck broken. What was curious, too, was that an 'andkerchief was bound round the brute's heyes, so that he must have been driven over the edge blindfold. Hodd, wasn't it? Well, folks say that the gent and his tax-cart pass along the road every hevening after the arrival of the 9.30 train. *I don't believe it. I ain't a bit superstitious—not I!*"

The next week, I was again disappointed in my expectation of being able to put my scheme in execution. However, on the third Saturday after my conversation with Corporal Ball, I walked into Brighton in the afternoon, the distance being about nine miles. I spent an hour on the shore watching the boats. I then sauntered round the Pavilion, ardently longing that fire might break forth and consume that architectural monstrosity.[6]

I believe that I afterwards had a cup of coffee at the refreshment rooms of the station, and capital refreshment rooms they are—or were—very moderate and very good. I think that I partook of a bun, but if put on my oath, I could not swear to the fact. A floating reminiscence of bun lingers in the chambers of memory, but I cannot be positive, and I wish in this paper to advance nothing but reliable facts. I squandered precious time in reading the advertisements of baby-jumpers—which no mother should be without—which are indispensable in the nursery and the greatest acquisition in the parlour, the greatest discovery of modern times, &c., &c. I perused a notice of the advantage of metallic brushes and admired the young lady with her hair white on one side and black on the other. I studied the Chinese letter commendatory of Horniman's tea and the inferior English translation, and I counted up the number of agents in Great Britain and Ireland.

At length, the ticket-office opened, and I booked for Hassock's Gate, second class, fare one shilling.

I ran along the platform till I came to the compartment of the second-class carriage which I wanted. The door was locked, so I shouted for a guard.

"Put me in here, please!"

"Can't there, s'r. Next, please. Nearly empty. One woman and baby."

"I particularly wish to enter *this* carriage," said I.

"Can't be. Lock'd. Comp'ny orders," replied the guard, turning on his heel.

"What reason is there for the public's being excluded, may I ask?"

"Dun 'ow. 'Spress orders—c'n't let you in. Next carriage, please. 'Ow then—quick, please."

I knew the guard, and he knew me by sight, for I often travelled to and fro on the line. I thought it best to be candid with him. I briefly told him my reason for making the request and begged him to assist me in executing my plan.

He then consented, though with reluctance.

"'Ave y'r own way," said he. "Only if an'thing 'appens, don't blame me!"

---

[6] Constructed between 1787 and 1823, Brighton's Royal Pavilion first served as a seaside pleasure palace for King George IV. Today, it's a tourist attraction and wedding venue. Photos available on the Internet might help one decide if the narrator's fiery opinion of the place is within reason.

"Never fear," laughed I, jumping into the carriage.

The guard left the carriage unlocked, and in two minutes, we were off.

I did not feel in the slightest degree nervous. There was no light in the carriage, but that did not matter as there was twilight. I sat facing the engine on the left side, and every now and then I looked out at the downs with a soft haze of light still hanging over them. We swept into a cutting, and I watched the lines of flint in the chalk and longed to be geologising among them with my hammer, picking out shepherds' crowns and sharks' teeth, the delicate rhynconella and the quaint ventriculite. I remembered a not very distant occasion on which I had actually ventured there and been chased off by the guard. This was after I had brought down an avalanche of chalk debris in a manner dangerous to traffic whilst endeavouring to extricate a magnificent ammonite which I found and—alas! left—protruding from the side of the cutting. I wondered whether that ammonite was still there. I looked about to identify the exact spot as we whizzed along.

And, at that moment, we shot into the tunnel.

There are two tunnels with a bit of chalk-cutting between them. We passed through the first, which is short, and in another moment plunged into the second.

I cannot explain how it was that now, all of a sudden, a feeling of terror came over me. It seemed to drop over me like a wet sheet and wrap me round and round.

I felt that someone was seated opposite me—someone in the darkness with his eyes fixed on me.

Many persons possessed of keen nervous sensibility are well aware when they are in the presence of another, even though they can see no one. I believe that I possess this power strongly. If I were blindfolded, I think that I should know when anyone was looking fixedly at me, and I am certain that I should instinctively know that I was not alone if I entered a dark room in which another person was seated, even though he made no noise.

I remember a college friend of mine, who dabbled in anatomy, telling me that a little Italian violinist once called on him to give a lesson on his instrument. The foreigner—a singularly nervous individual—moved restlessly from the place where he had been standing, casting many a furtive glance over his shoulder at a press which was behind him.[7]

---

[7] In this case, a "press" is a fairly tall, free-standing cabinet—something like a wardrobe—that typically held sheets, napkins, or clothing.

At last, the little fellow tossed aside his violin, saying, "I cannot give de lesson if someone weel look at me from behind! Dare is somebody in de cupboard, I know!"

"You are right, there is!" laughed my anatomical friend, flinging open the door of the press and revealing a skeleton.

The horror which oppressed me was numbing. For a few moments I could neither lift my hands nor stir a finger. I was tongue-tied. I seemed paralysed in every member. I fancied that I felt eyes staring at me through the gloom. A cold breath seemed to play over my face. I believed that fingers touched my chest and plucked at my coat. I drew back against the partition, and my heart stood still. My flesh became stiff, my muscles rigid.

I do not know whether I breathed—a blue mist swam before my eyes, and my head span.

The rattle and roar of the train dashing through the tunnel drowned every other sound.

Suddenly we rushed past a light fixed against the wall in the side, and it sent a flash—instantaneous as that of lightning—through the carriage. In that moment, I saw what I shall never, never forget. I saw a face opposite me, livid as that of a corpse, hideous with passion like that of a gorilla.

I cannot describe it accurately, for I saw it but for a second. Yet there rises before me now, as I write, the low broad brow seamed with wrinkles, the shaggy, over-hanging grey eyebrows. The wild ashen eyes, which glared as those of a demoniac. The coarse mouth with its fleshy lips compressed till they were white. The profusion of wolf-grey hair about the cheeks and chin. The thin, bloodless hands, raised and half-open, extended towards me as though they would clutch and tear me.

In the madness of terror, I flung myself along the seat to the further window.

Then I felt that *it* was moving slowly down and was opposite me again. I lifted my hand to let down the window, and I touched something. I thought it was a hand—yes, yes! it was a hand, for it folded over mine and began to contract on it. I felt each finger separately—they were cold, dully cold. I wrenched my hand away. I slipped back to my former place in the carriage by the open window. In frantic horror, I opened the door, clinging to it with both my hands round the window jamb and swinging myself out with my feet on the floor and my head turned from the carriage. If the cold fingers had but touched my clutching hands, mine would have given way. Had I but turned my head and seen that hellish countenance peering out at me, I must have lost my hold.

Ah! I saw the light from the tunnel mouth—it smote on my face. The engine rushed out with a piercing whistle. The roaring echoes of the tunnel died away. The cool fresh breeze blew over my face and tossed my hair. The speed of the train was relaxed, and the lights of the station became brighter.

I heard the bell ringing loudly. I saw people waiting for the train. I felt the vibration as the brake was put on. We stopped.

And then my fingers gave way. I dropped as a sack on the platform, and then, then—not till then—I awoke. There now! from beginning to end the whole had been a frightful dream caused by my having too many blankets over my bed.

If I must append a moral: Don't sleep too hot.

THE FOUR-FIFTEEN EXPRESS

AMELIA B. EDWARDS[1]

I.

The events which I am about to relate took place between nine and ten years ago. Sebastopol had fallen in the early spring, the peace of Paris had been concluded since March, and our commercial relations with the Russian empire were but recently renewed.[2] I, returning home after my first northward journey since the war, was well pleased with the prospect of spending the month of December under the hospitable and thoroughly English roof of my excellent friend, Jonathan Jelf, Esq., of Dumbleton Manor, Clayborough, East Anglia. Travelling in the interests of the well-known firm in which it is my lot to be a junior partner, I had been called upon to visit not only the capitals of Russia and Poland, but had found it also necessary to pass some weeks among the trading ports of the Baltic. The year was already far spent before I again set foot on English soil, and instead of shooting pheasants with my friend in October, as I had hoped, I came to be his guest during the more genial Christmas-tide.

My voyage over and a few days given up to business in Liverpool and London, I hastened down to Clayborough with all the delight of a schoolboy whose holidays are at hand. My way lay by the Great East Anglian line as far as Clayborough station, where I was to be met by one of the Dumbleton carriages and conveyed across the remaining nine miles of country. It was a foggy afternoon, singularly warm for the 4th of December, and I had arranged to leave London by the 4.15 express. The early darkness of

---

[1] This short story comes from *Every Saturday* 2.51 [Dec. 22, 1866] pp. 755-63. (Probably about the same time, it also appeared in *Routledge's Christmas Annual,* but I haven't found an extant copy of that publication.) It was reprinted in Edwards' *Monsieur Maurice, and Other Tales* (Hurst and Blackett, 1873) Vol. 3, pp. 67-133.

[2] These are references to the ending of the Crimean War, which had been waged between 1853 and 1856.

winter had already closed in, and the lamps were lighted in the carriages. A clinging damp dimmed the windows, adhered to the door handles, and pervaded all the atmosphere. The gas jets at the neighbouring bookstand diffused a luminous haze that only served to make the gloom of the terminus more visible. Having arrived some seven minutes before the starting of the train—and, by the connivance of the guard, taken sole possession of an empty compartment—I lighted my travelling lamp, made myself particularly snug, and settled down to the undisturbed enjoyment of a book and a cigar.

Great, therefore, was my disappointment when, at the last moment, a gentleman came hurrying along the platform, glanced into my carriage, opened the locked door with a private key, and stepped in.

It struck me at the first glance that I had seen him before—a tall, spare man, thin-lipped, light-eyed, with an ungraceful stoop in the shoulders and scant gray hair worn somewhat long upon collar. He carried a light waterproof coat, an umbrella, and a large brown japanned deed-box, which last he placed under the seat. This done, he felt carefully in his breast-pocket, as if to make certain of the safety of his purse or pocketbook, laid his umbrella in the netting overhead, spread the waterproof across his knees, and exchanged his hat for a travelling cap of some Scotch material. By this time, the train was moving out of the station and into the faint gray of the wintry twilight beyond.

I now recognised my companion. I recognised him from the moment when he removed his hat and uncovered the lofty, furrowed, and somewhat narrow brow beneath. I had met him, as I distinctly remembered, some three years before at the very house for which, in all probability, he was now bound like myself. His name was Dwerrihouse. He was a lawyer by profession and, if I was not greatly mistaken, was first cousin to the wife of my host. I knew also that he was a man eminently "well-to-do," both as regarded his professional and private means. The Jelfs entertained him with that sort of observant courtesy which falls to the lot of the rich relation, the children made much of him, and the old butler, albeit somewhat surly "to the general," treated him with deference.

Observing him by the vague mixture of lamplight and twilight, I thought that Mrs. Jelf's cousin looked all the worse for the three years' wear and tear which had gone over his head since our last meeting. He was very pale and had a restless light in his eye that I did not remember to have observed before. The anxious lines, too, about his mouth were deepened, and there was a cavernous, hollow look about his cheeks and temples which seemed to speak of sickness or sorrow. He had glanced at me as he came in, but without any gleam of recognition in his face. Now he glanced again, as I fancied, somewhat doubtfully. When he did so for the third or fourth time, I ventured to address him.

"Mr. John Dwerrihouse, I think?"

"That is my name," he replied.

"I had the pleasure of meeting you at Dumbleton about three years ago."

Mr. Dwerrihouse bowed.

"I thought I knew your face," he said, "but your name, I regret to say—"

"Langford—William Langford. I have known Jonathan Jelf since we were boys together at Merchant Taylor's, and I generally spend a few weeks at Dumbleton in the shooting season. I suppose we are bound for the same destination?"

"Not if you are on your way to the manor," he replied. "I am travelling upon business—rather troublesome business, too—while you, doubtless, have only pleasure in view."

"Just so. I am in the habit of looking forward to this visit as to the brightest three weeks in all the year."

"It is a pleasant house," said Mr. Dwerrihouse.

"The pleasantest I know."

"And Jelf is thoroughly hospitable."

"The best and kindest fellow in the world!"

After a moment's pause, Mr. Dwerrihouse pursued, "They have invited me to spend Christmas week with them."

"And you are coming?"

"I cannot tell. It must depend on the issue of this business which I have in hand. You have heard perhaps that we are about to construct a branch line from Blackwater to Stockbridge."

I explained that I had been for some months away from England and had, therefore, heard nothing of the contemplated improvement.

Mr. Dwerrihouse smiled complacently before saying, "It *will* be an improvement. A *great* improvement. Stockbridge is a flourishing town and needs but a more direct railway communication with the metropolis to become an important centre of commerce. This branch was my own idea. I brought the project before the board and have myself superintended the execution of it up to the present time."

"You are an East Anglian director, I presume?"

"My interest in the company," replied Mr. Dwerringhouse, "is threefold. I am a director, I am a considerable shareholder, and as head of the firm of Dwerrihouse, Dwerrihouse & Craik, I am the company's principal solicitor."

Loquacious, self-important, full of his pet project, and apparently unable to talk on any other subject, Mr. Dwerrihouse then went on to tell of the opposition he had encountered and the obstacles he had overcome in the cause of the Stockbridge branch. I was entertained with a multitude of local details and local grievances. The rapacity of one squire, and the impracticability of another. The indignation of the rector whose glebe was threatened, and the culpable indifference of the Stockbridge townspeople, who could not be brought to see that their most vital interests hinged upon a junction with the Great East Anglian line. The spite of the local newspaper, and the unheard-of difficulties attending the Common question. Each and all were laid before me with a circumstantiality that possessed the deepest interest for my excellent fellow traveller, but none whatever for myself.

From these, to my despair, he went on to more intricate matters: to the approximate expenses of construction per mile, to the estimates sent in by different contractors, to the probable traffic returns of the new line, to the provisional clauses of the new act as enumerated in Schedule D of the company's last half-yearly report, and so on and on and on, till my head ached and my attention flagged and my eyes kept closing in spite of every effort that I made to keep them open.

At length, I was roused by these words:

"Seventy-five thousand pounds, cash down."

"Seventy-five thousand pounds, cash down!" I repeated in the liveliest tone I could assume. "That *is* a heavy sum."

"A heavy sum to carry here," replied Mr. Dwerrihouse, pointing significantly to his breast pocket, "but a mere fraction of what we shall ultimately have to pay."

"You do not mean to say that you have seventy-five thousand pounds at this moment upon your person!" I exclaimed.

"My good sir, have I not been telling you so for the last half-hour?" said Mr. Dwerrihouse testily. "That money has to be paid over at half-past eight o'clock this evening at the office of Sir Thomas's solicitors on completion of the deed of sale."

"But how will you get across by night from Blackwater to Stockbridge with seventy-five thousand pounds in your pocket?"

The Four-Fifteen Express

"To Stockbridge!" echoed the lawyer. "I find I have made myself very imperfectly understood. I thought I had explained how this sum only carries us as far as Mallingford—the first stage, as it were, of our journey—and how our route from Blackwater to Mallingford lies entirely through Sir Thomas Liddell's property."

"I beg your pardon," I stammered. "I fear my thoughts were wandering. So you only go as far as Mallingford tonight?"

"Precisely. I shall get a conveyance from the Blackwater Arms. And you?"

"Oh, Jelf sends a trap to meet me at Clayborbough. Can I be the bearer of any message from you?"

"You may say—if you please, Mr. Langford—that I wished I could have been your companion all the way and that I will come over, if possible, before Christmas."

"Nothing more?"

Mr. Dwerrihouse smiled grimly. "Well," he said, "you may tell my cousin that she need not burn the hall down in my honour *this* time and that I shall be obliged if she will order the blue-room chimney to be swept before I arrive."

"That sounds tragic. Had you a conflagration on the occasion of your last visit to Dumbleton?"

"Something like it. There had been no fire lighted in my bedroom since the spring, the flue was foul, and the rooks had built in it. When I went up to dress for dinner, I found the room full of smoke and the chimney on fire. Are we already at Blackwater?"

The train had gradually come to a pause while Mr. Dwerrihouse was speaking, and on putting my head out of the window, I could see the station some few hundred yards ahead. There was another train before us blocking the way, and the guard was making use of the delay to collect the Blackwater tickets. I had scarcely ascertained our position when the ruddy-faced official appeared at our carriage door.

"Tickets, sir!" said he.

"I am for Clayborough," I replied, holding out the tiny pink card.

He took it, glanced at it by the light of his little lantern, and gave it back. Next, he looked at my fellow traveller—as I fancied, somewhat sharply—and disappeared.

"He did not ask for yours," I said with some surprise.

"They never do," replied Mr. Dwerrihouse. "They all know me, and I travel free, of course."

"Blackwater! Blackwater!" cried the porter, running along the platform beside us as we glided into the station.

Mr. Dwerrihouse pulled out his deed box, put his travelling cap in his pocket, resumed his hat, took down his umbrella, and prepared to be gone.

"Many thanks, Mr. Langford, for your society," he said with old-fashioned courtesy. "I wish you a good-evening."

"Good-evening," I replied, putting out my hand.

But he either did not see it or did not choose to see it. Slightly lifting his hat, he stepped out upon the platform. Having done this, he moved slowly away and mingled with the departing crowd.

Leaning forward to watch him out of sight, I trod upon something which proved to be a cigar case. It had fallen, no doubt, from the pocket of his waterproof coat. It was made of dark morocco leather with a silver monogram upon the side. I sprang out of the carriage just as the guard came up to lock me in.

"Is there one minute to spare?" I asked eagerly. "The gentleman who travelled down with me from town has dropped his cigar case—he is not yet out of the station."

"Just a minute and a half, sir," replied the guard. "You must be quick."

I dashed along the platform as fast as my feet could carry me. It was a large station, and Mr. Dwerrihouse had by this time got more than halfway to the farther end.

I, however, saw him distinctly, moving slowly with the stream. Then, as I drew nearer, I saw that he had met some friend, that they were talking as they walked, that they presently fell back somewhat from the crowd and stood aside in earnest conversation. I made straight for the spot where they were waiting.

There was a vivid gas jet just above their heads, and the light fell full upon their faces. I saw both distinctly—the face of Mr. Dwerrihouse and the face of his companion. Running, breathless, eager as I was, getting in the way of porters and passengers, and fearful every instant lest I should see the train going on without me, I yet observed that the newcomer was considerably younger and shorter than the director, and that he was sandy haired, mustachioed, small featured, and dressed in a close-cut suit of Scotch tweed. I was now within a few yards of them. I ran against a stout gentleman, I was nearly knocked down by a luggage truck, I stumbled over a carpetbag. I gained the spot just as the driver's whistle warned me to return.

To my utter stupefaction, they were no longer there. I had seen them but two seconds before—and they were *gone!* I stood still. I

The Four-Fifteen Express

looked to right and left. I saw no sign of them in any direction. It was as if the platform had gaped and swallowed them.

"There were two gentlemen standing here a moment ago," I said to a porter at my elbow. "Which way can they have gone?"

"I saw no gentlemen, sir," replied the man.

The whistle shrilled out again.

The guard, far up the platform, held up his arm and shouted to me to "come on!"

"If you're going on by this train, sir," said the porter, "you must run for it."

I did run for it, just gained the carriage as the train began to move, was shoved in by the guard, and left, breathless and bewildered, with Mr. Dwerrihouse's cigar case still in my hand.

It was the strangest disappearance in the world. It was like a transformation trick in a pantomime. They were there one moment—palpably there, walking, with the gaslight full upon their faces—and the next moment they were gone. There was no door near, no window, no staircase. It was a mere slip of barren platform, tapestried with big advertisements. Could anything be more mysterious?

It was not worth thinking about, and yet, for my life, I could not help pondering upon it—pondering, wondering, conjecturing, turning it over and over in my mind, and beating my brains for a solution of the enigma. I thought of it all the way from Blackwater to Clayborough. I thought of it all the way from Clayborough to Dumbleton, as I rattled along the smooth highway in a trim dogcart drawn by a splendid black mare and driven by the silentest and dapperest of East Anglian grooms.

We did the nine miles in something less than an hour, and pulled up before the lodge gates just as the church clock was striking half-past seven. A couple of minutes more, and the warm glow of the lighted hall was flooding out upon the gravel, a hearty grasp was on my hand, and a clear jovial voice was bidding me "welcome to Dumbleton."

"And now, my dear fellow," said my host, when the first greeting was over, "you have no time to spare. We dine at eight, and there are people coming to meet you, so you must just get the dressing business over as quickly as may be. By the way, you will meet some acquaintances: the Biddulphs are coming, and Prendergast—Prendergast of the Skirmishers[3]—is staying in the house. Adieu! Mrs. Jelf will be expecting you in the drawing room."

---

[3] A "Shirmisher" is a light infantry or cavalry soldier.

I was ushered to my room—not the blue room, of which Mr. Dwerrihouse had made disagreeable experience—but a pretty little bachelor's chamber hung with a delicate chintz and made cheerful by a blazing fire. I unlocked my portmanteau. I tried to be expeditious, but the memory of my railway adventure haunted me. I could not get free of it—I could not shake it off. It impeded me, worried me, it tripped me up, it caused me to mislay my studs, to mistie my cravat, to wrench the buttons off my gloves. Worst of all, it made me so late that the party had all assembled before I reached the drawing room. I had scarcely paid my respects to Mrs. Jelf when dinner was announced, and we paired off, some eight or ten couples strong, into the dining room.

I am not going to describe either the guests or the dinner. All provincial parties bear the strictest family resemblance, and I am not aware that an East Anglian banquet offers any exception to the rule. There was the usual country baronet and his wife, there were the usual country parsons and their wives, there was the sempiternal turkey and haunch of venison. *Vanitas vanitatum.*[4] There is nothing new under the sun.

I was placed about midway down the table. I had taken one rector's wife down to dinner, and I had another at my left hand. They talked across me, and their talk was about babies. It was dreadfully dull. At length, there came a pause. The entrees had just been removed, and the turkey had come upon the scene. The conversation had all along been of the languidest, but at this moment, it happened to have stagnated altogether. Jelf was carving the turkey. Mrs. Jelf looked as if she was trying to think of something to say. Everybody else was silent. Moved by an unlucky impulse, I thought I would relate my adventure.

"By the way, Jelf," I began, "I came down part of the way today with a friend of yours."

"Indeed!" said the master of the feast, slicing scientifically into the breast of the turkey. "With whom, pray?"

"With one who bade me tell you that he should, if possible, pay you a visit before Christmas."

"I cannot think who that could be," said my friend, smiling.

"It must be Major Thorp," suggested Mrs. Jelf.

I shook my head.

"It was not Major Thorp," I replied. "It was a near relation of

---

[4] "Sempiternal" means eternal, and *"vanitas vanitatum"* is Latin for vanities of vanities with a suggestion that life is empty. It seems our narrator's mood has very quickly shifted from mystification to ennui.

The Four-Fifteen Express

your own, Mrs. Jelf."

"Then I am more puzzled than ever," replied my hostess. "Pray tell me who it was."

"It was no less a person than your cousin, Mr. John Dwerrihouse."

Jonathan Jelf laid down his knife and fork. Mrs. Jelf looked at me in a strange, startled way, not saying a word.

"And he desired me to tell you, my dear madam, that you need not take the trouble to burn the hall down in his honour this time, but only to have the chimney of the blue room swept before his arrival."

Before I had reached the end of my sentence, I became aware of something ominous in the faces of the guests. I felt I had said something which I had better have left unsaid and, for some unexplained reason, my words had evoked a general consternation. I sat confounded, not daring to utter another syllable, and for at least two whole minutes, there was dead silence round the table. Then Captain Prendergast came to the rescue.

"You have been abroad for some months, have you not, Mr. Langford?" he said with the desperation of one who flings himself into the breach. "I heard you had been to Russia. Surely you have something to tell us of the state and temper of the country after the war?"

I was heartily grateful to the gallant Skirmisher for this diversion in my favour. I answered him, I fear, somewhat lamely. But he kept the conversation up, and presently one or two others joined in, and so the difficulty—whatever it might have been—was bridged over. Bridged over, but not repaired. A something, an awkwardness, a visible constraint remained. The guests hitherto had been simply dull, but now they were evidently uncomfortable and embarrassed.

The dessert had scarcely been placed upon the table when the ladies left the room. I seized the opportunity to select a vacant chair next to Captain Prendergast.

"In heaven's name," I whispered, "what was the matter just now? What had I said?"

"You mentioned the name of John Dwerrihouse."

"What of that? I had seen him not two hours before."

"It is a most astounding circumstance that you should have seen him," said Captain Prendergast. "Are you sure it was he?"

"As sure as of my own identity. We were talking all the way between London and Blackwater. But why does that surprise you?"

"*Because*" replied Captain Prendergast, dropping his voice to the lowest whisper, "*because John Dwerrihouse absconded three months ago with seventy-five thousand pounds of the company's money and has never been heard of since.*"

II.

John Dwerrihouse had absconded three months ago—but I had seen him only a few hours back! John Dwerrihouse had embezzled seventy-five thousand pounds of the company's money—yet he told me that he carried that sum upon his person! Were ever facts so strangely incongruous, so difficult to reconcile? How should he have ventured again into the light of day? How dared he show himself along the line? Above all, what had he been doing throughout those mysterious three months of disappearance?

Perplexing questions these. Questions which at once suggested themselves to the minds of all concerned, but which admitted of no easy solution. I could find no reply to them. Captain Prendergast had not even a suggestion to offer. Jonathan Jelf, who seized the first opportunity of drawing me aside and learning all that I had to tell, was more amazed and bewildered than either of us. He came to my room that night, when all the guests were gone, and we talked the thing over from every point of view—without, it must be confessed, arriving at any kind of conclusion.

"I do not ask you," he said, "whether you can have mistaken your man. That is impossible."

"As impossible as that I should mistake some stranger for yourself."

"It is not a question of looks or voice, but of facts. That he should have alluded to the fire in the blue room is proof enough of John Dwerrihouse's identity. How did he look?"

"Older, I thought. Considerably older, paler, and more anxious."

"He has had enough to make him look anxious, anyhow," said my friend gloomily, "be he innocent or guilty."

"I am inclined to believe that he is innocent," I replied. "He showed no embarrassment when I addressed him, and no uneasiness when the guard came round. His conversation was open to a fault. I might almost say that he talked too freely of the business which he had in hand."

"That again is strange, for I know no one more reticent on such subjects. He actually told you that he had the seventy-five thousand pounds in his pocket?"

The Four-Fifteen Express

"He did."

"Humph! My wife has an idea about it, and she may be right."

"What idea?"

"Well, she fancies—women are so clever, you know, at putting themselves inside people's motives—she fancies that he was tempted, that he did actually take the money, and that he has been concealing himself these three months in some wild part of the country, struggling possibly with his conscience all the time and daring neither to abscond with his booty nor to come back and restore it."

"But now that he has come back?"

"That is the point. She conceives that he has probably thrown himself upon the company's mercy, made restitution of the money, and, being forgiven, is permitted to carry the business through as if nothing whatever had happened."

"The last," I replied, "is an impossible case. Mrs. Jelf thinks like a generous and delicate-minded woman, but not in the least like a board of railway directors. They would never carry forgiveness so far."

"I fear not. And yet it is the only conjecture that bears a semblance of likelihood. However, we can run over to Clayborough tomorrow and see if anything is to be learned. By the way, Prendergast tells me you picked up his cigar case."

"I did so, and here it is."

Jelf took the cigar case and examined it by the light of the lamp. He said at once that it was beyond doubt Mr. Dwerrihouse's property. He remembered to have seen him use it.

"Here, too, is his monogram on the side," he added. "A big J transfixing a capital D. He used to carry the same on his notepaper."

"It offers, at all events, a proof that I was not dreaming."

"Ay, but it is time you were asleep and dreaming now. I am ashamed to have kept you up so long. Goodnight."

"Goodnight, and remember that I am more than ready to go with you to Clayborough or Blackwater or London or anywhere, if I can be of the least service."

"Thanks! I know you mean it, old friend, and it may be that I shall put you to the test. Once more, goodnight."

So we parted for that night and met again in the breakfast room at half-past eight next morning. It was a hurried, silent, uncomfortable meal. None of us had slept well, and all were thinking of the same subject. Mrs. Jelf had evidently been crying. Jelf was impatient to be off, and both Captain Prendergast and myself felt ourselves to be in the painful position of outsiders who are involuntarily brought into a domestic trouble. Within twenty minutes after we had left the breakfast table, the dogcart was brought round, and my friend and I were on the road to Clayborough.

"Tell you what it is, Langford," he said as we sped along between the wintry hedges, "I do not much fancy to bring up Dwerrihouse's name at Clayborough. All the officials know that he is my wife's relation, and the subject just now is hardly a pleasant one. If you don't much mind, we will make the 11.10 to Blackwater. It's an important station, and we shall stand a far better chance of picking up information there than at Clayborough."

So we took the 11.10, which happened to be an express and, arriving at Blackwater about a quarter before twelve, proceeded at once to prosecute our inquiry.

We began by asking for the stationmaster, a big, blunt, businesslike person, who at once averred that he knew Mr. John Dwerrihouse perfectly well and that there was no director on the line whom he had seen and spoken to so frequently.

"He used to be down here two or three times a week about three months ago," said he, "when the new line was first set afoot. But since then, you know, gentlemen—"

He paused significantly.

Jelf flushed scarlet.

"Yes, yes," he said hurriedly, "we know all about that. The point now to be ascertained is whether anything has been seen or heard of him lately."

"Not to my knowledge," replied the stationmaster.

"He is not known to have been down the line anytime yesterday, for instance?"

The stationmaster shook his head.

"The East Anglian, sir," said he, "is about the last place where he would dare to show himself. Why, there isn't a stationmaster, there isn't guard, there isn't a porter, who doesn't know Mr. Dwerrihouse by sight as well as he knows his own face in the looking glass, or who wouldn't telegraph for the police as soon as he had set eyes on him at any point along the line. Bless you, sir! There's been a standing order out against him ever since the 25th of September last."

"And yet," pursued my friend, "a gentleman who travelled down yesterday from London to Clayborough by the afternoon express testifies that he saw Mr. Dwerrihouse in the train and that

The Four-Fifteen Express

Mr. Dwerrihouse alighted at Blackwater station."

"Quite impossible, sir," replied the stationmaster promptly.

"Why impossible?"

"Because there is no station along the line where he is so well known or where he would run so great a risk. It would be just running his head into the lion's mouth. He would have been mad to come nigh Blackwater station, and if he *had* come, he would have been arrested before he left the platform."

"Can you tell me who took the Blackwater tickets of that train?"

"I can, sir. It was the guard, Benjamin Somers."

"And where can I find him?"

"You can find him, sir, by staying here, if you please, till one o'clock. He will be coming through with the up-express from Crampton, which stays in Blackwater for ten minutes."

We waited for the up-express, beguiling the time as best we could by strolling along the Blackwater Road till we came almost to the outskirts of the town, from which the station was distant nearly a couple of miles. By one o'clock, we were back again upon the platform and waiting for the train. It came punctually, and I at once recognised the ruddy-faced guard who had gone down with my train the evening before.

"The gentlemen want to ask you something about Mr. Dwerrihouse, Somers," said the stationmaster by way of introduction. The guard flashed a keen glance from my face to Jelf's and back again to mine.

"Mr. John Dwerrihouse, the late director?" said he interrogatively.

"The same," replied my friend. "Should you know him if you saw him?"

"Anywhere, sir."

"Do you know if he was in the 4.15 express yesterday afternoon?"

"He was not, sir."

"How can you answer so positively?"

"Because I looked into every carriage and saw every face in that train, and I could take my oath that Mr. Dwerrihouse was not in it. *This* gentleman was," he added, turning sharply upon me. "I don't know that I ever saw him before in my life, but I remember his face perfectly. You nearly missed taking your seat in time at this station, sir, and you got out at Clayborough."

"Quite true, guard," I replied, "but do you not remember the face of the gentleman who travelled down in the same carriage with me as far as here?"

"It was my impression, sir, that you travelled down alone," said Somers with a look of some surprise.

"By no means. I had a fellow traveller as far as Blackwater, and it was in trying to restore him the cigar case which he had dropped in the carriage that I so nearly let you go on without me."

"I remember your saying something about a cigar case, certainly," replied the guard, "but—"

"You asked for my ticket just before we entered station."

"I did, sir."

"Then you must have seen him. He sat in the corner next the very door to which you came."

"No, indeed. I saw no one."

I looked at Jelf. I began to think the guard was in the ex-director's confidence and paid for his silence.

"If I had seen another traveller, I should have asked for his ticket," added Somers. "Did you see me ask for his ticket, sir?"

"I observed that you did not ask for it, but he explained that by saying—" I hesitated. I feared I might be telling too much and so broke off abruptly.

The guard and the stationmaster exchanged glances. The former looked impatiently at his watch.

"I am obliged to go on in four minutes more, sir," he said.

"One last question, then," interposed Jelf with a sort of desperation. "If this gentleman's fellow traveller had been Mr. John Dwerrihouse—and he had been sitting in the corner next the door in which you took the tickets—could you have failed to see and recognise him?"

"No, sir. It would have been quite impossible."

"And you are certain you did not see him?"

"As I said before, sir, I could take my oath that I did not see him. And if it wasn't that I don't like to contradict a gentleman, I would say I could also take my oath that this gentlemen was quite alone in the carriage the whole way from London to Clayborough. Why, sir," he added dropping his voice so as to be inaudible to the stationmaster, who had been called away to speak to some person close by, "you expressly asked me to give you a compartment to yourself, and I did so. I locked you in, and you were so good as to give me something for myself."

"Yes. But Mr. Dwerrihouse had a key of his own."

"I never saw him, sir. I saw no one in that compartment but yourself. Beg pardon, sir. My time's up."

The Four-Fifteen Express

And with this, the ruddy guard touched his cap and was gone. In another minute, the heavy panting of the engine began afresh, and the train glided slowly out of the station.

We looked at each other for some moments in silence. I was the first to speak.

"Mr. Benjamin Somers knows more than he chooses to tell," I said.

"Humph! do you think so?"

"It *must* be. He could *not* have come to the door without seeing him. It's *impossible*."

"There is one thing not impossible, my dear fellow."

"What is that?"

"That you may have fallen asleep and dreamed the whole thing."

"Could I dream of a branch line that I had never heard of? Could I dream of a hundred and one business details that had no kind of interest for me? Could I dream of the seventy-five thousand pounds?"

"Perhaps you might have seen or heard some vague account of the affair while you were abroad. It might have made no impression upon you at the time and might have come back to you in your dreams, recalled perhaps by the mere names of the stations on the line."

"What about the fire in the chimney of the blue room—should I have heard of *that* during my journey?"

"Well, no. I admit there is a difficulty about that point."

"And what about the cigar case?"

"Ay, by Jove! there is the cigar case. That is a stubborn fact. Well, it's a mysterious affair, and it will need a better detective than myself, I fancy, to clear it up. I suppose we may as well go home."

III.

A week had not gone by when I received a letter from the secretary of the East Anglian Railway Company, requesting the favour of my attendance at a special board meeting not then many days distant. No reasons were alleged and no apologies offered for this demand upon my time, but they had heard, it was clear, of my inquiries about the missing director and had a mind to put me through some sort of official examination upon the subject. Being still a guest at Dumbleton Hall, I had to go up to London for the purpose, and Jonathan Jelf accompanied me.

I found the administration of the Great East Anglian line

represented by a party of some twelve or fourteen gentlemen seated in solemn conclave, round a huge green baize table, in a gloomy boardroom adjoining the London terminus. We were courteously received by the chairman, who at once began by saying that certain statements of mine respecting Mr. John Dwerrihouse had come to the knowledge of the administration and that they, in consequence, desired to confer with me on those points. We were placed at the table, and the inquiry proceeded in due form.

I was first asked if I knew Mr. John Dwerrihouse, how long I had been acquainted with him, and whether I could identify him at sight. I was then asked when I had seen him last.

To this, I replied, "On the 4th of this present month, December, 1856."

Then came the inquiry of where I had seen him on that fourth day of December, to which I replied that I met him in a first-class compartment of the 4.15 down-express, that he got in just as the train was leaving the London terminus, and that he alighted at Blackwater station.

The chairman then inquired whether I had held any communication with my fellow traveller, whereupon I related—as nearly as I could remember it—the whole bulk and substance of Mr. John Dwerrihouse's diffuse information respecting the new branch line. To all this, the board listened with profound attention while the chairman presided and the secretary took notes.

I then produced the cigar case. It was passed from hand to hand and recognised by all. There was not a man present who did not remember that plain cigar case with its silver monogram or to whom it seemed anything less entirely corroborative of my evidence.

When, at length, I had told all that I had to tell, the chairman whispered something to the secretary. The secretary touched a silver hand bell, and the guard, Benjamin Somers, was ushered into the room. He was then examined as carefully as myself. He declared that he knew Mr. John Dwerrihouse perfectly well, that he could not be mistaken in him, that he remembered going down with the 4.15 express on the afternoon in question, that he remembered me, and that—there being one or two empty first-class compartments on that especial afternoon—he had placed me in a carriage by myself in compliance with my request.

He was positive that I remained alone in that compartment all the way from London to Clayborough. He was ready to take his oath that Dwerrihouse was neither in that carriage with me nor in any

The Four-Fifteen Express

compartment of that train. He remembered distinctly to have examined my ticket to Blackwater, was certain that there was no one else at that time in the carriage, and could not have failed to observe a second person if there had been one. Had that second person been Mr. John Dwerrihouse, insisted the guard, he should have quietly double-locked the door of the carriage and have at once given information to the Blackwater stationmaster. So clear, so decisive, so ready was Somers with this testimony that the board looked fairly puzzled.

"You hear this person's statement, Mr. Langford," said the chairman. "It contradicts yours in every particular. What have you to say in reply?"

"I can only repeat what I said before. I am quite as positive of the truth of my own assertions as Mr. Somers can be of the truth of his."

"You say that Mr. Dwerrihouse alighted in Blackwater and that he was in possession of a private key. Are you sure that he had not alighted by means of that key before the guard came round for the tickets?"

"I am quite positive that he did not leave the carriage till the train had fairly entered the station and the other Blackwater passengers were alighting. I even saw that he was met there by a friend."

"Indeed! Did you see that person distinctly?"

"Quite distinctly."

"Can you describe his appearance?"

"I think so. He was short and very slight, sandy-haired with a bushy moustache and beard, and he wore a closely fitting suit of gray tweed. His age I should take to be about thirty-eight or forty."

"Did Mr. Dwerrihouse leave the station in this person's company?"

"I cannot tell. I saw them walking together down the platform, and then I saw them standing inside under a gas jet, talking earnestly. After that, I lost sight of them quite suddenly, and just then, my train went on and I with it."

The chairman and secretary conferred together in an undertone. The directors whispered to one another. One or two looked suspiciously at the guard. I could see that my evidence remained unshaken and that, like myself, they suspected some complicity between the guard and the defaulter.

"How far did you conduct that 4.15 express on the day in question, Somers?" asked the chairman.

"All through, sir," replied the guard, "from London to Crampton."

"How was it that you were not relieved at Clayborough? I thought there was always a change of guards at Clayborough."

"There used to be, sir, till the new regulations came in force last midsummer. Since then, the guards in charge of express trains go the whole way through."

The chairman turned to the secretary.

"I think it would be as well," he said, "if we had the daybook to refer to upon this point."

Again the secretary touched the silver hand bell and requested the porter in attendance to summon Mr. Raikes. From a word or two dropped by another of the directors, I gathered that Mr. Raikes was one of the undersecretaries.

He came, a small, slight, sandy-haired, keen-eyed man with an eager, nervous manner and a forest of light beard and moustache. He just showed himself at the door of the boardroom and, being requested to bring a certain daybook from a certain shelf in a certain room, bowed and vanished.

He was there such a moment, and the surprise of seeing him was so great and sudden, that it was not till the door had closed upon him that I found voice to speak. He was no sooner gone, however, than I sprang to my feet.

"That person," I said, "is the same who met Mr. Dwerrihouse upon the platform at Blackwater!"

There was a general movement of surprise. The chairman looked grave and somewhat agitated.

"Take care, Mr. Langford," he said. "Take care what you say."

"I am as positive of his identity as of my own."

"Do you consider the consequences of your words? Do you consider that you are bringing a charge of the gravest character against one of the company's servants?"

"I am willing to be put upon my oath, if necessary. The man who came to that door a minute since is the same whom I saw talking with Mr. Dwerrihouse on the Blackwater platform. Were he twenty times the company's servant, I could say neither more nor less."

The chairman turned again to the guard.

"Did you see Mr. Raikes in the train or on the platform?" he asked.

Somers shook his head.

"I am confident Mr. Raikes was not in the train," he said, "and

The Four-Fifteen Express

I certainly did not see him on the platform."

The chairman turned next to the secretary.

"Mr. Raikes is in your office, Mr. Hunter," he said. "Can you remember if he was absent on the 4th instant?"[5]

"I do not think he was," replied the secretary, "but I am not prepared to speak positively. I have been away most afternoons myself lately, and Mr. Raikes might easily have absented himself if he had been disposed."

At this moment, the undersecretary returned with the daybook under his arm.

"Be pleased to refer, Mr. Raikes," said the chairman, "to the entries of the 4th instant, and see what Benjamin Somers's duties were on that day."

Mr. Raikes threw open the cumbrous volume and then ran a practised eye and finger down some three or four successive columns of entries. Stopping suddenly at the foot of a page, he then read aloud that Benjamin Somers had on that day conducted the 4.15 express from London to Crampton.

The chairman leaned forward in his seat, looked the undersecretary full in the face, and said quite sharply and suddenly:

"Where were *you*, Mr. Raikes, on the same afternoon?"

"*I,* sir?"

"*You,* Mr. Raikes. Where were you on the afternoon and evening of the 4th of the present month?"

"Here, sir, in Mr. Hunter's office. Where else should I be?"

There was a dash of trepidation in the undersecretary's voice as he said this, but his look of surprise was natural enough.

"We have some reason for believing, Mr. Raikes, that you were absent that afternoon without leave. Was this the case?"

"Certainly not, sir. I have not had a day's holiday since September. Mr. Hunter will bear me out in this." Mr. Hunter repeated what he had previously said on the subject, but added that the clerks in the adjoining office would be certain to know. Whereupon the senior clerk, a grave, middle-aged person in green glasses, was summoned and interrogated.

His testimony cleared the undersecretary at once. He declared that Mr. Raikes had in no instance, to his knowledge, been absent during office hours since his return from his annual holiday in September.

I was confounded. The chairman turned to me with a smile, in which a shade of covert annoyance was scarcely apparent.

---

[5] "Instant" means of the current month.

"You hear, Mr. Langford?" he said.

"I hear, sir, but my conviction remains unshaken."

"I fear, Mr. Langford, that your convictions are very insufficiently based," replied the chairman with a doubtful cough. "I fear that you 'dream dreams' and mistake them for actual occurrences. It is a dangerous habit of mind and might lead to dangerous results. Mr. Raikes here would have found himself in an unpleasant position had he not proved so satisfactory an alibi."

I was about to reply, but he gave me no time.

"I think, gentlemen," he went on to say, addressing the board, "that we should be wasting time were we to push this inquiry further. Mr. Langford's evidence would seem to be of an equal value throughout. The testimony of Benjamin Somers disproves his first statement, and the testimony of the last witness disproves his second. I think we may conclude that Mr. Langford fell asleep in the train on the occasion of his journey to Clayborough and dreamed an unusually vivid and circumstantial dream, of which, however, we have now heard quite enough."

There are few things more annoying than to find one's positive convictions met with incredulity. I could not help feeling impatience at the turn that affairs had taken. I was not proof against the civil sarcasm of the chairman's manner. Most intolerable of all, however, was the quiet smile lurking about the corners of Benjamin Somers's mouth and the half-triumphant, half-malicious gleam in the eyes of the undersecretary. The man was evidently puzzled and somewhat alarmed. His looks seemed furtively to interrogate me. Who was I? What did I want? Why had I come there to do him an ill turn with his employers? What was it to me whether or not he was absent without leave?

Seeing all this, and perhaps more irritated by it than the thing deserved, I begged leave to detain the attention of the board for a moment longer. Jelf plucked me impatiently by the sleeve.

"Better let the thing drop," he whispered. "The chairman's right enough. You dreamed it, and the less said now the better."

I was not to be silenced, however, in this fashion. I had yet something to say, and I would say it. It was to this effect: dreams were not usually productive of tangible results, and I requested to know in what way the chairman conceived I had evolved from my dream so substantial and well-made a delusion as the cigar case which I had had the honour to place before him at the commencement of our interview.

"The cigar case, I admit, Mr. Langford," the chairman replied,

The Four-Fifteen Express

"is a very strong point in your evidence. It is your *only* strong point, however, and there is just a possibility that we may all be misled by a mere accidental resemblance. Will you permit me to see the case again?"

"It is unlikely," I said as I handed it to him, "that any other should bear precisely this monogram and yet be in all other particulars exactly similar."

The chairman examined it for a moment in silence. He then passed it to Mr. Hunter. Mr. Hunter turned it over and over, and shook his head.

"This is no mere resemblance," he said. "It is John Dwerrihouse's cigar case to a certainty. I remember it perfectly. I have seen it a hundred times."

"I believe I may say the same," added the chairman. "Yet how account for the way in which Mr. Langford asserts that it came into his possession?"

"I can only repeat," I replied, "that I found it on the floor of the carriage after Mr. Dwerrihouse had alighted. It was in leaning out to look after him that I trod upon it, and it was in running after him for the purpose of restoring it that I saw—or believed I saw—Mr. Raikes standing aside with him in earnest conversation."

Again I felt Jonathan Jelf plucking at my sleeve.

"Look at Raikes," he whispered. *"Look at Raikes!"*

I turned to where the undersecretary had been standing a moment before and saw him, white as death, with lips trembling and livid, stealing toward the door.

To conceive a sudden, strange, and indefinite suspicion, to fling myself in his way, to take him by the shoulders as if he were a child, and to turn his craven face, perforce, toward the board were with me the work of an instant.

"Look at him!" I exclaimed. "Look at his face! I ask no better witness to the truth of my words!"

The chairman's brow darkened.

"Mr. Raikes," he said sternly, "if you know anything, you had better speak!"

Vainly trying to wrench himself from my grasp, the undersecretary stammered out an incoherent denial.

"Let me go," he said. "I know nothing—you have *no* right to detain me—*let me go!*"

"Did you or did you not meet Mr. John Dwerrihouse at Blackwater station? The charge brought against you is either true or false. If true, you will do well to throw yourself upon the mercy of the board and make full confession of all that you know."

The undersecretary wrung his hands in an agony of helpless terror.

"*I was away!*" he cried. "I was *two hundred miles away* at the time! I know nothing about it—I have nothing to confess—I am innocent—I call God to witness I am innocent!"

"Two hundred miles away!" echoed the chairman. "What do you mean?"

"I was in Devonshire. I had three weeks' leave of absence—I appeal to Mr. Hunter—Mr. Hunter knows I had three weeks' leave of absence! I was in Devonshire all the time! I can prove I was in Devonshire!"

Seeing him so abject, so incoherent, so wild with apprehension, the directors began to whisper gravely among themselves. One got quietly up and called the porter to guard the door.

"What has your being in Devonshire to do with the matter?" said the chairman. "When were you in Devonshire?"

"Mr. Raikes took his leave in September," said the secretary, "about the time when Mr. Dwerrihouse disappeared."

"I never even heard that he had disappeared till I came back!"

"That must remain to be proved," said the chairman. "I shall at once put this matter in the hands of the police. In the meanwhile, Mr. Raikes, being myself a magistrate and used to dealing with these cases, I advise you to offer no resistance but to confess while confession may yet do you service. As for your accomplice—"

The frightened wretch fell upon his knees.

"I had no accomplice!" he cried. "Only have mercy upon me—only spare my life, and I will confess all! I didn't mean to harm him! I didn't mean to hurt a hair of his head! Only have mercy upon me, and let me go!"

The chairman rose in his place, pale and agitated.

"Good heavens!" he exclaimed, "what horrible mystery is this? What does it mean?"

"As sure as there is a God in heaven," said Jonathan Jelf, "it means that murder has been done."

"*No! no! no!*" shrieked Raikes, still upon his knees and cowering like a beaten hound. "Not *murder!* No jury that ever sat could bring it in *murder*. I thought I had only *stunned* him—I never meant to do more than *stun* him! Manslaughter! *Manslaughter!* Not *murder!*"

Overcome by the horror of this unexpected revelation, the chairman covered his face with his hand and, for a moment or two, remained silent.

"Miserable man," he said at length, "you have betrayed yourself."

"You bade me confess! You urged me to throw myself upon the mercy of the board!"

"You have confessed to a crime which no one suspected you of having committed," replied the chairman, "and which this board has no power either to punish or forgive. All that I can do for you is to advise you to submit to the law, to plead guilty, and to conceal nothing. When did you do this deed?"

The guilty man rose to his feet and leaned heavily against the table. His answer came reluctantly, like the speech of one dreaming.

"On the 22d of September!"

On the 22d of September! I looked in Jonathan Jelf's face, and he in mine. I felt my own smiling with a strange sense of wonder and dread. I saw his blanch suddenly, even to the lips.

"Merciful Heaven!" he whispered. *"What was it, then, that you saw in the train?"*

IV.

What was it that I saw in the train? That question remains unanswered to this day. I have never been able to reply to it. I only know that it bore the living likeness of the murdered man, whose body had then been lying some ten weeks under a rough pile of branches and brambles and rotting leaves at the bottom of a deserted chalk pit about halfway between Blackwater and Mallingford. I know that it spoke and moved and looked as that man spoke and moved and looked in life. That I heard, or seemed to hear, things revealed which I could never otherwise have learned. That I was guided, as it were, by that vision on the platform to the identification of the murderer. And that, a passive instrument myself, I was destined by means of these mysterious teachings to bring about the ends of justice. For these things, I have never been able to account.

As for that matter of the cigar case, on inquiry, it proved that the carriage in which I travelled down that afternoon to Clayborough had not been in use for several weeks and was, in point of fact, the same in which poor John Dwerrihouse had performed his last journey. The case had doubtless been dropped by him and had lain unnoticed till I found it.

Upon the details of the murder, I have no need to dwell. Those who desire more ample particulars may find them and the written confession of Augustus Raikes in the files of the *Times* for 1856. Enough that the undersecretary, knowing the history of the new line and following the negotiation step by step through all its stages, determined to waylay Mr. Dwerrihouse, rob him of the seventy-five thousand pounds, and escape to America with his booty.

In order to effect these ends, he obtained leave of absence a few days before the time appointed for the payment of the money, secured his passage across the Atlantic in a steamer advertised to start on the 23d, provided himself with a heavily loaded life-preserver, and went down to Blackwater to await the arrival of his victim. How he met him on the platform with a pretended message from the board, how he offered to conduct him by a short cut across the fields to Mallingford, how—having brought him to a lonely place—he struck him down with the life-preserver and so killed him, and how, finding what he had done, he dragged the body to the verge of an out-of-the-way chalk pit and there flung it in and piled it over with branches and brambles are facts still fresh in the memories of those who, like the connoisseurs in De Quincey's famous essay, regard murder as a fine art.[6]

Strangely enough, having done his work, the murderer was afraid to leave the country. He declared that he had not intended to take the director's life, but only to stun and rob him and that, finding the blow had killed, he dared not fly for fear of drawing down suspicion upon his own head. As a mere robber, he would have been safe in the States, but as a murderer, he would inevitably have been pursued and given up to justice. So he forfeited his passage, returned to the office as usual at the end of his leave, and locked up his ill-gotten thousands till a more convenient opportunity. In the meanwhile, he had the satisfaction of finding that Mr. Dwerrihouse was universally believed to have absconded with the money, no one knew how or whither.

Whether he meant murder or not, however, Mr. Augustus Raikes paid the full penalty of his crime, being hanged at the Old Bailey in the second week in January, 1857. Those who desire to make his further acquaintance may see him any day—admirably done in wax—in the Chamber of Horrors at Madame Tussaud's exhibition in Baker Street. He is there to be found in the midst of a select society of ladies and gentlemen of atrocious memory, dressed

---

[6] Thomas De Quincy's mock-lecture "On Murder, considered as one of the Fine Arts" first appeared in *Blackwood's Magazine* [Feb., 1827] pp. 200-13. It offers a satirical "artistic appreciation" of the finer points involved in committing such a ghastly crime.

in the close-cut tweed suit which he wore on the evening of the murder and holding in his hand the identical life-preserver, with which he committed it.

AN APPALLING MYSTERY

ANONYMOUS[1]

Since the last annual visit of the East Wheeling spirit, no spooks have walked above ground in this vicinity for several years, and the minds of our citizens had begun to run in the even tenor of their ways on this question, some even being so skeptical as to doubt the very presence of the spirits of dead men on this terrestrial ball.

The frightful revelations of a party who were eyewitnesses of the scene we are about to describe dispelled those dreams of security and cause the hearts of many to quake and their guilty consciences to tremble. The witnesses themselves have been in such a state of terror and dismay since the occurrence that it has been with great difficulty that we could gather the real facts in the case, their rolling eyes and chattering teeth, their ghastly countenances giving evidence of the truth of the asseverations, but preventing a connected repetition of the events as they occurred. The disconnected sentences and ejaculations of horror, which have been repeated as coming from their blanched and quivering lips, we feel convinced have been altered and exaggerated so that the accounts which prevailed yesterday in the city were totally incorrect—in fact, were garbled versions of the affair.

THE LOCATION.

The tunnel of the Hempfield Railroad has long been notorious as the scene of some of the most horrible murders which have been chronicled in the annals of our newspapers and in the criminal records of our country. Its situation is well known to most of our readers, but for the enlightenment of those who have not visited it, we will give a brief description which the new interest awakened by

---

[1] This article comes from West Virginia's *Wheeling Daily Intelligencer,* July 19, 1869, p. 4. Though the tracks are gone, the railroad tunnel remains and, in fact, can be traversed as a part of the Wheeling Heritage Trail.

the events of Thursday will sanction. The tunnel enters the hillside at the distance of about forty feet from the bridge over Wheeling Creek, behind the hill which forms the background to our thriving and prosperous city. It immediately enters a bed of rock and coal, which if the darkness occasioned by the exclusion of the sun's rays were not sufficient to render it gloomy and dismal, would of itself have that effect.

Its sides and ceiling are covered with dampness and moisture. Directly overhead is situated the Peninsula Cemetery, so that the green and poisonous slime which oozes from the fissures and crevices in the overhanging rocks, with but little effort of the imagination, may be attributed to the graves and coffins of the dead who lie mouldering above.

At the mouth of the tunnel is a sequestered spot known as Berry's Hole. Its name is significant, and its record shows it to be the watery grave of many poor fellows. In the memory of many of our readers, the history of Schaffer, the blood thirsty and brutal murderer who expiated his crimes on the scaffold at Parkersburg, is still fresh.[2] That the slaughter of one of his victims took place in the tunnel is well known and is supposed to have immediate reference to the appearance of the ghost last week. The murdered man entered the tunnel when he was attacked by Shaffer with a hatchet. Unarmed and inoffensive, the victim was dealt a ferocious blow on the temple. Holding his supplicating hands before his face, he received the second blow upon his arms and fingers. The deed having been accomplished, the victim was dragged and concealed in a culvert near the east mouth of the tunnel, where it was afterwards discovered.

Other deeds of this kind are too well known to bear repetition—so that it has been an unceasing wonder that the scene of so many horrible crimes has not been continually haunted by the spirits of the murdered men. The place is therefore a most fitting one for the scene which transpired on Thursday.

LET THE DEAD REST.

Thursday evening, about 6 o'clock, a party of four men were proceeding through the tunnel on their way to the country beyond.

---

[2] In January of 1868, Joseph Eisele (a.k.a. John Shaffer, though the press often varied the spelling of this surname) confessed to murdering Joseph Lilienthal, Aloys Ulrich, and Rudolph Tsutor. Ulrich had been the one murdered in this tunnel. The confession came after Eisele was arrested for attempting to also murder John White. He was hanged on March 6th of that year.

Having spent the day in Wheeling and imbibed the usual amount of fusel oil, they were rather hilarious than otherwise, though none of them were sufficiently under the influence of liquor to be unable to accurately perceive anything that transpired. The subject of the reappearance of spirits after death had been mooted, but was scoffed and laughed at more in a tone of bravado than real conviction. The topic was still under consideration while they were in the tunnel, but no sooner had they reached the point where the light from the outer world becomes dim and obscure than an ominous silence fell upon all and every one of them.

The darkness of the cavern had settled into an appalling gloom, but still they held their way. Soon groans and supplications for mercy fell upon their startled ears. The usual cavernous echo was doubly apparent, as the tone of the voice was unnatural and sepulchral—the men stood transfixed with horror and fright, the atmosphere was close and stifling.

All at once, issuing from the solid rock which forms the ceiling directly over the spot where the murderer slaughtered his victim, a ghastly form appeared. All around, as we have said, was impenetrable darkness, but the spectre itself was as clearly visible as in the noon day. It descended feet first, till it reached a place about equidistant from the floor and ceiling of the tunnel, where it stopped and remained for a few seconds.

Although covered with the slime and earth of the grave, the features of the ghastly spectre were distinctly visible, clad in the habiliments of the tomb. Its appearance was horrible in the extreme. One arm was extended with the bloody fingers of the hand hanging half severed from their stems. With the forefinger of the other hand, it pointed to a gaping wound in his temple. The wound seemed fresh, but the drops of blood seemed clotted and stood out in bold relief on the face of the ill-starred wretch. Without a movement of the lips, a voice apparently issuing from the throat of the ghost exclaimed in a tone so unnatural as to be totally indescribable: "Let the dead rest!"

The horror stricken witnesses of this appalling spectacle rushed from the scene. At the mouth of the tunnel, they met other parties whose credulity was not sufficient to believe the story of the witnesses. They therefore obtained a lantern and returned to the spot where the apparition was first seen. They were not long waiting when the spirit, in the same place, repeated the words he had before used—if possible, in a more horrifying tone. The spectre then glided rapidly through the air toward the western mouth of the tunnel. The individuals thus had made sure of the authenticity of the apparition. They were deprived of the power of speech for some hours, and even after the intervention of days, their fearful recollections are so vivid as to render them almost afraid of speaking on the subject.

A SECOND APPEARANCE.

The persons who witnessed this appalling spectacle in the tunnel being men of respectable and truthful characters, their statements created a widespread and profound sensation in the eastern part of the city, where they reside. This was intensified by facts which were disclosed yesterday morning by a gentleman who lives a couple of miles east of the city and which are related as follows:

He was coming into the city afoot, by way of the railroad, late in the evening. He was approaching the tunnel on the east and had noticed a couple of persons walking about a hundred yards ahead. A short distance this side of the schoolhouse, while walking on the track and looking down to guard his steps, he suddenly felt a strange shiver and sensation of horror. Looking up, he saw a man standing a few yards ahead directly over the stone culvert (where Ulrich's body had been hidden). His arms were held up above his head as if guarding against apprehended blows and the blood was streaming down his face and neck. There was an awful stony glare in the eyes, which rooted the beholder to the ground.

His first thought was that it was one of the men who had been walking ahead of him, who had been assaulted by the other. But before he had time to follow out the thought, he glanced past the horrid spectacle and saw the two men just about to pass into the tunnel. At that instant, the man, spectre, or whatever it was vanished and was nowhere to be seen. Utterly confounded, the frightened and horror stricken beholder stood gazing at the vacant air, trying to comprehend what he had seen.

In a moment or two, he had recovered sufficiently to think connectedly. He looked carefully around. Nothing whatever was to be seen, though it was still light enough to see objects with perfect distinctness. He says he thought at one moment of running forward to tell the men who were ahead and to ask them if they had seen anything. But of course, he reflected, the apparition was not there when they had passed. Besides, he felt sure he would be ridiculed and called a fool for his fright. He found it impossible, however, to go forward over the spot. Turning about, he returned home (we judge, with a good deal precipitancy).

Yesterday morning, he came into the city by the pike, and hearing of the appearance in the tunnel, he told one or two friends in confidence what he had witnessed. He is an intelligent person and given to credulity, but he expresses himself unable to explain the mystery. His account of the appearance of the apparition corresponds substantially with that of Ulrich, the murdered man.

Since these terrifying events have been made public, hints are thrown out that this is not the first time blood-chilling sights have been seen and strange sounds heard in and about the tunnel, generally about dark in the evening, but at least once in the middle of the day. Many dark rumors are afloat that don't seem worth repeating. We give the leading circumstances as they were related to us and leave our readers to judge for themselves of their probability.

B EIGHTY-EIGHT

ANONYMOUS[1]

I was on duty as head guard of the up-north train when what I am about to tell you took place. It happened one wet and stormy autumn evening just about dusk. How well I remember the time! My journey for the day was over, and the train was just drawing up to the platform at Park End Station—Park End is a very busy place now, as I daresay you are aware, and it was a busy place even then—when I heard a sudden sharp cry of *"Man down!"* from some of the porters. The very same moment, as it seemed, my van, which was at the tail end of the train, gave a strange sort of jolt, as though the wheels had been lifted off the metals and had gone over something *soft*.

I turned cold from head to foot and, letting go the handle of my brake, was out of my van in a couple of seconds. There the poor fellow was, sure enough, lying about a yard away from the hindmost wheels, a heap of clothes and broken bones. In attempting to get out before the train had come to a standstill, he had slipped down between the carriages and the platform. One carriage and my heavy brake-van had gone over him.

I was the first man that leaped down onto the line to lift him up. We got him onto the platform as tenderly as we could, a ring of porters, guards, and passengers forming round us. A couple of lanterns held aloft lighted up the ghastly scene.

He whom I held in my arms was a man between fifty and sixty years old. His sandy hair and his sandy beard were fast turning gray. He had a sharp foxy-looking face, like that of a man keen at a bargain and well able to take care of his own interests. He was plainly dressed in black and gray, but with a certain stamp about him which showed that he was both a gentleman and a man well to do.

Poor fellow! he was very near his end. He had given utterance to no cry when he first fell, and one or two low moans were all that

---

[1] This short story was taken from *Chamber's Journal* 8.396 [July 29, 1871] pp. 470-75.

now told his agony. His lips moved as though he wanted to speak to me, but only a faint murmur came from them. I bent my ear close to his mouth, but even then I could not make out what he wanted to say. He groaned and shut his eyes, and I thought he was gone.

In a moment or two, however, his eyes reopened, and again he tried to speak. But in vain. Then, for about as long a time as it would take me to count twenty, his gaze met mine with an expression in it of such yearning anxiety and terrible despair as I had never seen before and hope never to see again. Then a sudden spasm crossed his face, changing its whole expression. He flung one arm out quickly, his head fell back, and he was dead.

A stretcher was brought, on which the body was carried to the dead-house at the hospital, there to await the inquest. The dead man had no luggage with him except a small black bag. But there were papers about him sufficient to prove his identity. His name was Muxloe, and he lived in London. He was a bachelor and had chambers in the Temple.[2] His business, as far as I could make out, seemed a sort of cross between that of a lawyer and a money-lender. After the inquest, at which I was called as one of the chief witnesses, the body was claimed by the relatives, and I thought that I had seen and heard the last of Mr. Muxloe.

I went about my work as usual, but I could not get out of my memory that look of terrible despair which had flashed from the dead man's eyes into mine during the last minute of his life. It haunted me by day, and it haunted me by night, when I was at work and when I was asleep. Do what I would, I could not get that ghastly face, with its strange yearning gaze, out of my mind. Poor as I was, I would have given much to know what it was that Mr. Muxloe was so despairingly anxious to tell me.

A month or more passed away, and although the poor dead gentleman was often in my thoughts, I had quite recovered my cheerfulness, when the strangest thing happened to me. I was acting as guard that week to the 9 a.m. down express. We had stopped at Claywoods, a station about thirty miles north of Park End. I had got out of my van as usual to see after the passengers. I had made everything right and was just about to give the starting signal with my whistle, when as I walked alongside the train, glancing into a compartment here and there, whom should I see sitting in one of the carriages—as plainly as ever I saw anything in my life—but the dead man, Mr. Muxloe!

---

[2] "The Temple" is one of London's major legal districts, deriving its name from the local landmark Temple Church.

You might have knocked me down with a feather, as the saying is. My blood turned cold to see in his eyes that same strange look of which I have already spoken. It was a look that went through me and chilled my heart with horror. How I contrived to give the signal for the train to start and got back into my van, I never knew—but we had got half-a-dozen of miles from Claywoods before I seemed to come to my proper sense. All that I could, as soon as I was fit to think more calmly, was to doubt the evidence of my own eyes. I was an utter disbeliever in ghosts or apparitions of any kind. I would not believe that I had seen anything out of the common way in the present case. I chose rather to think that I had been a victim to some freak of my imagination—that Mr. Muxloe had been so much in my thoughts of late that I had come, at length, to believe that I saw Mr. Muxloe again in proper person.

I had quite persuaded myself that such must be the case by the time we drew up at our next station. Still, it was not without a little shrinking of the nerves that I walked quickly past the carriage where I had seen the ghost or whatever it was. There was no ghost there now—and I laughed a little spiteful laugh to myself. In fact, two old ladies had just had the door of the very compartment opened for them and were being thrust in with their boxes and bundles. I saw the old ladies comfortably seated and shut the door on them myself, and as I did so, I unthinkingly read off the number of the carriage in which they had taken their places.

That number was B 88.

There seemed to me a familiar ring about designation B 88, and I kept repeating it over to myself after the train was fairly underway again, puzzling my memory to think where I had heard it before. At last, it all flashed across my mind: B 88 was the number of the carriage from which Mr. Muxloe was in the act of alighting when he missed his footing and fell! It had been brought up among the evidence at the inquest and had there impressed itself on my memory. There was something odd about the affair that I didn't like. Perhaps the apparition was my death-token and had been sent to warn me.

For the remainder of that day, my thoughts were far from comfortable.

Next day, I was ordered away in charge of a special, and I did not go out anymore that week with the 9 a.m. express. The week following, it was my turn to go out with the 9.15 p.m. mail. It was a train that, as a rule, carried very few passengers. White Ash was one of the stations, and at it, we stopped for three minutes to pick up and set down post-office bags. We were just on the point of starting again, and I had just taken my usual look along the length of the train to see that everything was secure, when—as you will already have guessed—I was again startled by seeing the ghost of Mr. Muxloe sitting all alone in the middle compartment of a first-class carriage. That carriage was the hateful *B 88!*

The light from the roof shone down full and clear on the dead man's face. It was stony and expressionless, except for the vivid light in those deep-set eyes, which gazed into mine with that same terrible yearning of which I have spoken before, as though it has some dread secret on its mind and could obtain no rest till it had revealed it to me. I was still looking—breathless, spellbound—and I seemed to have been looking for minutes instead of seconds, when it slowly uplifted a lean forefinger and beckoned me to approach.

This was more than I could bear. I fainted clean away on the platform. When I came to myself, the train had been sent forward in the charge of another guard, and I was lying in one of the waiting rooms, where the stationmaster and his daughter had been doing their best to bring me round.

Well, my nerves were so upset that it was almost a week before I was fit to go on duty again. I had plenty of time, while sitting at home, to turn the whole affair over and over in my mind. I came to the conclusion that it was very likely I should see Mr. Muxloe again—perhaps *often* again. But, arguing from all I had heard and read about ghosts, they had no power given them to harm one. All that they could do was to appear unexpectedly at strange times and places, and so make themselves as unpleasant as possible. The upshot of it was that, having made up my mind that I should see Mr. Muxloe again, I tried to so nerve myself as to be able to look on him without being overmuch afraid.

After I got to work again, you may be sure that I looked carefully before starting on each journey to see whether that confounded B 88 formed part of my train. I had got an idea that I should never see Mr. Muxloe except in connection with that particular carriage, and as the event proved, I was right.

The first time that I found B 88 made up as part of my train was about five days after my recovery. There it was, one morning, when on duty, staring at me as brazen as you please. I seemed to pick it out instinctively from all the other carriages. I won't say that my heart didn't flutter a little when I first marked it. I kept my eye on it and was not a little pleased to see a gentleman and his two sons get into it about two minutes before starting. A glance at their tickets showed me that they had booked through to a point about fifty miles beyond where I gave up charge of the train. Not being able to have the carriage to himself, Mr. Muxloe did not, on that occasion, put in an appearance.

Two days later, B 88 was again included in my train. This time, the middle compartment remained unoccupied. From the moment that fact was clear to me, I felt sure that I should see Mr. Muxloe before the end of my journey. Knowing this, you might perhaps ask me what need there was for me to go near that particular carriage at all? Or even, if I had to pass it, why I could not keep my eyes turned another way? If such questions were put to me, my only answer would be that I couldn't, for the life of me, keep away from the carriage. As often as the train came to a stand, my feet seemed to drag me past it against my will. My eyes would turn and look, whether I wished them to or not.

Well, I did see Mr. Muxloe several times before the end of that journey. We stopped at four stations—the train was an express one—and four separate times did I see him. But if I had seen him a thousand times, I felt that I could never become familiar with him— never regard him with anything but a mixed feeling of the deepest awe and aversion—a feeling too intense for me to describe to you in any words. He seemed to be always on the lookout for me and for nobody else. The moment I came in sight of him, his terrible eyes would meet mine, and then my heart would shrink within me and every nerve in my body would quiver with dread unspeakable. Always, too, he beckoned me with his long lean forefinger—but I took good care never to obey the summons.

I don't want to trouble you with too many details. It is enough to say that, every time I took out B 88 as a part of my train and every time the middle compartment was unoccupied, so sure was I to see the ghost of Mr. Muxloe. You see, it was a thing I dared not talk about for fear the Company should say that a man who was in the habit of seeing ghosts was not fit to be guard of a train and should send me about my business in consequence.

I did, however, talk about the ghost once or twice to my wife and got called a fool for my pains. But what else could a married man expect? Wives, as a rule, don't like other people to call their husbands fools, but they don't object to make use of that objectionable little word themselves.

Well, sir, time went on, and my life almost became a burden to me. I was a haunted man, and I had no means of getting rid of my tormentor. I went off my feed. I no longer enjoyed my dinners as I had been used to do. My evening pipe no longer soothed me. I began to go more into company and to frequent the bar-parlour of an evening oftener than was good for me. You see, I could not bear the company of my own thoughts. I never liked to sit by myself after dark. Even my sleep was broken and disturbed with dreams of that terrible ghost.

It was soon after Mr. Muxloe first began to trouble me in this way that I made up my mind to ascertain whether he could be seen by anyone besides myself. One day, when he had travelled with me all the way from Park End to the end of my journey and we had drawn up for the collection of tickets, I approached one of the collecters, who had passed *his* compartment as though it were empty.

Having my eye on the ghost all the time, says I: "Bill, you have forgotten to collect that old gent's ticket in the middle compartment of B 88."

"Have I?" says Bill, and with that he goes back and opens the door of B 88. "Why, you duffer, the compartment's empty," says he next moment, giving the door an extra bang.

"Empty is it?" said I, innocent-like. "Ah! now I recollect. The old gent got out at the last station." But the dread that was upon me deepened when I found that the apparition could be seen by no one but myself.

Four or maybe five months had gone by from the date of Mr. Muxloe's death when my health broke down—so much so that I was ordered away for a month to my native air. Change of air and rest, the doctor said, would probably make a man of me again. I had not given him the least hint as to the real cause of my illness. I was afraid I should only be laughed at for my pains.

Well, I went away down north, and there I picked up appetite and strength wonderfully. Mr. M. never troubled me once. Indeed, I had not expected that he would so do, B 88 being far away from me. So it fell out that by the end of my holiday, I had grown so strong and hearty as almost to be able to laugh at myself as a whimsical fool who had allowed himself to be frightened by a shadow. I fully made up my mind that rather than let myself get into such a low nervous way again, I would give up my situation as guard and set up in some other line of life.

So the end of my holiday came, and I started back home one cold frosty afternoon in early springtime, looking forward with pleasure to seeing my old woman and the two lads again, and wondering how my mates at the station had been getting on while I had been away.

It was eight o'clock and had long been dark when I reached Carnhope Junction—that is, the junction with our own line, a place eighty miles from Park End. The guard who had charge of the train from Carnhope was an old mate of mine. For the first twenty miles, I travelled with him in his brake, and we had a quiet smoke and a chat together. Then, feeling inclined for a snooze, I left him and got into an empty second-class compartment. Here, I wrapped myself well up and was asleep in three minutes.

I must have slept for about an hour, when I awoke with start. I could not make out for a minute or two where I was. I was still rubbing my eyes and looking round with a gape, when I saw something that brought me to my senses with a shock as if I had been suddenly thrust overhead with ice-cold water!

Inside the door of the carriage in which I was sitting was marked up the fatal number: B 88!

All the feeling and fears which I had flattered myself for having conquered forever came back in a rush as I read over the number to myself in a frightened whisper. The thought that B 88 would form part of the train in which I should travel back home after my holidays had never entered into my calculations. I had never thought to look at the carriages before getting into the train at Carnhope Junction, and in consequent of this neglect, a strange fate had led me into the very place of all others where I would least have wished to be. B 88 was a composite carriage—that is to say, the middle compartment was a first-class one while the two end compartments were second-class. It was in one of these latter compartments that I was now sitting. The middle first-class compartment was the one haunted by the ghost of Mr. Muxloe.

I hardly know how to describe to you the feeling that now took possession of me. It was neither more nor less than an intense longing to leave the compartment in which I was sitting and make my way, by means of the footboard outside the carriage, as far as the window of the next compartment, then peep in and see whether the ghost were already there waiting for me. I tried to fight against this insane desire—I *did* fight against it with all my strength—but in vain. There was some power within me that I found it impossible to resist. I was like a man walking in his sleep, whose actions are beyond his own control, except that I knew quite well what I was about. In all respects but one, I was collected and as much in my proper senses as ever I had been in my life.

I could not stop to argue with myself. I could not stop to reflect. The impulse that was upon me grew stronger with every moment's delay. Almost before I knew that I had stirred from my seat, I had opened the carriage door and was out on the footboard with the cold night air blowing keenly around me. We were going along at a tidy pace—about thirty miles an hour—but I had no fears as to my safety. I had passed along the footboards when the trains were at full speed too often for that.

Very few steps brought me close to the window of the middle compartment. The window was open, and I could see everything inside as plainly as I can now see you who are sitting beside me. There was only one passenger in the compartment.

Mr. Muxloe.

Yes, there he sat, his dreadful eyes staring straight into mine—looking bluer, colder, more ghost-like than ever. Then his long lean forefinger was slowly raised, beckoning me to enter. All power of resistance had been taken from me. Slowly, I opened the door, and slowly, I got inside—never taking my eyes from off his for a moment—then I shut the door behind me and sat down opposite to him.

The night was a cold one, but I was strong and hearty and had scarcely felt it. But the moment I sat down opposite the ghost, I became conscious of a coldness far exceeding any that I had ever experienced before. I became chilled to the very marrow. The air of the compartment seemed as though it had swept over a thousand icebergs. My hair seemed to lift, and my whiskers to crisp and tangle with the intense cold. And I found afterwards that my watch had stopped at the very moment of my entering the carriage.

I sat down and waited for what might happen next.

My companion's hand had gone down on to his knee when I opened the carriage door. He now sat opposite to me, neither stirring nor speaking, doing nothing, in fact, but gaze with mournful intensity straight into my very soul. The cold grew more extreme, if such a thing were possible. A numbness that had begun with my feet was now creeping slowly up my body. I could feel it creep and spread little by little, stealing gradually upward to my heart and slowly freezing the life out of me. I had no power to move a muscle. I sat like a man turned to stone.

At length, the cold touched my heart—or seemed to do so. A deathlike faintness crept over me. The light in the roof grew dimmer. The figure opposite me lost its sharpness of outline, becoming faded and indistinct. But through everything, I could feel those piercing eyes fixed immovably on mine, till eventually life itself seemed to be rubbed slowly and softly out, and I knew nothing more.

I knew nothing more—that is, till I came to my senses in a dream, and strange to say, I knew from the first moment that my dream was nothing more than a dream. I found myself in an old-fashioned, oak-paneled room, which had evidently been a state apartment in some aristocratic mansion in years gone by. It was now, however, furnished in a spare and meagre manner with a few articles of commonplace furniture. In the huge fireplace, the sides of which were inlaid with blue and white Dutch tiles, a few dying cinders had been raked carefully together. It was night, for the wide window-place was curtained and the large room was dimly lighted by a couple of candles. On each side of the chimneypiece, a candle was held by a griffin's claw in bronze that protruded from the wall. But all of these were details that I seemed to feel rather than to see.

My attention was at once concentrated on the occupants of the room, two in number. One of them was a young man about five-and-twenty years old, with sandy hair and beard, and keen foxy-looking face—none other, in fact, than Mr. Muxloe himself as he must have appeared when a young man. The other inmate of the room was a man both younger and handsomer than Mr. Muxloe, but he was at that moment lying dead across the hearth, with ghastly face and wide-staring eye, and with a ragged wound in his forehead. Close by the dead man lay a heavy riding-whip.

Mr. Muxloe was down on one knee with one had clasped tightly in the other, gazing with a sort of frenzied horror at the terrible piece of work before him. It was a look that has come back to me in my dreams many a time since then.

"My friend—the only friend I ever had," I heard him mutter, "and yet I, of all men, must be his murderer!" He pressed his hands to his eyes, and great sobs shook him from head to foot.

After a time, he grew calmer, and then he rose sadly to his feet.

"There is no help for it," he said. "I cannot face the world—I dare not risk the gallows."

He went out, but returned presently with a spade, a pickaxe, and one or two other implements from the garden. Then he turned back the faded carpet and proceeded with workmanlike dexterity to take up a portion of the oaken flooring. In the ground thus exposed to view, he dug a deep and narrow trench, throwing up the earth onto the boards as he did so. It was a work that took some time, and long before he had done it, great beads of sweat rolled down his haggard face. But they fell unheeded, and he never ceased digging till the hole was to his satisfaction. Then he got out of it and rested for a little while.

But presently he was up and examining the contents of a dusty old box that lay neglected in one corner of the room. From the box, he produced a sheet of parchment, and going to a table on which stood pen and ink, he proceed slowly and with much deliberation to write out a statement. Once finished, he signed and dated it. Next, from a cupboard, he brought a small tin canister. As soon as the writing was dry, he folded the parchment and shut it up in the canister.

Next, from the same cupboard, he brought a large travelling cloak, which he proceeded to spread out at the bottom of the trench. Then, but not without some inward shrinking, as I could see, he went up to the body and raised it in his arms. Before placing it in the hole he had dug, he kissed it tenderly on the forehead twice.

"Oh, Arthur! Oh, my friend," he murmured, "if by the sacrifice of my life I could bring back a smile to those white lips, I swear to heaven that I would gladly die this minute. To think that I should make a murderer of myself for any woman's sake—least of all, for *her!*"

In three minutes more, the body was in the rude grave that had been dug to receive it, the canister and the riding-whip had been laid beside it, and some folds of the travelling cloak had been thrown over the whole. Mr. Muxloe, spade in hand, was standing with anguished face, gazing his last on the man whom his fierce passions had blotted so suddenly out of existence.

I saw no more. I think it must have been the loud whistling of the engine as we shot into Fell Side Tunnel that awoke me so suddenly. Anyhow, at this point, I did awake, finding myself still sitting in the middle compartment of B 88, but with no Mr. Muxloe opposite me. I was alone. My limbs were so numbed and stiff with cold that, for a few minutes, I seemed to have no use of them. Gradually, some warmth crept back into my veins, and as soon as I felt that my strength and nerve were equal to the task, I made the best of my way back to my own compartment.

We were but five miles from Park End by this time. A few minutes later, I was on the platform with the old woman and the youngsters, all shaking me by the hand at once. It is almost worth one's while to leave home for a time just to see how pleased the missis and the bairns are to get back again.

I said nothing to anybody about what I had seen and gone through in B 88. I kept it shut up close in my own mind, but I could not help thinking it all over at least twenty times a day. That scene in the oak-paneled room was so deeply impressed on my memory that, after all these years, I can recall every feature of it as clearly as if it had happened but yesterday. Had it been a scene in real life, I should doubtless have half-forgotten it years ago. But the surrounding circumstances were so strange and out of the common way that, if I should live to be a hundred, it would all be as fresh in memory as if was the morning after it happened.

A week came and went without my seeing or hearing anything more of Mr. Muxloe. One evening, as I was going off duty, I was met and stopped by a gentleman dressed all in black.

"Can you tell me," said he, "whether your Company has a guard of the name of Preston in its employ?"

"*My* name is John Preston, at your service, sir," answered I.

"Then you are probably the man I want," said he. "My name is Keppel, and I am a nephew of the Mr. Muxloe who was so unfortunately killed at this station about six months ago. I was out of England at the time and was obliged to depend on a brief newspaper report for the details of the occurrence. I am greatly desirous of having full particulars from someone who was on the spot at the time. If you be the man I take you for, it was you who lifted up my uncle from the spot where he fell, and it was in your arms that he died."

"I am the man you mean, sir, and to any information I can give you, you are quite welcome."

"Then here is my address—and if you will come to my house for an hour this evening, you shall have no cause to regret having obliged me."

I promised to be at his house by nine o'clock. With that, we parted.

I was there to my time. The house was in the outskirts of the town and stood in its own grounds. It was too dark for me to see much of the outside, but the moment I got indoors, I saw that the whole place was very old. I was admitted by a servant who, after telling me that Mr. Keppel would be down in two or three minutes, threw open a side door and showed me into a long, low, old-fashioned room—into no other room, in fact, than the oak-paneled room of my dream! I knew it again in a moment, although it was now furnished very differently, and I sank into a chair all of a tremble.

Yes, there was the very oak-paneling with its quaint, zigzag-carved pattern. There, the wide old fireplace, inlaid with blue and white Dutch tiles. There, the huge window-place, in which half a dozen people might have sat with comfort. I recognized them all!

I could not describe to you the cold, sickening feeling that crept over me as I looked round. Had that gruesome tragedy, as seen by me in my dream, ever been really enacted in that room? Did the murdered man's bones still lie uncoffined under the boards of that old floor? I shuddered like a frightened child as I put these questions to myself.

Fortunately, I had time to pull myself together a bit before Mr. Keppel came into the room. He was very kind and affable, and had the decanters and a cold fowl brought out before ever he asked me a question. Just then, I could not eat, but a stiff tumbler of brandy-and-water helped me to get my nerve back again. After that, Mr. Keppel began to question me, and I gave him a full, true, and particular account of all the circumstances, so far as I knew them, in connection with his uncle's death. He was greatly interested. But when I had got through everything that he wanted to know, and he had nothing further to ask me, I plucked up my heart of grace and determined to tell how Mr. Muxloe had appeared to me several times since death and of my strange dream in B 88.

I never saw anyone more astonished than Mr. Keppel was by the time I had finished my story. For a little while, he seemed almost too overcome to speak.

At last, he said: "If what you say be true—and I have no reason to doubt your word—it apparently points to one of those mysteries which seem purposely sent now and then as if to baffle the utmost exercise of human reason. This house, which now belongs to me, was certainly my uncle's property for a great number of years. Although he lived for the most part in London, he used to come down here for one or two days almost every month, ostensibly for the sake of the excellent fishing with which the neighbourhood abounds. He would never let the house, despite the potential to have had tenants by the score. One old woman had the sole charge of it when he was away. She waited upon him when he was here.

"There is one fact in connection with my uncle's residence here which seems in some measure to bear out the most singular point of your narrative: this very room in which we are sitting—in which, according to your account, a dreadful tragedy took place many years ago—was never, so long as I can remember, made use of by my uncle. It was always kept locked and shuttered. Though I was here often during my uncle's lifetime, I never saw inside the door of this room till after his death. Enough, however, for the present. I must have time to carefully think over this strange story of yours. Come and see me at eight the evening after tomorrow, if you have no better engagement."

Punctual to the time, I was there. I was shown into the oak-paneled room. There, I found Mr. Keppel, two gentlemen, and the gardener. The last, whose name I learned was Donald, waited beside a crowbar, a shovel, and other such tools.

"I have told these two gentlemen, who are particular friends of mine," said Mr. Keppel, "all that you told me the other evening. We have consulted together and have decided, not without hesitation, to investigate the matter, so far as it is in our power to do so after so great a lapse of time. As a matter of course, our first step is to ascertain whether anyone has been buried in the way described by you, under the flooring of this room. Donald here, who is discretion itself, will proceed to make the necessary search. Please point out the exact spot, as nearly as you can remember it, where you saw the body put away."

I had no difficulty in doing this—everything was fixed too clearly in my memory for that. So Donald set to work under my directions. I took off my coat and gave him a helping hand while the three gentlemen looked quietly on. I need not trouble you with details. It will be sufficient to say that, before long, we came upon a skeleton intermixed with some fragments of clothing and some rusted jewelry. Near at hand were the remains of what had at one time been a riding-whip, loaded with lead, while not a great distance away was the rusted tin canister which I felt certain from the first that we should not fail to find.

Mr. Keppel opened the canister and drew from it a strip of parchment. We all crowded round the table. After glancing through the paper himself, he proceeded to read aloud what was there written. This is what was written:

> Park End, November 9, 18—; 11 p.m.
> I, John Muxloe, of the Inner Temple, barrister-at-law, having this night done a deed which, if made public, would in all probability bring me to the gallows, hereby and solemnly depose to the truth of the undermentioned facts:
> At nine o'clock this evening, being at that time busy over my law books, I was disturbed by a knock at the front

door. My servant having left me to attend the deathbed of her mother, I was constrained to open the door myself. The person who knocked was my friend, Arthur Clevedon, the dearest friend I had on Earth. He had his riding boots on and was splashed with mud. In one hand, he carried a heavy whip. He walked past me without a word of greeting into the oak-panelled room, and I followed, wondering what could possibly be the matter with him. His first words to me were: 'John Muxloe, you are an infernal villain!' I was thunderstruck!

'Those are very hard words, Arthur,' I said. 'You must be either crazy or drunk.'

'Neither one nor the other,' he answered. 'I repeat that you are an infernal villain, and I have come to horsewhip you!'

I laughed a little scornfully. 'It is possible for two people to play at that game, *amigo mio,*' I said.

He was poising his riding whip in his hand, and his eyes looked as if they would burn me through.

'Arthur, my friend,' I said, suddenly softening, 'what is it?—what is the meaning of these hard words? As true as there is a heaven above us, I do not understand you.'

'Liar and scoundrel, you understand me but too well!' he answered. Then he gave vent to a wild torrent of words, in which he accused me of having surreptitiously stolen away the affections of a certain lady, whose name need not be mentioned here. He declared that I had been fully aware that her troth had already been plighted in secret to *him*. Never was there a more unfounded accusation! It is true that the lady had promised to become mine, but—and I swear it here most solemnly—I had not the remotest idea that Arthur Clevedon had ever been anything more to her than an ordinary friend. She had deceived him and hoodwinked me, for what purpose was known to her own false heart alone. All this I tried to tell Arthur, but he would not hear me. Once again, he called me a liar, and as he did so, he lashed me across the face with his whip.

With a cry of rage, I sprang at his throat. I know scarcely anything of what followed till I saw him lying dead at my feet, with blood streaming from a great wound in his forehead. I had smitten him down with his own heavy whip.

All this happened but one short hour ago, but what an hour has that been to me! What other terrible hours has the future in store for me! But I dare not look forward. Another thing I dare not do: I dare not let the world know the deed I have this night done. My story would never be believed. They would say I had murdered him—they would hang me! No, I must keep my own counsel. I must lock up the secret forever in my own breast.

I have dug a hole under the flooring of this room in which to dispose of the body. By its side, I shall place this document so that, in case this night's dark deed should ever be brought to light in time to come, all dispute and inquiry may be obviated. Should it ever be brought to light during my lifetime, I shall have but one resource. I should kill myself.

O Arthur! dearest friend that ever man had, how I— But I can write no more for tears. My eyes are blinded, my heart weeps tears of blood. In that world beyond the grave where all that is dark here is made clearer than day, we maybe perhaps meet again. Then will thy hand clasp mine in friendship as of old—only it will be a friendship that will last forever. Then wilt thou know how innocent I was of wronging thee in thought, word, or deed. Till that time shall come—Farewell!

John Muxloe

The reading of this strange document filled everyone present with horror and surprise. It was, of course, considered a confirmation of the statement I had made to Mr. Keppel. Nothing more was done that night. Mr. Keppel said he must have time to consider what steps it would be most advisable to take under such peculiar circumstances.

The result may be stated in very few words. The bones were taken up, placed in a coffin, and interred with the customary solemnities in consecrated ground. The world was never told that it had been discovered whose bones they were, but I think it not unlikely that Mr. Keppel made some private communication to the friends of Mr. Clevedon. Be that as it may, the affair was quietly hushed up, and the real facts of the case never spread beyond a very limited circle.

I need scarcely add that Mr. Muxloe never troubled me again. On the other hand, Mr. Keppel did not lose sight of me. He had been a good friend to me in twenty different ways between then and now.

And so ends this full, true, and particular account of the only ghost I ever saw—or wish to see—till the time comes when I shall be a ghost myself.

THE ENGINEER'S STORY

EBEN E. REXFORD[1]

Yes, sir, I *do* believe in ghosts. *Why?*

Well, sir, because I saw one once. *Tell you about it?* Well, sir, I will, if you'll set down an' listen. 'Taint very much to tell, but it was a good deal to see, you can jest bet your life, an' I never go by the place when I see it without feelin' kind o' scary.

Lemme see. 'Twas in '60. I was jest beginnin' my work on this road that year. I'd been on a road out west, but a friend got me the position here that I've kep' ever sence.

It was a rainy, disagreeable day when the affair I'm goin' to tell you about happened. Jest one o' them days that makes a feller feel blue in spite of himself, an' he can't tell why, neither, 'less he lays it all to the weather. I don't know what made me feel so, but it seemed as if there was danger ahead ever after we left Wood's Station. An' what made it seem so curious was that the feelin' o' danger come on me all to once. It was jest about four o'clock, as near as I can tell. Anyway, jest about the time when the down express must have got safely by the place where what I'm goin' to tell you about happened, I was a-standin' with one hand on a lever, a-lookin' ahead through the drizzlin' rain, feelin' chilly an' kinder downhearted, as I've said, though I didn't know why. All of a sudden, the idea come to me that somethin' was wrong somewhere. It took hold o' me, an' I couldn't git red of it, nohow.

It got dark quite early, on account o' the fog an' the rain. It was dark as pitch afore we left Holbrook, which was the last station we passed afore we come to the place where I see the ghost.

"I never felt so queer in my life afore," said Jimmy, the fireman, to me all of a sudden.

As I was feelin' queer myself, he kinder startled me, a-sayin' what he did.

---

[1] Attributed to the *Chicago Ledger,* this short story appeared in a newspaper from Ebensburg, Pennsylvania, called *The Cambria Freeman,* May 31, 1878, p. 1.

"Why! What d'ye mean?" said I without lettin' on that I felt uneasy myself.

"Do' know," answered Jimmy. "Can't tell how I do feel—on'y as if somethin' was goin' to happen."

That was jest it! I felt the same thing, an' I told him so, an' we talked about it till we both got real fidgety.

There's a purty sharp curve about twenty miles from Holbrook. The road makes a turn round a mountain, an' the river runs below ye about forty feet or sech a matter. It is a pokerish-lookin' place when you happen to be goin' over it an' think what 'ud be if the train should pitch over the bluff inter the river.

Wall, we got to the foot o' the mountain just where the curve begins. The light from the headlamp lit up the track an' made it bright as day about as fur as from me to the fence yonder ahead o' the engine. Outside o' that spot, all was dark as you ever see it, I'll bet.

All to once, I see somethin' right ahead in the bright light. We allers run slow round this curve, so I could see distinct. My hair riz right up, I tell you, fer what I see was a man a-standin' right in the middle o' the track, a-wavin' his hands! An' I grabbed hold o' the lever an' whistled down brakes an' stopped the train as fast as ever I could, fer you see, I thought 'twas a *live* man. An' Jimmy, he see it too an' turned round to me with an awful scart face, fer he thought sure he'd be run over.

But I began to see 'twa'n't any flesh-and-blood man afore the train come to a stop, fer it seemed to glide right along over the track, keepin' jest about so fer ahead of us all the time.

"It's a *ghost*," cried Jimmy, a-grabbin' me by the arm. "You can see right *through* him!"

An' we could!

Yes, sir, we could. When I come to notice it, the figger ahead of us was a kind of foggy-lookin' thing, and it only half hid anything that was behind it. But it was jest as much like a man as you be, an' you'da said the same thing if you'da seen it.

The train stopped. An' then, sir, what d'ye think happened?

Well, sir, that *thing* just grew thinner an' thinner, till it seemed to blend right in with the fog that was all around it, and the fust we knew 'twas gone!

"It *was* a ghost!" said Jimmy in a whisper. "I knew somethin' was a-goin' to happen 'cause I felt so queer like."

They come a-crowdin' up to find why I'd stopped the train, an' I swear I never felt so kind o' queer an' foolish as I did when I told

The Engineer's Story

'em what I'd seen 'cause I knew they didn't b'lieve in ghosts, most likely, an' they'd think I was drunk or crazy.

"He see it, too," sez I, a-pointin' to Jimmy.

"Yes, 'fore God, I did," sez Jimmy, solemn as if he was a witness on the stand.

"This is a pretty how-d'ye-do," sez the conductor, who didn't b'lieve we'd seen anything. "I'm surprised at you, Connell—I thought you was a man o' sense."

"I thought so, too," sez I, "but I can't help what I see. If I was a-dyin' this minute I'd swear I see a man on the track—or leastwise the *ghost* of one. I thought 'twas a real man when I whistled."

"An' so would I," sez Jimmy.

The conductor couldn't help seein' that we was in earnest an' b'lieved what we said.

"Take a lantern an' go along the track," sez he to some o' the men.

An' they did. An' what d'ye s'pose they found?

Well, sir, they found the rails all tore up jest at the spot where the train woulda shot over the bluff into the river if it had gone on!

Yes, sir, they found that, an' I tell you there was some pretty solemn lookin' faces when it got among the passengers how near we'd been to death.

"I never b'lieved in ghosts," sez the conductor, "but I b'lieve you see *somethin'*, Connell, an' you've saved a precious lot o' lives. That's a sure thing."

Well, sir, they went to huntin' round, an' they found a lot o' tools an' things that the men who'd tore up the rails had left in a hurry, when they found the train wasn't goin' over the bluff as they'd expected. An' they found, too, when it come light, the body o' the man whose business it was to see to the curve, where it had been hid away after bein' *murdered*.

An' *that* man was the man whose ghost we had seen.

Yes, sir. He'd come to warn us o' the danger ahead after the men had killed him an' was a-waitin' for us to go over the rocks to destruction. An' he'd saved us.

I found out afterward that there was a lot o' money onboard, an' I s'pose the men who tore up the track knew it.

So that's my ghost story. An' it's a true one, sir.

UNTITLED

ANONYMOUS[1]

From time to time, hints have been thrown out concerning the haunted engine of the Detroit, Lansing and Northern railroad. Of late so much has been said that your correspondent determined to inquire into the matter. The engine (No. 20) is run at Edmore as a yard engine by Cal Piatt, from whom I learned that the locomotive had been the means of causing the death of several people, and only last spring, it ran over and killed a man near Portland. The side which has run over the bodies keeps up a constant groaning and moans like a human being in distress. It has since been oiled and everything done to stop this noise, but it has no effect whatever.

The latest freak in which it has indulged occurred one day last week. The engine was standing on the track and the engineer standing beside it, but no one was touching any part of the machinery when the bell commenced ringing and continued for several seconds. Several persons standing by witnessed this and say they would swear that it was a fact.

Engineer Piatt says that he is not naturally superstitious, but he doesn't know what to make of it.

---

[1] Attributed to Michigan's *Detroit Free Press,* this report was reprinted in *The Railroad Age* 8.35 [Aug. 30, 1883] p. 540. I was pleasantly surprised to discover that the editors of journals such as this—despite targeting readers in the railroad business—included this kind of unnerving article with some regularity.

TERROR OF HAUNTED LOCOMOTIVES

ANONYMOUS[1]

Locomotive engineers are almost, if not altogether, as superstitious in regard to haunted locomotives as sailors are in regard to haunted ships. About ten years ago, the engine *Matt Morgan* blew up while standing on the track of the Shore Line road near the station in Providence, R.I., killing the engineer. The engine was subsequently rebuilt and put on the road.

On the first trip that she made after being rebuilt, she went tearing into Providence in the night with the train swinging behind and the sleeping town echoing to the shrill whistle. On approaching the station, the engineer leaned forward to shut off the steam, but to his horror, a ghostly form appeared at his side and a ghostly hand grasped his wrist and held him fast. When the station was reached the ghost disappeared, and the engineer stopped the train some distance beyond. At least, this is what the engineer tells.

Many people have not forgotten the terrible Richmond Switch disaster several years ago on the Providence and Stonington road. A little brook became swollen by the rain and carried away a railroad bridge. The train came rushing along that night and was hurled into the chasm. Giles, the engineer, when he saw the danger ahead, instead of leaping from the engine as his fireman did, grasped the lever and reversed the engine. But it was too late. The train was going at such speed that the locomotive leaped clear across the stream, and they found Giles lying under his overturned engine with the lever driven through his body and one hand clutching the throttle valve with the grasp of death.[2]

---

[1] Attributed to the *New York Tribune*, this article was reprinted in various periodicals, including Virginia's *Richmond Dispatch*, Nov. 4, 1885, p. 4, and *Locomotive Firemen's Magazine* 10.1 [Jan. 1886] p. 26.

[2] Newspaper reports on the April 19, 1873, wreck add details and suggest corrections. Heavy rains burst a dam in the Rhode Island town of Richmond Switch

Giles, when he came into Providence, was accustomed to give two peculiar whistles as a signal to his wife, who lived near the railroad where it enters the suburbs of the city, that he was all right and would soon be home. The absence of those whistles was the first intimation which was received at Providence of the disaster. When the engine, which made the terrible leap on that stormy night, was rebuilt and put on the road again, there was at first great trouble in getting engineers for it, with such a superstitious horror was it regarded. Today, there are people ready to swear that they have heard whistles, such as Giles used to blow signals to his wife, sound through the suburbs of Providence, when no train was coming up the road.

(now Wood River Junction), which washed away the railway bridge. The number of fatalities reported varied from seven to twenty, but later articles said early estimates were too high. The fireman, George Eldrigde, was killed at his post, and the engineer was named William Guile. Both "remained in an upright position even after death, the former with his hand on the throttle," according to *The New York Herald,* April 20, 1873, p. 7.

GHOST WITHOUT A HEAD:
A MIDNIGHT PHANTOM THAT IS TERRORIZING EMPLOYEES OF THE LAKE ERIE & WESTERN ROAD

ANONYMOUS[1]

Findlay, Ohio, Jan. 16. Trainmen on the Lake Erie & Western railroad, between Findlay and Fostoria, are greatly disturbed over what they claim is the ghost of a dead freight conductor. The conductor was killed one night last November, about eight miles east of this city, by this train breaking into two sections in such a manner that he was thrown to the track from the car on which he was standing and beheaded by the wheels before the train could be controlled.

This accident occurred near the little town of Arcadia, at a point where dense woods nearly arch the track above the rails, and here it is, the trainmen assert, the ghost of the mutilated conductor who was known in life as Jimmie Welsh makes its appearance nearly every night as the midnight train going west from Sandusky reaches the spot where Welsh met his fate. The engineer and other officials of the train say that, when these woods are reached, an object looking like a headless man comes walking slowly out towards the track with a lantern in its hand, which it waves backwards and forwards as if searching for something. The trainmen are positive that it is the ghost of Welsh hunting for the head, which was severed from the body by the car-wheels. They insist that this object is plainly visible until the engine passes by, when the phantom slowly turns and fades away among the trees.

Two crews have already abandoned this run and have been transferred to other divisions of the road on account of this alleged ghost, and the engineer who brought this train through last night

---

[1] This report appeared on the front page of Indiana's *Indianapolis Journal*, January 17, 1890.

was so terrified over encountering this headless conductor that, when he reached this city, it was with difficulty that he was persuaded to stay on his engine until relieved at Lima. He said that he would not pass through another such experience for any sum of money.

No other trains are annoyed by this ghostly conductor, but this is explained by the fact that no other crew passes the spot where poor Welsh lost his life at the time of night where he was decapitated by the wheels of his train. The story has thoroughly alarmed all the employees of the road, and unless the spirit of Jimmie Welsh is appeased in some way, this midnight train will have to be abandoned.

FROM REAL GHOST STORIES

W. T. STEAD[1]

One of the best and, at the same time, one of the simplest ghost stories I have heard from my friends was that which was told me by the manager of Mr. Burgess, who used to print the *Review of Reviews*. Mr. Archer is a brother Tynesider. When he was a youth, he was employed as telegraphist at the Gateshead railway station.

At the end of the platform stood, and possibly still stands, the dead house,[2] which was an eerie and unpleasant object to young Archer, who was on night duty at the station. When he left his office in the early hours of the morning, he was always uneasy in passing the dead house and was always exceedingly glad when he could find anyone to accompany him while he was in the immediate vicinity.

One morning, about two o'clock, he came out upon the platform and was walking in the direction of the dead house, feeling that he would have to go past it alone. To his great delight, he saw standing on the platform, at a short distance in front of him, the familiar figure of a man in the employ of the railway company. Hoping to secure the company of the workman past the dead house, he stepped up to him, when—to his utter astonishment and no little dismay—the figure *vanished into thin air.*

Feeling very uncomfortable, but not knowing what to make of it, he went to the signalman at Greenfield and told him he could not understand it: he had just seen —— standing on the platform, and

---

[1] This anecdote comes from *Real Ghost Stories: A Revised Reprint of the Christmas Numbers of the "Review of Reviews," 1891-92* (Grant Richards, 1897) p. 150. This book is a compendium of reputedly authentic ghost stories. *Review of Reviews* was Stead's magazine featuring reviews of books and magazines mixed with celebrity featurettes and commentary on current events. Along with publishing, Stead was deeply interest in Spiritualism and other psychical subjects. He died on the *Titanic* after giving his life jacket to another passenger.

[2] As one might guess, a "dead house" is a structure used to house the recently deceased prior to, say, burial.

when he went up to him, he suddenly disappeared.

The signalman looked rather astonished and said, "You have seen ——? It is impossible. Did you not know that he was killed yesterday, and his body is lying in the dead house at this moment?"

It was now Mr. Archer's turn to be dismayed. He was perfectly certain he had seen the man—yet the man was dead.

A GHOST-HAUNTED RAILWAY

ANONYMOUS[1]

No little sensation has been aroused amongst the residents of a locality intersected by the main line of the London, Chatman, and Dover Railway, at Sittingbourne, by the assertion that a level-crossing at that spot is haunted by ghosts. The tale goes that, at the witching hour of midnight, the apparition takes its ghostly walk, heedless of passing trains.

Of recent years, the level-crossing which used to exist at this spot has proved fatal to one or two persons, and in consequence, a foot bridge has been erected. It is stated that the spirit of one of the victims now haunts the crossing, and numbers of people who reside in the immediate vicinity may be seen out of doors at nighttime waiting for the apparition.

The rumours arise, no doubt, from the fact that a few days since, as a goods train was passing the spot at about two a.m., the driver thought he saw someone on the line, and he believed that he had run over the person. The train was brought to a standstill and a search made, but no one was to be found. Superstition was rife at once, and the driver is credited with the belief that the apparition foretells impending danger. The supposed ghostly visitations continued from that date, and this part of the line now enjoys quite a local notoriety.

---

[1] This report was run in North Yorkshire's *North-Eastern Daily Gazette,* Oct. 31, 1893, pg. 4. I'm unsure whether it being printed on Halloween makes it less—or *more*—discomforting.

A RAILROAD GHOST

ANONYMOUS[1]

"*Ghosts!*" snorted the conductor scornfully. "Why, man alive, the woods are full of 'em in these mountains. Just wait till we take the siding for No. 3 to pass, and I'll tell you about Granny Whittaker and her cow, whose spooks I seen with my own eyes. *Ghosts!* There's at least one full grown spook for every mile post on the division."

So it was I held my peace until the train was safely on the siding, and we were gathered around the stove in the caboose. The wind was howling wildly through the gorges, making the windows rattle and the doors creak. Meanwhile, the unusual draught caused the iron stove to glow redly in the semi-twilight. One felt mighty comfortable inside the cab that evening.

"Now, about them spooks," remarked the conductor, putting away his dinner pail and lighting his pipe. "I'm not goin' to tell you any fancy tales, but just give you a short account of what I seen with my own eyes one winter about ten years ago, and you can believe it or not as you see fit. At that time, I was front brakeman on old Bill Staley's crew, and we had the name of bein' the toughest gang on the division all through, includin' the engineer and fireman. Pete Smith was at the throttle, and I do solemnly believe he was the most impious man on the face of the Earth. Swear? Why, profanity came to his lips easier than anything else. I've seen him sit down on a log and curse the road, from president to apprentice, because a nut got loose or a couplin' broke.

"And he was as *cranky* as he was profane. For instance, one day, he got it into his head the telegraph operator at Big Tunnel kept the red signal up a few seconds longer than necessary, which raised

---

[1] This short story appeared in Maine's *Portland Daily Press,* Sept. 1, 1895, p. 6. Like many newspaper pieces in the era, this one traveled far and wide. I found an earlier version, titled "The Haunted Engineer," in *The Evening Express* (Dec. 27, 1894, p. 4), a paper published in Cardiff, Wales.

A Railroad Ghost

his wrath so, when the board finally dropped, old Pete wouldn't start. Instead, he got a wrench and began takin' off a cylinder head. We knew it wasn't any use remonstratin' with him, as he'd use his own sweet will about the matter. Meantime, train after train drew up behind us, and the dispatcher at the other end of the division was nearly crazy. He asked by wire several times what was the matter—and, at last, sent a message threatenin' to suspend Pete unless he got started within ten minutes.

"When he got this word, Pete, who all the time had been tinkerin' with the cylinder as if he was makin' big repairs, began to swear. He set down on the pilot and salivated that dispatcher until words actually failed him. Then he told the operator to tell the dispatcher to go to a warm place, and he renewed his leisurely work on the engine. At last, he got in the mood to start, after we had laid there two hours and twenty minutes. The worst of it was nobody could say positively that the cylinder didn't need repairs, so nothing could be done.

"I mentioned this just to show what a mean, cantankerous cuss Pete was, and so you'd better understand what I'm going to tell you. Ten years ago, the country hereabouts wasn't near as well settled as it is now. The old residenters weren't over-good, either. They had the name of bein' a bad lot, and about the worst was Granny Whittaker, who lived in a rickety little log house in a clearing near the top of the mountain. It was said she was a witch, and most people avoided her as they would the devil.

"She had an old mooley cow that used to run free all over the mountain, often as not takin' the railroad for a short cut home. That cow caused lots of trouble, for there wasn't an engineer on the division who wouldn't a blame sight rather stop his train and chase the brute away than incur Granny Whittaker's anger by killin' it—that is, exceptin' Pete. One day, the cow got on the track ahead of him when he was in an extra bad humor, and he tried to run it down, sayin' he'd send the cow to kingdom come if he got the chance. He got it. The next day, the cow wasn't quick enough, and Pete caught it square in the center, knockin' it down the bank like a feather. Then he laughed. I think it was the first time I ever heard him laugh, and along with the rest of the trainmen, I didn't like it a bit, for we was afeared of Granny Whittaker.

"The followin' day, when we reached that spot again, there was a red flag stickin' up between the rails. Contrary as Pete was, he didn't dare run past a danger signal, so he blowed for brakes, and the train came to a stop. All at once, old Granny Whittaker rose up from somewhere and opened on Pete. She called down the most blood-curdlin' curses on him I ever heard, her skinny finger pointin' at him and her eyes flashin' sulphur and brimstone. Old Pete wriggled and tried to answer, but she didn't give him a chance until she ran out of breath. I was lookin' for him to do some swearin' himself, but he only said, 'Shet up, ye old hag, or I'll send ye to jine the cow.' Then he started his engine.

"She ran alongside his cab, screamin', 'I'll put a spell on you and your engine, you murderer!'

"She threw a little bottle of what looked like ink at him. It hit the window and busted, flyin' all over him and the engine. She cackled and yelled with delight.

"'You'll die by your own engine, you wretch, and me and my cow'll haunt you,' she yelled as we moved away.

"Pete wiped the stuff off with some waste and said nothin'. I saw the old woman standin' and pointin' after us until we turned the bend.

"About a week after that, we were changed from a day to a night run. In spite of old Pete's crankiness, he was one of the best engineers on the road and had one of the best engines, too. So when things began to go wrong with the machinery of 290, the master mechanic couldn't understand it. The engine would run all right for a spell and then get balky. At such times, it wouldn't steam, the valves would stick, drawheads would be jerked out,[2] or the fire would get choked up—all apparently without any cause.

"Of course, at first, everybody blamed it on Pete, but after the road foreman of engines made two or three trips in her, it was seen Pete wasn't responsible. So they sent her to the shop for general repairs, and Pete was given an engine on another run.

"It was about two months before 290 was turned out for service again. In the meantime, old Granny Whittaker was found dead in her shanty and buried in her garden, the church people refusing to allow her to rest in consecrated ground.

"For a week after 290 was repaired, another engineer had her and she worked like a charm. Then they put her back on our run, and Pete took her again. We started out the first night with a heavy train, and as I told you, bein' front brakeman, my place was on the cars next the engine. It was raw and foggy, the kind of weather to make a man feel nervous in spite of himself, especially goin' through these mountain wilds. I was thinkin' of this when I heard Pete blow

---

[2] A "drawhead" sits at the rear of an engine or car, and a drawbar or other coupling device is attached to it to haul the next car behind.

A Railroad Ghost

for brakes—or rather as if there was somethin' on the track. I edged over to the side of the boxcars between which I was standin', and holdin' on to the grab-irons, I tried to see what was the matter. Just then I felt a soft bump and saw somethin' tumble down the bank. *That's an animal,* thought I. But when the train stopped and we all went back to look for it, not a thing could be found.

"'That's mighty funny,' said Pete. 'I'm sure I hit a cow.'

"'Cow!' said the flagman. 'Why, there ain't a cow within twenty miles of here since Granny Whittaker's was killed.'

"Then the same thought seemed to strike us all as the fireman remarked that *this was the exact spot* where the old woman's cow had been killed. Nobody wanted to seem afeared, but we all hustled back to the train not sayin' a word, exceptin' Pete, who began cursin' the old woman, her cow, and cows in general.

"All of a sudden, the underbrush rattled, and *there stood Granny Whittaker!*

"Now, I'm not tellin' you a fairy tale or makin' anything up. I'm just tellin' what I saw—and I don't mean to try to explain it—but there stood the old woman who had been dead for weeks, pointin' that skinny finger at Pete. Then she disappeared as quickly as she came.

"Grabbin' a lamp, Pete rushed into the woods and searched all around, but not a sign of a human bein' could be found. I tell you, that sort of frightened us all but Pete. He swore that it was a trick and that he'd get even with whoever it was tryin' to fool him.

"Next night, the *same thing* happened, exceptin' that no one but Pete tried to find the mysterious cow or the old woman, who appeared at the ditch as before. Pete fired a pistol at her, but she only hissed at him and vanished.

"The third night Pete asked me to ride in the engine, and although it was against the rules, I did as he wanted, for—to tell the truth—I was afeared to stay by myself.

"Everything seemed to go wrong that night. We were nearly an hour late gettin' started, and before we had gone ten miles, a coal car jumped the track, causin' forty minutes' delay. In tryin' to yank it on, a drawhead was pulled out, and we had to rig up a chain couplin'. Then somethin' beneath the boiler worked loose, and Pete tinkered at it twenty minutes before he made the repairs. Of course, all this didn't tend to improve his temper, and by the time we finally got on a steady run again, he was grumblin' and cursin' pretty lively.

"Well, when we reached the stretch of track where we'd killed the cow, there was the brute on the ties as usual—except old Granny

Whittaker was standin' beside it. I saw that just as plain as I see you sittin' on that keg this minute. Pete was crazy mad, and instead of reversin', he ripped out a curse, put on a full head of steam, and the engine give a jerk which nearly knocked me off the tank. I reckon we were goin' fifty mile an hour when the pilot struck 'em.

"Zip! Bump! The cow went flyin' down the bank. Then Pete give a yell. Lookin' past him, I saw somethin' crawlin' over the pilot and steam chest. *It was Granny Whittaker!* She reached up and grasped the sand rod and turned her eyes on Pete. God, how horrible she looked!

"Then she beckoned to him, and—would you believe it—he got up and crawled out on the footboard towards her. The fireman and me was paralyzed. We couldn't say a word or move a finger. The engineer slowly moved towards the old woman, and she stepped backward, seemin' to influence him by her eyes. Back, back, on to the steam chest, then on to the pilot, and then around in front of the boiler—out of our sight, she led him.

"A second later we heard a yell. God forbid I ever hear another like it.

"That broke the spell, and between the fireman and me, we shut off steam and blowed for brakes. The terrific speed at which we were movin' caused us to go a considerable distance before we stopped, but as soon as the train slackened, we jumped off and run forward. Pete wasn't there. We didn't think he would be.

"We found him a mile *back,* and there wasn't a whole bone in his body.

"The next day, engine No. 290 exploded within fifty feet of where we found Pete.

"Now, as I said, I saw those things with my own eyes, and I'm not tellin' you any hearsay yarns, but the downright truth. Sometime, if I get the chance, I'll tell you about a spook Jack Clements claims he saw—but I guess you don't want any more tonight?"

I did not.

THE GHOSTS OF SAG BRIDGE

213[1]

In the year of '73, during the month of June, there occurred upon the —— railway, a catastrophe almost without parallel and attended with loss of life, among whom were two well-known Illinois state penitentiary officials, several prominent people of the city of Joliet, and one unfortunate man whose body was never identified.

This accident was termed, in railway parlance, "a head end collision" between a northbound stock train and the southbound express. The time of the occurrence was about 10 o'clock at night, and the location of the accident was at a place called Sag Bridge, about twenty miles from Chicago.[2]

Strange to relate, none of the employees on the freight train or on either of the engines was killed, although the passengers occupying the smoker and the employees of the mail and baggage cars were cut, bruised, and some mangled into unrecognizable shape or literally cooked by the escaping steam and hot water.

The passengers occupying the coach and rear sleepers escaped with many slight bruises and a severe shaking up.

The stock on the northbound freight was cruelly crushed and tortured beyond description, and scattered in every possible direction.

The cause of the accident was attributed to negligence of the freight crew, as they were endeavoring, by rapid and reckless

---

[1] This report appeared in *The Railway Conductor* 13.10 [Oct., 1896] pp. 595-96. This was the journal of the Order of Railway Conductors of America, a fraternity-turned-union. Perhaps this explains why the author choose "213"–a member number?—as a byline. (Several other writers in the publication remain anonymous by simply appearing unnamed.)

[2] While there is still a crossing called the Sag Bridge in Lemont, Illinois, near the spot discussed here, it is not the same bridge. Also nearby is St. James at Sag Bridge, which is among northern Illinois's very oldest Catholic churches and reputed by some to be a hotspot for paranormal activity.

running, to gain Willow Springs siding for the southbound express and also to an imperfect system of train orders used on the line at that time.

The feeling against the conductor, whose name will not be mentioned, as he is a quiet, respectable citizen and still engaged as a railroad conductor within the limits of the state, was so intense at the time that he was obliged to immediately "flee for life" and remain hidden in straw stacks or timber, till the indignation against him subsided.

The railroad company offered a reward of $1000 for his capture, and although he was surrendered by a relative who divided the reward with him, no proceedings were instituted against him or the engineer.[3]

The locomotive of the ill-fated stock train was of the pattern which railroad men call a "gunboat" on account of the peculiar driving wheels and being capable of pulling heavy trains.

The disaster was gossip for weeks following, and the place looked upon with horror by passengers and trainmen alike.

In due course of time, engine 122 came out of the repair shops as good as new, but her career as a combination of machinery had just commenced: her first night's trip was marked by her cab lamps and headlights suddenly being extinguished by some supernatural agency just as the train passed the eventful point. At first, the enginemen thought but little of it except as a singular coincidence, but as time rolled along and the circumstances continued occurring at the same point upon all night runs, it became evident that there must be some invisible agency that marked engine 122 because of her connection with the great disaster.

In a short time, these unaccountable freaks of this engine caused considerable talk and excitement among the railroad employees, and in consequence of the numerous ghosts which were reported to exist in the locality of Sag Bridge, the night track watchman at the ill-fated place tendered his resignation, saying he

---

[3] The collision of 1873 is authentic. It happened on the Chicago and Alton Railroad on August 16th (not during June, as this writer states). The conductor of the freight train was Edward Beane, who failed in his obligation to wait for the slightly delayed southbound passenger train to pass before heading north. Neither engineer saw the other coming due to a curve in the road. About twenty people died, and several more were injured. After Beane turned fugitive out of fear of mob retaliation, his father "surrendered" him. There was a $1000 reward, but I found nothing to verify that the Beanes split that money. Newspapers confirm, though, that the younger Beane and the freight train's engineer, Joshua Puffenberger, were arrested for manslaughter and that both men were then acquitted.

could "shtand it no more." "Stand what?" interrogated his superiors. "Why, the ghosts! Sure, ivery Sathurday night, when I comes to me shanty, down forninst 'the bridge,' for a spell, there do be sittin' Mr. and Mrs. ——, who were killed in the big smashup, as natural as life, and talkin'."[4]

Although very few gave credence to his story in full, no amount of persuasion induced him to remain. He had seen ghosts, and his superstition compelled him to resign.

This fact, reaching the ears of the trainmen, caused them to relate their thrilling experience at this same place, much to the astonishment of the officials, who soon were convinced that Sag Bridge was haunted.

At "the bridge" stood a water tank which supplied most of the passing trains with water, and while thus stopping, many of the train hands were confronted by spooks and other apparitions. One freight conductor was so frequently met by these strange sights that he resigned as a consequence and is now one of Chicago's prominent businessmen. Conductor R. had no connection with the wreck, and why he should have been selected as a victim was unexplained, but so it was, and every trip that he ventured over his train while stopping at the Sag, his nerves sustained many shocks by forms flitting to and fro, ahead of and behind him, as he clambered over the freight cars comprising his train.

The engineer in charge of the 122, when nearing the Sag, would often see a man and woman climb upon the pilot of the locomotive, and when he ventured an attempt to investigate, they would jump off while the train was moving and suddenly disappear.

Two brakemen, "partners" on a night run, formed an investigating society of their own to pry into the causes for the wonderful phantoms at the Sag, and it happened one night, after they "had made the stop" for water, both discovered a ghostly looking object seated on the caboose steps. Arming themselves with stout clubs, they gave chase. The phantom fled and scaled the fence in full view of its pursuers, who followed and discovered, at the exact spot where the ghost disappeared from the fence, some cows quietly sleeping and undisturbed, showing plainly no earthly form in flesh and blood could have escaped by jumping into their midst.

One old railroad man related his experience to the reporter as follows: "I was a brakeman those days, and as true as I talk, the

---

[4] Following the stereotypes of the period, the watchman's dialect indicates he's Irish. The term "forninst" indicates the spectral couple sit close to or opposite from the bridge.

ghosts were plenty. Why, I've seen them time and again. Often, when walking by the train, examining the running gear, I could hear the chattering of teeth and the outcries of someone as if in anguish, till the chills would penetrate my very bones, and I would hasten back to the caboose to get rid of the mockery, and there I would see faces peering into the windows at me and, with a moan, quickly disappear. One night, I shot at a form, and, to my horror, the form looked like a boiling mass of burning Sulphur, and, with a fiendish laugh, it sank into the ground. That was too much for me. Half an hour afterward, when the train stopped at the next station and the conductor returned from the engine, I was found on the floor of the caboose in a dead faint."

The curse of the Sag Bridge has never been raised. Even today, train crews regard it with awe, mingled with a slight degree of fear, and they have reason for it: accident upon accident has occurred at that unlucky place, generally of a trivial nature, but upon several occasions since '73, these accidents have been attended by loss of life and destruction to property.

MISS SLUMBUBBLE— AND CLAUSTROPHOBIA

ALGERNON BLACKWOOD[1]

Miss Daphne Slumbubble was a nervous lady of uncertain age who invariably went abroad in the spring. It was her one annual holiday, and she slaved for it all the rest of the year, saving money by the many sad devices known only to those who find their incomes after forty "barely enough," and always hoping that something would one day happen to better her dreary condition of cheap tea, tin loaves, and weekly squabbles with the laundress.

This spring holiday was the only time she really *lived* in the whole year, and she half-starved herself for months immediately after her return, so as to put by quickly enough money for the journey in the following year. Once those six pounds were safe, she felt better. After that, she only had to save so many sums of four francs, each four francs meaning another day in the little cheap *pension* she always went to on the flowery slopes of the Alps of Valais.[2]

Miss Slumbubble was exceedingly conscious of the presence of men. They made her nervous and afraid. She thought in her heart that all men were untrustworthy, not excepting policemen and clergymen, for in her early youth she had been cruelly deceived by a man to whom she had unreservedly given her heart. He had suddenly gone away and left her without a word of explanation, and some months later had married another woman and allowed the announcement to appear in the papers. It is true that he had hardly once spoken to Daphne. But that was nothing. For the way he looked at her, the way he walked about the room, the very way he avoided her at the tea-parties where she used to meet him at her

---

[1] This short story appeared in Blackwood's collection *The Listener and Other Stories* (Eveleigh Nash, 1907) pp. 313-35.

[2] *"Pension"* is a French term for accommodations and, probably in this case, a boarding house that includes meals with a room.

rich sister's house—indeed, everything he did or left undone—brought convincing proof to her fluttering heart that he loved her secretly and that he knew she loved him. His near presence disturbed her dreadfully, so much so that she invariably spilt her tea if he came even within scenting-distance of her, and once, when he crossed the room to offer her bread and butter, she was so certain the very way he held the plate intimated his silent love that she rose from her chair, looked straight into his eyes, and took the *whole* plate in a state of delicious confusion!

But all this was years ago, and she had long since learned to hold her grief in subjection and to prevent her life being too much embittered by the treachery—she felt it *was* treachery—of one man. She still, however, felt anxious and self-conscious in the presence of men, especially of silent, unmarried men, and to some extent it may be said that this fear haunted her life. It was shared, however, with other fears, probably all equally baseless. Thus, she lived in constant dread of fire, of railway accidents, of runaway cabs, and of being locked into a small, confined space. The former fears she shared, of course, with many other persons of both sexes, but the latter, the dread of confined spaces, was entirely due, no doubt, to a story she had heard in early youth to the effect that her father had once suffered from that singular nervous malady, claustrophobia (the fear of closed spaces), the terror of being caught in a confined place without possibility of escape.

Thus it was clear that Miss Daphne Slumbubble—this good, honest soul with jet flowers in her bonnet and rows of coloured photographs of Switzerland on her bedroom mantelpiece—led a life unnecessarily haunted.

The thought of the annual holiday, however, compensated for all else. In her lonely room behind Warwick Square, she stewed through the dusty heat of summer, fought her way pluckily through the freezing winter fogs, and then, with the lengthening days, worked herself steadily into a fever heat of joyous anticipation as she counted the hours to the taking of her ticket in the first week of May.

When the day came, her happiness was so great that she wished for nothing else in the world. Even her name ceased to trouble her, for, once on the other side of the Channel, it sounded quite different on the lips of the foreigners while she was known as "Mlle. Daphne" in the little *pension,* and the mere sound brought music into her heart. The odious surname belonged to the sordid London life. It had nothing to do with the glorious days that Mlle. Daphne spent

Miss Slumbubble—and Claustrophobia

among the mountain tops.

The platform at Victoria was already crowded when she arrived a good hour before the train started, and got her tiny faded trunk weighed and labelled. She was so excited that she talked unnecessarily to anyone who would listen—to anyone in station uniform, that is. Already, in fancy, she saw the blue sky above the shining snow peaks, heard the tinkling cowbells, and sniffed the odours of pinewood and sawmill. She imagined the cheerful *table d'hôte* room with its wooden floor and rows of chairs; the *diligence*[3] winding up the hot white road far below; the fragrant *café complet* in her bedroom at 7.30—and then the long mornings with sketchbook and poetry book under the forest shade, the clouds trailing slowly across the great cliffs, and the air always humming with the echoes of falling water.

"And you feel sure the passage will be calm, do you?" she asked the porter for the third time as she bustled to and fro by his side.

"Well, there ain't no wind 'ere, at any rate, Miss," he replied cheerfully, putting her small box on a barrow.

"Such a lot of people go by this train, don't they?" she piped.

"Oh, a tidy few. This is the season for foreign parts, I suppose."

"Yes, yes. And the trains on the other side will be very full, too, I dare say," she said, following him down the platform with quick, pattering footsteps, chirping all the way like a happy bird.

"Quite likely, Miss."

"I shall go in a 'Ladies only,' you know. I always do every year. I think it's safer, isn't it?"

"I'll see to it all for yer, Miss," replied the patient porter. "But the train ain't in yet, not for another 'arf hour or so."

"Oh, thank you. Then I'll be here when it comes. 'Ladies only,' remember, and second class, and a corner seat facing the engine—no, back to the engine, I mean—and I do hope the Channel will be smooth. Do you think the wind—?"

But the porter was out of hearing by this time, and Miss Slumbubble went wandering about the platform watching the people arrive, studying the blue and yellow advertisements of the *Côte d'azur,* and waggling her jet beads with delight—with passionate delight—as she thought of her own little village in the high Alps where the snow crept down to a few hundred feet above the church and the meadows were greener than any in the whole wide world.

"I've put yer wraps in a 'Lidies only,' Miss," said the porter at

---

[33] A "diligence" is a stagecoach.

length, when the train came in, "and you've got the corner back to the engine all to yerself, an' quite comfortable. Thank you, Miss."

He touched his cap and pocketed his sixpence, and the fussy little traveller went off to take up her position outside the carriage door for another half hour before the train started. She was always very nervous about trains—not only fearful of possible accidents to the engine and carriages—but of untoward happenings to the occupants of corridor-less compartments during long journeys without stops. The mere sight of a railway station, with its smoke and whistling and luggage, was sufficient to set her imagination in the direction of possible disaster.

The careful porter had piled all her belongings neatly in the corner for her: three newspapers, a magazine and a novel, a little bag to carry food in, two bananas and a Bath bun in paper, a bundle of wraps tied with a long strap, an umbrella, a bottle of Yanatas, an opera-glass for the mountains, and a camera. She counted them all over, rearranged them a little differently, and then sighed a bit, partly from excitement, partly by way of protest at the delay.

A number of people came up and eyed the compartment critically and seemed on the point of getting in, but no one actually took possession. One lady put her umbrella in the corner and then came tearing down the platform a few minutes later to take it away again, as though she had suddenly heard the train was not to start at all. There was much bustling to and fro, and a good deal of French was audible, and the sound of it thrilled Miss Daphne with happiness, for it was another delightful little anticipation of what was to come. Even the language sounded like a holiday and brought with it a whiff of mountains and the subtle pleasures of sweet freedom.

Then a fat Frenchman arrived and inspected the carriage, and attempted to climb in. But she instantly pounced upon him in courageous dismay.

"Mais, c'est pour dames, m'sieur!" she cried, pronouncing it "dam."

"Oh, damn!" he exclaimed in English. "I didn't notice." And the rudeness of the man—it was the fur coat over his arm made her think he was French—set her all in a flutter, so that she jumped in and took her seat hurriedly and spread her many parcels in a protective and prohibitive way about her.

For the tenth time, she opened her black beaded bag and took out her purse and made sure her ticket was in it, and then counted over her belongings.

"I *do* hope," she murmured, "I do hope that stupid porter *has* put in my luggage all right, and that the Channel won't be rough. Porters *are* so stupid. One ought never to lose sight of them till the luggage is actually in. I think I'd better pay the extra fare and go first class on the boat if it is rough. I can carry all my own packages, I think."

At that moment, the man came for tickets. She searched everywhere for her own, but could not find it.

"I'm certain I had it a moment ago," she said breathlessly while the man stood waiting at the open door. "I know I had it—only this very minute. Dear me, what *can* I have done with it? Ah! here it is!"

The man took so long examining the little tourist cover that she was afraid something must be wrong with it, and when at last he tore out a leaf and handed back the rest, a sort of panic seized her.

"It's all right, isn't it, guard? I mean I'm all right, am I not?" she asked.

The guard closed the door and locked it.

"All right for Folkestone, ma'am," he said, and was gone.[4]

There was much whistling and shouting and running up and down the platform, and the inspector was standing with his hand raised and the whistle at his lips, waiting to blow and looking cross. Suddenly her own porter flew past with an empty barrow. She dashed her head out of the window and hailed him.

"You're sure you put my luggage in, aren't you?" she cried.

The man did not or would not hear, and as the train moved slowly off, she bumped her head against an old lady standing on the platform who was looking the other way and waving to someone in a front carriage.

"Ooh!" cried Miss Slumbubble, straightening her bonnet, "you really should look where you're looking, madam!"—and then, realising she had said something foolish, she withdrew into the carriage and sank back in a fluster on the cushions.

"Oh!" she gasped again, "oh dear! I'm actually off at last. It's too good to be true. Oh, that horrid London!"

Then she counted her money over again, examined her ticket once more, and touched each of her many packages with a long finger in a cotton glove, saying, "*That's* there, and that, and that, and—*that!*" And then turning and pointing at herself, she added, with a little happy laugh, "*and that!*"

The train gathered speed, and the dirty roofs and sea of ugly

---

[4] Folkestone is a port town in southeast England. Presumably, this is where Miss Slumbubble will transfer to a ferry headed to France.

chimneys flew by as the dreary miles of depressing suburbs revealed themselves through the windows. She put all her parcels up in the rack and then took them all down again—and, after a bit, she put a few up—a carefully selected few that she would not need till Folkestone—and arranged the others, some upon the seat beside her and some opposite. She kept the paper bag of bananas in her lap, where it grew warmer and warmer and more and more dishevelled in appearance.

"Actually off at last!" she murmured again, catching her breath a little in her joy. "Paris, Berne, Thun, Frutigen"—she gave herself a little hug that made the jet beads rattle—"then the long diligence journey up those gorgeous mountains"—she knew every inch of the way—"and a clear fifteen days at the *pension,* or even eighteen days, if I can get the cheaper room. Wheeeee! Can it be true? Can it be really true?" In her happiness, she made sounds just like a bird.

She looked out of the window, where green fields had replaced the rows of streets. She opened her novel and tried to read. She played with the newspapers in a vain attempt to keep her eye on any one column. It was all in vain. A scene of wild beauty held her inner eye and made all else dull and uninteresting.

The train sped on—slowly enough to her—yet every moment of the journey, every turn of the creaking wheels that brought her nearer, every little detail of the familiar route, became a source of keenest anticipatory happiness to her. She no longer cared about her name, or her silent and faithless lover of long ago, or of anything in the world but the fact that her absorbing little annual passion was now once again in a fair way to be gratified.

Then, quite suddenly, Miss Slumbubble realized her actual position and felt afraid. Unreasonably afraid. For the first time, she became conscious that she was alone, alone in the compartment of an express train and not even of a corridor express train.

Hitherto, the excitement of getting off had occupied her mind to the exclusion of everything else, and if she had realised her solitude at all, she had realized it pleasurably. But now, in the first pause for breath as it were, when she had examined her packages, counted her money, glared at her ticket, and all the rest of it for the twentieth time, she leaned back in her seat and knew with a distinct shock that she was alone in a railway carriage on a comparatively long journey, alone for the first time in her life in a rattling, racing, shrieking train. She sat bolt upright and tried to collect herself a little.

Of all the emotions, that of fear is probably the least susceptible

Miss Slumbubble—and Claustrophobia

to the power of suggestion, certainly of *auto*-suggestion. Of vague fear that has no obvious cause, this is especially true. With a fear of known origin one can argue, humour it, pacify, turn on the hose of ridicule—in a word, *suggest* that it depart. But with a fear that rises stealthily out of no comprehensible causes, the mind finds itself at a complete loss. The mere assertion "I am not afraid" is as useless and empty as the subtler kind of suggestion that lies in affecting to ignore it altogether. Searching for the cause, moreover, tends to confuse the mind and, searching in vain, to terrify.

Miss Slumbubble pulled herself sharply together and began to search for what made her afraid, but for a long time she searched in vain.

At first, she searched externally: she thought perhaps it had something to do with one of her packages, and she placed them all out in a row on the seat in front of her and examined each in turn, bananas, camera, food bag, black bead bag, &c., &c. But she discovered nothing among them to cause alarm.

Then she searched internally: her thoughts, her rooms in London, her *pension,* her money, ticket, plans in general, her future, her past, her health, her religion, anything and everything among the events of her inner life she passed in review. Yet she found nothing that could have caused this sudden sense of being troubled and afraid.

Moreover, as she vainly searched, her fear increased. She got into a regular nervous flurry.

"I declare if I'm not all in a perspiration!" she exclaimed aloud, shifting down the dirty cushions to another place and looking anxiously about her as she did so. She probed everywhere in her thoughts to find the reason of her fear, but could think of nothing. Yet in her soul there was a sense of growing distress.

She found her new seat no more comfortable than the one before it, and shifted in turn into all the corners of the carriage, and down the middle as well, till at last she had tried every possible part of it. In each place, she felt less at ease than in the one before.

She got up and looked into the empty racks, under the seats, beneath the heavy cushions, which she lifted with difficulty. Then she put all the packages back again into the rack, dropping several of them in her nervous hurry and being obliged to kneel on the floor to recover them from under the seats. This made her breathless. Moreover, the dust got into her throat and made her cough. Her eyes smarted, and she grew uncomfortably warm. Then, quite accidentally, she caught sight of her reflection in the coloured picture of Boulogne under the rack,[5] and the appearance she presented added greatly to her dismay. She looked so unlike herself and wore such an odd expression.

It was almost like the face of another person altogether.

The sense of alarm, once wakened, is fed by anything and everything, from a buzzing fly to a dark cloud in the sky. The woman collapsed onto the seat behind her in a distressing fluster of nervous fear.

But Miss Daphne Slumbubble had pluck. She was not so easily dismayed after all. She had read somewhere that terror was sometimes dispersed by the loud and strong affirmation of one's own name. She believed much that she read, provided it was plainly and vigorously expressed, and she acted at once on this knowledge.

"I am Daphne Slumbubble!" she affirmed in a firm, confident tone of voice, sitting stiffly on the edge of the seat. "I am not afraid—*of anything.*" She added the last two words as an afterthought. "I am Daphne Slumbubble, and I have paid for my ticket and know where I am going, and my luggage is in the van, and I have all my smaller things here!" She enumerated them one by one. She omitted nothing.

Yet the sound of her own voice, and especially of her own name, added apparently to her distress. It sounded oddly like a voice *outside* the carriage. Everything seemed suddenly to have become strange and unfamiliar and unfriendly. She moved across to the opposite corner and looked out of the window: trees, fields, and occasional country houses flew past in endless swift succession. The country looked charming. She saw rooks flying and farm-horses moving laboriously over the fields. What in the world was there to feel afraid of? What in the world made her so restless and fidgety and frightened?

Once again, she examined her packages, her ticket, her money. All was right.

Then she dashed across to the window and tried to open it. The sash stuck. She pulled and pulled in vain. The sash refused to yield. She ran to the other window with a like result. Both were closed. Both refused to open. Her fear grew. She was locked in! The windows would not open. Something was wrong with the carriage. She suddenly recalled the way everyone had examined it and refused to enter. There must be something the matter with the carriage—something she had omitted to observe. Terror ran like a

---

[5] Boulogne-sur-Mer, a.k.a. Boulogne, is a port city in northern France. This is the probable destination of Miss Slumbubble's ferry from Folkstone.

Miss Slumbubble—and Claustrophobia

flame through her. She trembled and was ready to cry.

She ran up and down between the cushioned seats like a bird in a cage, casting wild glances at the racks and under the seats and out of the windows. A sudden panic took her, and she tried to open the door. It was locked. She flew to the other door. That, too, was locked. Good Heavens, both were locked! She was locked in. She was a prisoner. She was caught in a closed space. The mountains were out of her reach—the free open woods—the wide fields, the scented winds of heaven. She was caught, hemmed in, celled, restricted like a prisoner in a dungeon. The thought maddened her. The feeling that she could not reach the open spaces of sky and forest, of field and blue horizon, struck straight into her soul and touched all that she held most dear.

She screamed.

She ran down between the cushioned seats and screamed aloud.

Of course, no one heard her. The thunder of the train killed the feeble sound of her voice. Her voice was the cry of the imprisoned person.

Then quite suddenly she understood what it all meant. There was nothing wrong with the carriage or with her parcels or with the train. She sat down abruptly upon the dirty cushions and faced the position there and then. It had nothing to do with her past or her future, her ticket or her money, her religion or her health. It was something else entirely. She knew what it was, and the knowledge brought icy terror at once. She had at last labelled the source of her consternation, and the discovery increased rather than lessened her distress.

It was the fear of closed spaces. It was *claustrophobia!*

There could no longer be any doubt about it. She was shut in. She was enclosed in a narrow space from which she could not escape. The walls and floor and ceiling shut her in implacably. The doors were fastened, the windows were sealed, there was no escape.

"That porter *might* have told me!" she exclaimed inconsequently, mopping her face. Then the foolishness of the saying dawned upon her, and she thought her mind must be going. That was the effect of claustrophobia, she remembered: the mind went, and one said and did foolish things. Oh, to get out into a free open space, uncornered! Here she was trapped, horribly trapped.

"The guard man should *never* have locked me in—*never!*" she cried. She ran up and down between the seats, throwing her weight first against the door and then against the other. Of course, fortunately, neither of them yielded.

Thinking food might calm her, perhaps, she took down the banana bag and peeled the squashy over-ripe fruit, munching it with part of the Bath bun from the other bag and sitting midway on the forward seat.

Suddenly the right hand window dropped with a bang and a rattle. It had only been stuck after all, and her efforts, aided by the shaking of the train, had completed its undoing, or rather its unclosing. Miss Slumbubble shrieked and dropped her banana and bun.

But the shock passed in a moment when she saw what had happened. The window was open and the sweet air was pouring in from the flying fields.

She rushed up and put her head out. This was followed by her hand, for she meant to open the door from the outside if possible. Whatever happened, the one imperative thing was that she *must get into open space*.

The handle turned easily enough, but the door was locked higher up. She could not make it budge. She put her head farther out, so that the wind tore the jet bonnet off her head and left it twirling in the dusty whirlwind on the line far behind, and this sensation of the air whistling past her ears and through her flying hair somehow or other managed to make her feel wilder than ever. In fact, she completely lost her head and began to scream at the top of her voice.

"I'm locked in! I'm a prisoner! Help, help!" she yelled.

A window opened in the next compartment, and a young man put his head out.

"What the deuce is the matter? Are you being murdered?" he shouted down the wind.

"I'm locked in! I'm locked in!" screamed the hatless lady, wrestling furiously with the obdurate door handle.

"Don't open the door!" cried the young man anxiously.

"I can't, you idiot! I can't!"

"Wait a moment, and I'll come to you. Don't try to get out. I'll climb along the footboard. Keep calm, madam, keep calm. I'll save you."

He disappeared from view. Good Heavens! He meant to crawl out and come to her carriage by the window! A man, a *young* man, would shortly be in the compartment with her. Locked in, too! No, it was impossible. That was *worse* than the claustrophobia, and she could not endure such a thing for a moment. The young man would certainly kill her and steal all her packages.

She ran once or twice frantically up and down the narrow floor. Then she looked out of the window.

"Oh, bless my heart and soul!" she cried out, "he's out already!"

The young man, evidently thinking the lady was being assaulted, had climbed out of the window and was pluckily coming to her rescue. He was already on the footboard, swinging by the brass bars on the side of the coach as the train rocked down the line at a fearful pace.

But Miss Slumbubble took a deep breath and made a sudden determination. She did, in fact, the only thing left to her to do. She pulled the communication cord once, twice, three times, and then drew the window up with a sudden snap just before the young man's head appeared round the corner of the sash. Then, stepping backwards, she trod on the slippery banana bag and fell flat on her back upon the dirty floor between the seats.

The train slackened speed almost immediately and came to a stop. Miss Slumbubble still sat on the floor, staring in a dazed fashion at her toes. She realised the enormity of her offence and was thoroughly frightened. She had actually pulled the cord!—the cord that is meant to be seen but not touched, the little chain that meant a £5 fine and all sorts of dire consequences.

She heard voices shouting and doors opening, and a moment later, a key rattled near her head, and she saw the guard swinging up onto the steps of the carriage. The door was wide open, and the young man from the next compartment was explaining volubly what he had seen and heard.

"I thought it was murder," he was saying.

But the guard pushed quickly into the carriage and lifted the panting and dishevelled lady onto the seat.

"Now, what's all this about? Was it you that pulled the cord, ma'am?" he asked somewhat roughly. "It's serious stoppin' a train like this, you know, a mail train."

Now, Miss Daphne did not mean to tell a lie. It was not deliberate, that is to say. It seemed to slip out of its own accord as the most natural and obvious thing to say, for she was terrified at what she had done and *had* to find a good excuse. Yet, how in the world could she describe to this stupid and hurried official all she had gone through? Moreover, he would be so certain to think she was merely drunk.

"It was a man," she said, falling back instinctively upon her natural enemy. "There's a man somewhere!" She glanced round at the racks and under the seats.

The guard followed her eyes. He declared, "I don't see no man. All I know is you've stopped the mail train without any visible or reasonable cause. I'll be obliged with your name and address, ma'am, if you please." He took a dirty notebook from his pocket and wet the blunt pencil in his mouth.

"Let me get air—at once," she said. "I must have air first. Of course, you shall have my name. The whole affair is disgraceful." She was getting her wits back. She moved to the door.

"That may be, ma'am," the man said, "but I've my duty to perform, and I must report the facts and then get the train on as quick as possible. You must stay in the carriage, please. We've been waiting 'ere a bit too long already."

Miss Slumbubble met her fate calmly. She realised it was not fair to keep all the passengers waiting while she got a little fresh air. There was a brief confabulation between the two guards, which ended by the one who had first come taking his seat in her carriage while the other blew his whistle. The train started off again and flew at great speed the remaining miles to Folkestone.

"Now, I'll take the name and address, if you please, ma'am," he said politely. *"Daffney,* yes, thank you. All right, Daphny without a *hef.* Thank you."

He wrote it all down laboriously. The hatless little lady sat opposite, indignant, excited, ready to be voluble the moment she could think what was best to say, and above all fearful that her holiday would he delayed, if not prevented altogether.

Presently, the guard looked up at her and put his notebook away in an inner pocket. It was just after he had entered the number of the carriage.

"You see, ma'am," he explained with sudden suavity, "this communication cord is only for cases of real danger, and if I report this, as I should do, it means a 'eavy fine. You must 'ave just pulled it as a sort of hexperiment, didn't you?"

Something in the man's voice caught her ear—there was a change in it. His manner, too, had altered somehow. He suddenly seemed to have become apologetic. She was quick to notice the change, though she could not understand what caused it. It began, she fancied, from the moment he entered the number of the carriage in his notebook.

"It's the delay to the train I've got to explain," he continued, as if speaking to himself. "I can't put it all onto the engine-driver—"

"Perhaps we shall make it up, and there won't be any delay," ventured Miss Slumbubble, carefully smoothing her hair and rearranging the stray hairpins.

"—and I don't want to get no one into any kind of trouble, least of all myself," he continued, wholly ignoring the interruption. Then he turned round in his seat and stared hard at his companion with rather a worried, puzzled expression of countenance and a shrug of the shoulders that was distinctly apologetic.

Plainly, she thought, he was preparing the way for a compromise—for a tip!

The train was slackening speed. Already it was in the cutting where it reverses and is pushed backwards onto the pier. Miss Slumbubble was desperate. She had never tipped a man before in her life except for obvious and recognised services, and this seemed to her like compounding a felony or some such dreadful thing.

Yet so much was at stake: she might be detained at Folkestone for days before the matter came into court, to say nothing of a £5 fine, which meant that her holiday would be utterly stopped. The blue and white mountains swam into her field of vision, and she heard the wind in the pine forest.

"Perhaps you would give this to your wife," she said timidly, holding out a sovereign.

The guard looked at it and shook his head.

"I 'aven't got a wife, exackly," he said, "but it isn't money I want. What I want is to 'ush this little matter up as quietly as possible. I may lose my job over this—but if you'll agree to say nothing about it, I think I can square the driver and t'other guard."

"*I* won't say anything, *of course*," stammered the astonished lady. "But I don't think I quite understand—"

"You couldn't understand either till I tell you," he replied, looking greatly relieved. "The fact is, I never noticed the carriage till I come to put the number down, and then I see it's the very one—the very same number—"

"What number?"

He stared at her for a moment without speaking. Then he appeared to make a great decision.

"Well, I'm in your 'ands anyhow, ma'am, and I may as well tell you the lot, and then we both 'elps the other out. It's this way, you see. You ain't the first to try and jump out of this carriage—not by a long ways. It's been done before by a good number—"

"Gracious!"

"The *first* who did it was that German woman, Binckmann—"

"Binckmann, the woman who was found on the line last year,

and the carriage door open?" cried Miss Slumbubble, aghast.

"That's her. This was the carriage she jumped from, and they tried to say it was murder, but couldn't find anyone who could have done it, and then they said she must have been crazy. And since then, this carriage was said to be 'aunted, because so many other people tried to do the same thing and throw theirselves out too, till the company changed the number—"

"To this number?" cried the excited spinster, pointing to the figures on the door.

"That's it, ma'am. And if you look you'll see this number don't follow on with the others. Even then the thing didn't stop, and we got orders to let no one in. That's where I made my mistake. I left the door unlocked, and they put you in. If this gets in the papers, I'll be dismissed for sure. The company's awful strict about that."

"I'm terrified!" exclaimed Miss Slumbubble, "for that's exactly what I felt—"

"That you'd got to jump out, you mean?" asked the guard.

"Yes. The terror of being shut in."

"That's what the doctors said Binckmann had—the fear of being shut up in a tight place. They gave it some long name, but that's what it was: she couldn't abide being closed in. Now, here we are at the pier, ma'am, and, if you'll allow me, I'll help you to carry your little bits of luggage."

"Oh, thank you, guard, thank you," she said faintly, taking his proffered hand and getting out with infinite relief onto the platform.

"Tchivalry ain't dead yet, Miss," he replied gallantly as he loaded himself up within her packages and led the way down to the steamer.

Ten minutes later, the deep notes of the syren echoed across the pier, and the paddles began to churn the green sea. And Miss Daphne Slumbubble, hatless but undismayed, went abroad to flutter the remnants of her faded youth before the indifferent foreigners in the cheap *pension* among the Alps.

APPENDIX: ARRIVAL AND DEPARTURE OF A PHANTOM TRACK WALKER

W.W. ADAIR[1]

These final two works deal with the ghost of an engineer who had worked for the Peanut Line. This railroad served western New York State from 1853 to 1933. Both narratives were published in Railroad Men, *a magazine that described itself as "A Publication Devoted to the Railroad Service." The first article appeared in 1902 with W.W. Adair noted as author, and the second in 1912 with W.W.A. in the byline. This is almost certainly the same person, a claim reinforced by how the second article—unfortunately but understandably—repeats information almost word-for-word from the article published a decade earlier. Together, the two chronicles offer a rare "life story" of a ghost, starting with its origin and ending with its relinquishing of earthly ties.*

— Tim Prasil

I: "The Phantom Track Walker"

In the network of railroads that intersects the western part of New York is an old single-tracker commonly known as the "The Peanut." This old switch begins the uneven tenor of its way in classic Batavia and ends abruptly in Tonawanda, N.Y. These terminals are a shade better than those of Colonel Carter's famous road of fiction,[2] but they have never produced sufficient traffic to keep the rust off the rails. Circumstances being favorable, it is the custom to start a mixed train of about a dozen cars out of Batavia each morning after

---

[1] The first article is "The Phantom Track Walker," *Railroad Men* 15.6 [March, 1902] pp. 235, 238. The second is "The Passing of a Railroad Ghost," *Railroad Men* 25.7 [April, 1912] pp. 203-05.

[2] This is an allusion to F. Hopkinson Smith's novel *Colonel Carter of Cartersville* (Grosset & Dunlap, 1891). The title character aspires to revitalize his Southern town by bringing a railroad to it.

breakfast. With any kind of luck, the crew will make the round trip and get back to the bosom of their families by midnight. The "schedule" is entirely an optional matter with the crew, and they are easy-going fellows.

The heavy snows that came in early 1882 disarranged matters to some extent on "The Peanut." The old "Red Line Limited" was reported five hours late at Richville on the first night of the storm, and when she struck Donovan's Grade, that piece of machinery which the crew reverently called "the engine" simply quit and went into winter quarters amid those rural surroundings. The three passengers were sent back to the village while the crew ordered a week's provisions and proceeded to make themselves comfortable.

For ten days, they were at home to their friends on Donovan's Grade, and the snowstorm continued for most of that time. Then the weather cleared, and word came that the roadmaster had started a snowplow from the west with four engines behind it. How the train was dug out and sent back—and how Engineer Bill McKean, of the snowplow crew, went down with his engine a mile further up the road—are familiar facts in local history. The country people were as much affected by the brave fellow's death as though he had been one of their own circle instead of an entire stranger.

It was just five years later when Jake Dibble drove into our yard one January morning and, with much illuminated English, told us that the Peanut track was being patrolled nightly near the culvert in the Black Ash Swamp by a ghost with a lantern. He declared that himself and the neighbors had watched it every night for a week—and for hours each night. He cited the fact that it was just beyond the culvert that McKean had met his death, and said he had not the least doubt that the mysterious track walker was the spirit of the departed engineer. I pretended to take his tale lightly, but my interest was aroused nonetheless.

A few days later, when the news came that Clark Gates had been set upon at the crossing by a demon with eyeballs of fire and a lantern in his hand, my curiosity overcame my discretion. Calling into confidence two other daredevil youngsters in the school named Sumner and Carrier, we soon outlined a plan of campaign. We would take our girls sleigh-riding the next night to the haunted district and investigate the stranger with the lantern.

The Peanut crossed the Black Ash Swamp at a point five miles distant, and we figured that, by starting at nine o'clock, we would arrive at a favorable hour for making the acquaintance of the ghostly track walker. Shortly after nine the following evening, we

Arrival and Departure of a Phantom Track Walker

were packed in three cutters and sped on our way to the music of sleigh bells. The night was clear and bitter cold. The moon was just past the full, and we could easily see a mile ahead.

As we dipped over the hill and came into sight of the railroad half a mile distant, our nerves were on a tingle and our eyes strained for the lantern. We saw nothing, however, until we had proceeded about a third of the distance. There, in full view, a lantern flashed forth near the culvert and almost instantly went out.

"You see it!" yelled Sumner, who was driving ahead.

We answered that we had and went forward as fast as we could. We tied our horses to the very snow-fence from which Gates had been attacked, but no fire-eyed demon appeared. The culvert was the point of interest, and that lay thirty rods up the track. The girls preferred to go with us rather than wait at the haunted crossing, and forming a line, we marched on the track walker's beat.

We searched every rod of track, examined the snow for footprints, and inspected the famous culvert. We stood around until benumbed with cold, but there was no accommodation about the ghost, and our reception was a decided "frost." We slowly returned to our sleighs and started for home in a very dissatisfied frame of mind. We had seen the lantern and, therefore, were sure that the stories had some foundation. What could it all mean?

As we rounded the hill, we instinctively looked back—and there, just west of the culvert, was the track walker taking up his nightly patrol. A lantern seemed to swing along as naturally as if carried by a human hand. After proceeding a short distance, the lamp would suddenly shoot toward the sky and go out, reappearing a little later at some other point on the beat. For an hour, we watched it as the maneuvers were repeated. Then we left for home with the mystery unexplained.

About a week later, the mysterious patrol ceased as suddenly as it had begun. It was not seen again until another five years had rolled by, but when the tenth anniversary of the great storm came, the track walker again took up his lonely vigil. The vicinity of the culvert was still his base of operation, and he patrolled the district faithfully for four weeks. The fifteenth anniversary witnessed the same proceeding, and now that the twentieth year had come, the lonely trackman has revisited the old scenes.

Word comes from that section that the farmers are terrorized by the unnatural occurrence and are looking for blood spots on the face of the moon. They are full of ominous forebodings and believe that the track walker will yet wreak vengeance by bringing some sort of disaster upon the neighborhood. As for Clark Gates, he has his nightly chores done regularly before sundown. When darkness falls, it finds him bivouacked in his domicile—with doors and windows securely barred—and *nothing* can induce him to venture without until the return of daylight.

II: "The Passing of a Railroad Ghost"

The average reader whose list of periodicals does not embrace the *Clarence Weekly Compass* probably missed the brief and altogether inadequate mention that was recently made in that paper concerning the passing of the historic ghost of the Peanut Railroad, which lately gave reasonable evidence of formally retiring from business. The story that has to do with the coming of the ghost—and with his February patrol of that part of the Peanut Railroad that runs through the Black Ash Swamp—dates back to the great snowstorm of 1881 and the disastrous wreck that occurred in connection with it.

The kind of railroading done on the Peanut in the olden days is familiar to all railroad men. Circumstances being favorable, it was the custom to start a mixed train of about a dozen cars out of Batavia each morning shortly after breakfast. With any kind of luck, the crew was expected to make the trip to Tonawanda and return sometime within the twenty-four hours. The schedule was largely an optional matter, and the crew was composed of easy-going fellows.

Early in February, 1881, came the heaviest snowstorm that had visited western New York with the memory of the oldest inhabitant.[3] Beginning shortly before noon, the snow fell continuously in such volume that, for hours, it was impossible to see across the street with any distinctness. The old "Red Line Limited" was reported five hours late at Richville Station, and when she struck Donovan's Grade at about 9 o'clock in the evening, the tired engine quit for the night, and the crew went into winter

---

[3] In the earlier piece, Adair sets the scene by recalling the "heavy snows that came in early 1882," not 1881. The discrepancy is not resolved by the historical record. In 1881, one newspaper reported heavy snow from the East Coast to the Great Plains, noting that "the blockading of trains was frequent" (*Mineral Point Tribune,* Feb. 3, 1881, p. 2). A year later, the news from New York read: "The snow continues. Trains are blocked on Long Island, in the interior of the state and New England" (*Salt Lake Herald,* Feb. 5, 1882, p. 13). "Bill McKean" also becomes "Bill McKeon" here, but—if Adair isn't spreading (or inventing) a legend—he might be respecting the family's privacy by using an alias.

Arrival and Departure of a Phantom Track Walker

quarters amid those rural surroundings. The three passengers were sent back to the village while the train crew ordered a week's provisions and proceeded to make themselves comfortable. For ten days, they were at home to their friends on Donovan's Grade, and the snowstorm continued for the greater part of that time.

Then the weather cleared, and word came that the roadmaster had started a snowplow from the west with four engines behind it. Those who were boys at that time will not soon forget how the massive engines crashed into the snowdrifts, making the plow hurl great chunks of snow far up on either side of the track. As a battleship might ram an adversary, so the snowplow crews would back away for a fresh start and come thundering into the solid whiteness, cutting their way a few rods at a time toward the imprisoned train.

Nor was their task finished when the train had been released and switched out on the siding. Before them still lay two miles of drifts between high board fences, and upon this embargo of traffic, they continued their attack with dogged persistence.

Finally, as the victory was almost won, the four engines and the snowplow went off the track as they struck the drift at a culvert in the Black Ash Swamp, and brave Bill McKeon, engineer of the snowplow crew, was buried under his engine. The country people were as much affected by his death as though he had been one of their own circle instead of an entire stranger.

It was exactly a year later that strange tales began to emanate from the farmer folk living on the ridge overlooking the Black Ash Swamp. Their stories agreed in every detail and were to the effect that the track near the culvert was being patrolled nightly by a ghost with a lantern. Several of them declared that they had watched it every night for weeks and that it had walked the track for hours each night. They cited the fact that it was just beyond the culvert that Bill McKeon had met his death, and none of them seemed to doubt that the mysterious track walker was the spirit of the departed engineer. One farmer, returning late from Indian Falls, told a hair-raising story of having been waylaid at the crossing by a demon with eyeballs of fire, who carried a lantern in his hand.

These tales stirred the adventurous spirit of the young men of that vicinity, and sleigh-riding parties began to make excursions to the haunted region. The experience of these curiosity seekers varied greatly. Some of them saw the light at a distance. Others did not see it at all. Those who saw it complained that it invariably vanished when they attempted to get within a quarter of a mile of the culvert.

The principal result of these sleigh rides was a number of happy weddings.

Every fifth year since that time, the ghost of the Black Ash Swamp has returned to the scene of his vigil on the first day of February. He has patrolled the track for an entire month, then his labors have ceased as suddenly as they have begun. The maneuvers have not varied in any essential particular. A lantern, describing the same arcs as if carried by a human hand, has appeared regularly at midnight and carried on that wearied patrol up and down a mile of track for hours at a time.

The scene of this phenomenon, coupled with the fact that the visit bore such a close relation to the great snowplow wreck, has admitted of only one theory that might be put forward as an explanation. The spirit of the Black Ash Swamp has never been conceived as other than the shade of the dead engineer. The question the natives have always asked, when the ghost quit work along toward morning, has been: "What did he want?"

At first, country folk treated these mysterious visits lightly, but as they have been repeated with such monotonous regularity every fifth year, the more superstitious of the native have become greatly worried. Some have professed to see other uncanny manifestations, such as fiery stars shaped like daggers and blood-spots on the face of the Moon. Even the more conservative among them have anxiously wondered whether some delayed disaster would not eventually be visited upon them through the wrath of this weird patrolman.

Last month, there came what appears to be a very happy end to these nocturnal manifestations. An amateur student of the occultism was spending the Christmas holidays with a college chum, who is a son of one of the farmers on the ridge. Hearing the strange tales of the railroad ghost, the young collegian was reminded of the oriental theories respecting such visits. He began asking questions.

"Did he lose anything of value at the time of his death?" he asked after hearing of the accident to the brave engineer.

"Oh yes!" replied the farmer, "now that you speak of it, I remember that a hunting-case watch was found by one of the boys up at the next house the summer after the accident."

The collegian knew the sentimental fondness of a railroad engineer for a good watch, and he at once formulated an application of the oriental theory—that the visits would cease the moment the desire of the ghost was gratified.

"Do you want to be rid of these visits that are the cause of so much terror in the neighborhood?" he asked.

"Why, certainly," replied his host. "We would do anything to restore the peace of the neighborhood so that we might feel secure from this evil omen."

"Then let me tell you what to do," said the collegian. "If these visits are resumed in February, have the young man take the watch which he found and lay it on the track some clear night where it might easily be seen by anyone looking for such an object. If the result is what I anticipate, it will relieve the neighborhood of this annoyance."

"Then you think he is looking for his watch?" asked the farmer with an expectant thrill in his voice.

"At least," replied the student, "such a possibility can be imagined, and I think the interest attached to the experiment might make it well worth trying."

True to his custom, the spirit of the swamp returned to his vigil the first night in February of the present year. Again his tireless tramp over the snow went on night after night in the vicinity of the culvert.

Soon after his return came a beautifully clear winter's night, and trembling with excitement over the possible result, the young man left the house early in the evening, took the watch of the dead engineer, and laid it on the snow crust between the rails, where it must surely be seen by any passerby.

That night, there was little sleep among the farmers on the ridge. The lights were out in the houses at midnight, but the faces of parents and children alike were pressed against the window panes, watching for the first appearance of the phantom track walker. Presently, his light appeared half a mile east of the culvert and swung along at a good gait toward the scene of the wreck.

Suddenly, as it neared the spot where the watch was lying, the lantern seemed to be set down in the snow—an unprecedented occurrence. After a moment, it seemed as though a hand again picked up the lamp, swung it three times around in a circle, and shot it towards the sky, where it was lost to sight among the stars. Up in the farmhouses, the natives hugged each other, for they felt sure that it marked the last visit of the lonely patrolman of the swamp.

They sat on sentry again the next midnight, but the specter with the lantern did not appear, nor has he returned since. The young student who conceived the plan of banishing the ghost was hailed a hero, and it is reported that a substantial purse has been raised for him by the grateful people of the neighborhood, who feel that in ridding their section of an undesirable guest, he has not only contributed to their peace of mind—but enhanced the value of real estate.

ABOUT THE EDITOR

With a doctorate degree in English, Tim Prasil has taught at the university level, specializing in American literature from the 1800s and early 1900s and in popular genres, such as ghost stories and science fiction. He researches the histories of quirky genres of narrative with the goal of compiling the entertaining yet informative anthologies that make up the Phantom Traditions Library (of which this is the fifth volume).

Prasil also writes fiction about a ghost hunter named Vera Van Slyke. She appears in three novels: *Help for the Haunted, Guilt Is a Ghost,* and *The Hound of the Seven Mounds.* Interested readers can start with any novel, each of which is available from Brom Bones Books.

Brom Bones Books has also released Prasil's *The Lost Limericks of Edgar Allan Poe,* a collection of 100 limericks inspired by the great author's work, life, and spirit. The same publisher offers *Spectral Edition: Ghost Reports in U.S. Newspapers, 1864-1917,* in which Prasil presents the best of his extensive collection of actual articles about haunted houses and graveyards, haunted roads and rivers, even haunted people.

One more thing: "Tim Prasil" rhymes with *grim fossil.* Flattering, ain't it?

ALSO FROM
BROM BONES BOOKS

Can a hypnotist entrance a subject from across a room? Could a mesmerized person be compelled to commit murder? What if a hypnotic spell were extended *beyond death?* Such mysteries are explored—and the farthest-reaching possibilities of hypnotism are imagined—by Edgar Allan Poe, Louisa May Alcott, Arthur Conan Doyle, Ambrose Bierce, and fourteen more authors in *Entranced by Eyes of Evil: Tales of Mesmerism and Mystery*.

This is the first volume in the Phantom Traditions Library. Visit BromBonesBooks.com for audio readings and more.

ALSO FROM
BROM B🎃NES BOOKS

Echoing Ghost Stories: Literary Reflections of Oral Tradition
Edited by Tim Prasil
Phantom Traditions Library

For centuries, storytellers recited ghost stories aloud. As magazine production grew in the 1800s, *reading* spooky tales rose in popularity, and many authors preserved on paper the experience of *listening* to an account of the supernatural. Ambrose Bierce, Edith Wharton, M.R. James, and others put their stamps on this distinctive tradition. *Echoing Ghost Stories: Literary Reflections of Oral Tradition* showcases such tales, establishing their place within the wider genre of the Victorian ghost story.

This is the second volume in the Phantom Traditions Library. Visit BromBonesBooks.com for audio readings and more.

ALSO FROM
BROM B🎃NES BOOKS

SPECTRAL EDITION

Ghost Reports from U.S. Newspapers 1865-1917

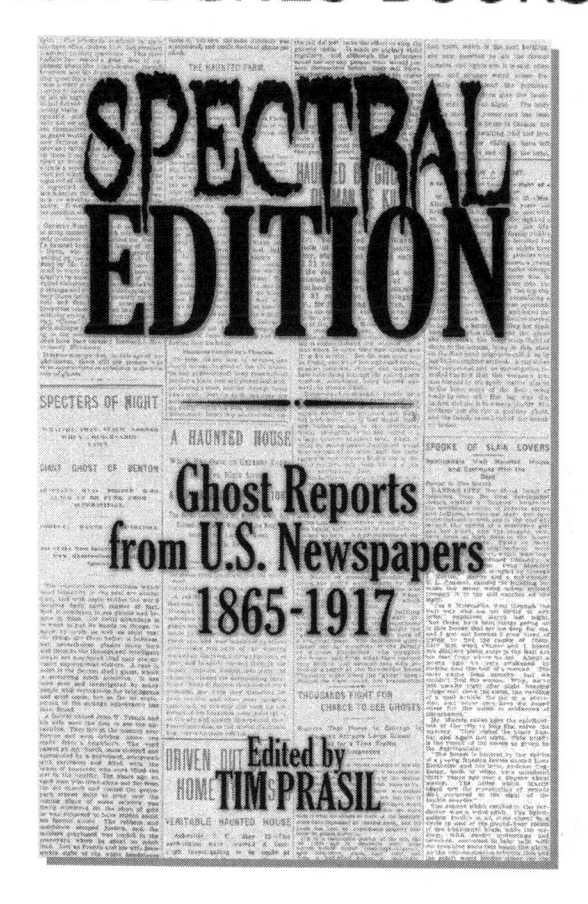

Edited by TIM PRASIL

Between the American Civil War and the nation's entry into World War I, a wave of ghost reports appeared in U.S. newspapers. Haunted houses and cemeteries, haunted roads and rivers, and even haunted people were treated as legitimate news. Tim Prasil has collected hundreds of these articles, and *Spectral Edition: Ghost Reports from U.S. Newspapers, 1865-1917* displays the scariest, strangest, funniest, and most intriguing of them.

Visit BromBonesBooks.com for sample ghost reports, audio readings, and more information.

ALSO FROM
BROM BONES BOOKS

GUILT IS A GHOST
A VERA VAN SLYKE GHOSTLY MYSTERY
TIM PRASIL

Desperate to contact his murdered friend, millionaire Roderick Morley held a séance. Things went horribly wrong, though, and he left the room—to commit *suicide*. Afterward, Morley Mansion was deemed haunted. Ghost hunter Vera Van Slyke and her assistant, Lucille Parsell, were summoned. But there was *another* shadow cast over that house. A fake medium had conducted that séance, a shame-ridden woman calling herself: "Lucille Parsell." And, sometimes, *guilt is a ghost* that can never be banished.

This novel is part of the Vera Van Slyke Ghostly Mysteries series. Visit BromBonesBooks.com for reviews, details, and more!